SAMMY:

Women

Troubles

Robin Hardy

Westford Press

The characters and circumstances in this book are fictitious, and any resemblance to people living or dead is coincidental. As fiction, it is not intended to portray the actual workings of any institution or organization in Dallas.

Sammy: Women Troubles, 2nd edition

© 2003 Robin Hardy. All rights reserved.

Westford Press
6757 Arapaho Rd., Suite 711, PMB 236
Dallas, TX 75248-4073

ISBN: 0-9745829-2-1
LCCN: 2003113632

To lovable jerks everywhere. You know who you are.

one

Sammy held his wife, Marni, close on the country club dance floor as they swayed to the gentle beat of "To a Dream" played by the hot new band Backlash at this special occasion. There was a loud pop near his shoulder right before they were sprayed with champagne. Marni ducked to safety behind Sammy. "Pruett!" he uttered, turning.

A good-looking, sandy-haired man in a tuxedo similar to Sammy's grinned mischievously as the champagne bubbled from the bottle in his hands. "I wasn't *aiming* for you, Sambo. You just always seem to get in the line of fire."

A blonde woman in an ankle-length ivory dress and veil turned Sammy by the shoulder. "I owe you something. Excuse us, Marni—" and she kissed Sammy full on the lips.

Marni sighed and rolled her eyes, smiling. Such was life with black-haired, blue-eyed Sammy, who drew feminine attention from anywhere within a three-mile radius. He couldn't help it. "That's okay, Kerry," she murmured.

"Two can play at that game," announced Pruett, and turned Marni around for a kiss.

"Get your mitts off my wife, animal," Sammy ordered, disengaging from the bride. Then he turned back to say, "Congratulations, Kerry. He's a great guy."

A waiter brought up champagne glasses and peremptorily separated Pruett from the bottle. Hannibal, the band's lead singer, announced from the dais, "Okay, people, listen up! Time to toast the bride and groom. Will the best man come take the mike, please?—if you can find your way around on a stage."

A light burst of laughter followed Sammy as he took a glass and trotted up to the dais. Marni watched with a full heart. In the four months since that near-fatal gunshot wound, she had watched Sammy struggle back to health with single-minded determination. All that remained of the trauma was a small scar beneath his left breast, an aversion to breathing cold air, and, a Medal of Honor for placing himself in the line of fire to protect Marni, Kerry, and her son Chris. As a cop, Sammy accepted guns discharging in his direction as an occupational hazard.

"Kerry—Dave," he said at the mike, lifting his glass, "may you find the happiness together you so deserve. May laughter fill your days and love your nights, and may God watch over you and Chris with the shield of His peace." He drained the glass and all those in the room did likewise as Kerry Pruett leaned in her new husband's arms.

Ten-year-old Chris caught Sammy as he was coming down from the dais. "Mom says our house is not far from your new apartment!"

"Right around the corner," Sammy grinned, offering his hand for their new secret handshake.

"When I grow up," Chris sighed, holding his hand, "I'm gonna be a cop just like you and dad. I wish I'd'a been the one to arrest Grip for shooting you."

"That was some trial. Short and sweet," muttered Mike Masterson, coming up behind them. He was Sammy's and Dave's boss, the sergeant in charge of the Targeted Activity Section of the Special Investigations Bureau of the Dallas Police. Mike, an African American, had an authoritative air that masked his deep affection for the officers under his command. "When you walked real slowlike into the courtroom and sat in the witness stand," he said to Sammy, "a couple of the jurors were wiping their eyes. And when the defense started hammering you about provoking Grip, I thought the judge was going to have a coronary."

"Easiest conviction I ever nailed," Sammy said, a corner of his mouth turning up. "All I had to do was look wounded."

"Well then, you could've stayed in Dallas—you didn't have to go on vacation to get all shot up. Then I wouldn't've had to keep hopping back and forth to San Antone," Mike griped, to forestall an alarming slide into sentimentality.

"You love me," Sammy grinned.

"Like a migraine," Mike retorted. "I couldn't care less, but the lieutenant was wondering how you'd feel about returning to work in TAS." Targeted Activity was a proactive, free-ranging section that investigated a broad range of illegal activities.

"Sure," Sammy replied, interest clicking in his eyes. "What've you got?"

"Come on in Monday and I'll lay it out for you. This one's gonna take two, Sambo—a man and a woman," Mike said.

"Perfect. Marni and I will be there first thing Monday," Sammy replied, glancing at her across the room.

Mike paused. "That—won't work, Kidman. Marni's been helpful to us, but she's a civilian. This one calls for a professional."

Sammy inhaled. "I know she doesn't have the paperwork, Mike, but we don't work like you think. Marni doesn't touch a gun or try to make arrests. She's my eyes and ears, and she's got unbelievable instincts. I'd'a never pulled off that job at the theater without her—not that the results made you look top notch, or anything, not to mention all the publicity we got on rescuing that baby and all," he casually elaborated.

Mike shook his head heavily. "I'm sorry, Sammy; you can't bring a civilian into official police business. The liability is unacceptable."

Sammy eyed Mike coolly. "I work with Marni, or not at all."

"Don't start giving me ultimatums, Sammy," Mike warned. "The lieutenant—"

"You tell the lieutenant," Sammy said with a stony edge, "that if it weren't for Marni, I'd be spread across several cemeteries by now. That may not seem like such a big deal to *him,* but it is to me. You let me work alone, and bring in Marni however it suits me, or I walk."

"Sammy—"

"Did you know the chief of police of the San Antonio department came to see me while I was in the hospital down there? They offered me a detective's position, with complete freedom *and* more money. Whether we went would depend on Marni, of course. By the way, she hasn't stopped talking about San Antonio since we came home. All I have to do to make her pliable, if you know what I mean, is talk about taking her back," Sammy said, a silly grin spreading across his face.

Mike drooped in resignation. "Let me call the lieutenant, but I'll probably have to take it up to the captain or deputy chief to get approval on this one."

"Whatever suits you," Sammy said aloofly, and turned to claim his dance with the bride as Mike left the banquet room to make his call in private.

By the time Sammy had relinquished Kerry with an affectionate kiss on her cheek, Mike had reentered the room. He gave Sammy a curt nod, then collared him to add firmly, "But Lieutenant Kerr wants it understood that the city assumes no responsibility for Marni. Officially, he doesn't even know what you're doing."

"My man!" Sammy exulted, grabbing Mike's head and planting a kiss on his bristly face.

"Cut that out!" Mike demanded, glancing around self-consciously.

"I'm jealous," purred Marni, sidling up. "You've been ignoring me for the last thirty minutes."

Sammy looked down at his kittenish wife, with her shoulder-length brown hair and almond eyes. "Ignoring you? Not possible. Mike here was just telling me that he's got a special assignment for us."

"*Us?*" Marni cocked a brow skeptically at him.

"Uh-huh. Ain't that so, Mike?" Sammy beamed triumphantly at him.

"Sammy's getting away with murder, Marni," Mike confessed in a mutter. "Just *please* don't get hurt. And—we'll need passport photos of you both."

Monday morning Sammy and Marni were sitting down in Mike's office in the Big Building Downtown, the Police and Courts Building. As an undercover unit, Targeted Activity was supposed to be housed along with Narcotics, Vice, and Criminal Investigations in another downtown building that had no external connection with the police department. However, there wasn't room, and until the building space could be reallocated or another one leased, TAS was stuck in the first available space in the Big Building.

Meeting with Sammy, Marni, and Mike was another gentlemen whom Mike introduced as an investigative agent with a large insurance company. "This will be a fact-gathering assignment, Sammy," Mike said, laying a file in front of him and Marni. "Mutual Life asked us for local support in the initial phase of investigation. Whatever you uncover needs to be turned over to Foster here."

"I thought you people conducted your own investigations. Why should Dallas taxpayers foot the bill for this?" Sammy asked, perusing the folder, and Marni shifted in discomfort.

"Good question. Maybe your superiors agreed that the problem was serious enough to warrant it," Foster said. Then he added drily, "Congratulations on your Medal of Honor, coming on top of your lifesaving award. This department is mighty generous with the awards, isn't it?" Sammy looked at him over the folder.

"Yes, well—you're familiar with the Threlkelds, aren't you?" Mike continued.

"Anybody who reads the *Sun-Times* knows the Threlkelds," Sammy muttered. "Wealthy oil family. Real estate developers. High society and investments. What's this about art?"

Mike opened his mouth but Foster answered, "We've gotten a tip that the Threlkelds have had their hands on some major art works that have been stolen from museums and private collections. However, we can't verify this without some inside help. That's you." Foster leaned back, looking from Sammy to Marni. He was a lean, self-confident man with a hawklike demeanor.

"The Threlkelds have requested domestics from a local employment agency—specifically, they need a maid and a chauffeur. We've got the paperwork all set up for you and Marni to go over there this afternoon at three," Mike said, pointing out some forms in the file. "Sammy, your name is Jim Brandon. Marni is your wife Melody." Marni smiled up at Mike. "You've got driver's licenses, social security cards, passports—the works," Mike pointed out.

Sammy slowly closed the file and leaned forward on his knees in his contemplating-the-distasteful posture. "Since when did we start placing cops in families on the basis of a tip?" he asked.

"There have been three heists from major collections in the past six weeks alone," Foster said, jabbing the file with a forefinger. "The Threlkelds have been strongly implicated as having possession of two of those pieces."

"By whom?" Sammy asked skeptically.

"That's not for you to know, cop. You just do your job and leave the rest to us." Foster glanced at Mike as if to say, *This is the best you've got?*

"Sammy," Mike said, forestalling Foster with a look, "it's really important to a lot of people to get these thefts cleared up. Nobody's asking you to go on a fishing expedition—the art is our sole target. And, if you're there long enough, you can just as well clear the Threlkelds."

Sammy looked at Mike for a moment, then stood with the file. "We'll see what we can do."

At three o'clock that afternoon, Sammy and Marni were driving up to the Threlkeld estate in Sammy's classic '66 Mustang convertible. He pulled up to the huge wrought-iron gates and leaned over to push the intercom button. "Yes?" came the response.

"Jim and Melody Brandon. We're from the employment agency," Sammy said. A moment later there was a click and the gates laboriously opened. Sammy drove up a long cobbled driveway past a fountain and sculptured gardens to the front of the whitewashed mansion. They got out of the car, Marni straining to look everywhere at once, and mounted broad, flat steps toward twenty-foot-tall doors.

Sammy rang the doorbell and stepped back with an "ain't-this-something" look at Marni. A uniformed butler opened the door. "I'm Jim Brandon, and this is my wife, Melody. The employment agency sent us," Sammy said.

"Where are your papers?" the butler asked severely, and Sammy withdrew them from his sports coat pocket and handed them over. The butler scrutinized the documents while they waited at the door, then stepped back to let them in. Marni's jaw dropped as she gazed around the vast white marble floor, thirty-foot ceilings, and elaborate oaken wall moldings.

"You will *never* come through the front door again, unless you are escorting one of the Family in or out. You will use the rear entrance exclusively, and you will not be seen in any part of the house in which you have not been summoned. Is that clear?" the butler said ominously.

"Yes, sir," Sammy replied, and Marni managed a nod.

The butler took them to the rear of the house and sat them at a long wooden table in the kitchen. "Wait here. Mrs. Threlkeld will be down presently to interview you," he instructed, then departed. Marni and Sammy looked at each other, and waited.

For a while, the house was as quiet as if she and Sammy were the only living beings in it. The kitchen wall clock ticked loudly. A clothes dryer in the laundry room nearby hummed. A leaf blower growled faintly from the back lawn. Suddenly there were piercing screams and running footsteps.

Sammy and Marni sat up and looked out the doors to the sunroom beyond. "You jerk!" a girl's voice screamed. There was a crash, young masculine laughter, and a lanky teenaged boy shot out the back door and disappeared past the startled gardener on the exquisite grounds.

His pursuer, a young woman, halted at the door, disheveled and panting. "I'm gonna flush everything you own, you—" She then caught sight of Sammy and Marni staring from the kitchen, and she marched into the kitchen, demanding of Sammy, "Who are you?"

He stood, and Marni did, too. "I'm Jim Brandon, the new chauffeur. This is—"

"You've got to be the most gorgeous man I've ever seen. Do you work out?" she demanded.

"A little," he admitted. She appraised him and he shifted. She looked about eighteen, with carefully frizzled dark brown hair, painstaking makeup, and a skillfully bobbed nose. She smiled in satisfaction (or anticipation), then glimpsed the object of her wrath lurking behind the hedges around the pool. "Bobby! You pervert!" she screamed from the kitchen, causing

Marni to flinch. With that, she ran out in pursuit of feckless Bobby.

Sammy and Marni dropped back to the hard wooden chairs to wait. Over the next forty minutes, they heard nothing human other than muted footsteps and occasional disembodied voices.

All at once the butler appeared in the kitchen and stepped aside. Following him was obviously Mrs. Threlkeld—a woman with precisely coiffed silver-gray hair, stern eyes, and tight skin. Sammy and Marni stood, and he held out his hand. "Mrs. Threlkeld, I'm Jim Brandon, and this is my wife—"

"Let's begin with some basic ground rules," she said curtly, ignoring his hand. He quietly withdrew it. "You are not a person here. You are a piece of equipment necessary in the service of this Family. You and your wife will be given quarters here in this house, and you will be on call twenty-four hours a day, seven days a week. You may not have anyone over without special permission. You may take one day off every two weeks, when requested in writing three days in advance.

"You will take your meals here in the kitchen and you will confine yourselves to whatever area you have been assigned to work. You and your wife will receive a combined salary of seven-hundred-fifty a week, with the usual deductions for taxes, insurance, and social security. You may be dismissed at any time for any reason, and no explanation need be given. Do you understand?"

"Yes, ma'am," Sammy said with a masked face.

Mrs. Threlkeld gestured at the butler, who withdrew two pages from a file and handed one each to Marni and Sammy. Marni gazed at the single-spaced type. "This is a copy of your employment contract, specifying everything I have just told you. In addition, you agree never to speak with anyone from the media and never to publish anything in any form about the Threlkeld Family. Do you understand?"

"Yes, ma'am," Sammy repeated.

"As servants, you will be available to perform any duty which the Family requires of you. In addition, the chauffeur will maintain all cars in perfect running condition at all times. If you should have any grievances, you will convey them to Mr. Hellier here. At no time will you presume to speak to any member of the Family other than to answer questions. You will never use the front entrance nor the elevator unless *I* tell you to.

"Your uniforms are provided for you in your quarters, and you will be expected to wear them between the hours of eight A.M. and nine P.M.—longer if you are on special duty. It will be your responsibility to see that they are altered to fit you, if necessary, and kept clean. After you sign your contracts, you are to move your—vehicle to the back of the house and report in uniform to Mr. Hellier. Are we clearly understood?"

"Yes, Mrs. Threlkeld," Sammy said softly, his face inscrutable.

"Very well." She turned and marched out of the kitchen.

Hellier produced a pen from his jacket pocket, saying, "The contracts are to be signed and dated on the bottom line." Sammy and Marni each signed their copy and handed it to him. Then Hellier directed, "Go get your car and bring it around back. I'll show you where."

As the two headed out to Sammy's convertible, Marni whispered, "Can you believe this?"

"What a trip," he muttered. "As long as we're here, I'm only Jim and you're just Melody," he reminded her.

"The domestic equipment," she snickered in disbelief, and he shook his head.

Sammy started the car and guided it around back, where they saw Hellier motion them beside a five-car garage. Several other cars were scattered around the vehicle court.

While Sammy and Marni got out, Hellier said, "As soon as you change, the vehicles need attention. This way." They followed him to a back door between the sunroom and the kitchen. "This is the service entrance." He went down a hallway and opened a door—"And these are your quarters."

They looked into a bedroom and bath, humbly furnished and left in disarray. Their uniforms were in a rumpled heap on the floor. "Come to the kitchen when you are dressed," Hellier instructed, and left them to themselves.

Sammy shut the door as Marni bent to collect the clothes from the floor. She shook out the chauffeur's jacket and pants and laid them on the unmade bed with the hat as Sammy took off his sports coat. Then she picked up the blue zippered dress and apron. Far from the French maid's uniform she had feared, it was safely dowdy and several sizes too large.

Sammy had less luck: the coat strained around his chest and the pants hung over his feet. "Can you move some buttons and hem these?" he whispered.

"As soon as I find a needle and thread," she answered softly. He nodded, bending to cuff them in the meanwhile.

When they were dressed, they scrutinized each other ruefully. Then Sammy slipped his arms around her and teased, "Mrs. Brandon, we'll make a housewife of you yet."

"I consider it more of an inoculation," she returned, reaching up for a kiss.

"At least we're in this together. I wouldn't want to be an appliance with anybody but you," he murmured.

"You say the sweetest things," she purred.

They went up the hall to the kitchen, where a roly-poly little woman was beginning dinner preparations. She wore her graying hair in a very tight bun, which seemed to emphasize the narrow, suspicious slant of her eyes. Sammy glanced at Marni and nodded toward the cook, so Marni hesitantly approached her. "Hello. I'm Melody Brandon, the new maid."

"I don't have anything to do with you. Mrs. Cox will tell you what to do," the woman said brusquely. Marni nodded and backed off, glancing at Sammy. He cocked a brow.

Several minutes later Hellier was back with the same Mrs. Cox—slender, forty-five, with sleek black hair, she exuded the aura of Friends of the Symphony Co-Chairman. "Hello, dear; you must be Melody," she said, taking Marni's hand in both of hers. "I am Audrey Cox, the Threlkeld family's household manager. Welcome to our little extended family! If you have any questions or problems, please do not hesitate to bring them to myself or Mr. Hellier. Now, here is a list of your daily responsibilities. All cleaning supplies are located in the laundry room here off the kitchen. I know you'll do your very best for us, since you understand what an honor it is to be employed by the oldest, wealthiest family in Dallas."

Without waiting for a reply to her reverential little speech, she squeezed Marni's hand and turned out of the kitchen. As Marni looked over the lengthy list of chores, her jaw went slack. It was enough to overwhelm a young bride who had never so much as cleaned an oven.

Hellier nodded at Sammy: "The cars must be cleaned and tuned up. You'll find supplies in the garage."

"Yes, sir," Sammy said, turning to the back door. He went out to survey the cars parked pell-mell in the court. Leaning on the Rolls Royce, he looked in the window, then opened the driver's side door and sat.

"Wow," he muttered, glancing around the interior. He laid a tentative hand on the gearshift, then wiped his mouth nervously.

Getting out, he checked over the other cars and returned to the kitchen. While the cook's back was turned, he picked up the telephone and dialed a number. It was answered, "Masterson."

"Hello, grease breath," Sammy said.

"Hello, Jim. What can I do for you?" Mike asked cordially.

"I need you to patch me in to somebody right away who can walk me through the gear pattern on a Rolls Royce Silver Shadow," Sammy said, glancing at the cook as she glanced at him. "And I need shop manuals for—have you got a pencil, darlin'?—the Rolls, which is about three years old, and: a Jaguar XJS, a Bi Turbo Maserati, and a BMW 535i. Those three are this year's models."

". . . and a BMW 535i. Gotcha. Okay, Jim, stand by and I'll transfer you to somebody in motor vehicles."

"Thanks, sweetheart," Sammy said, winking at the cook. She turned away in a huff, but looked back a moment later.

Meanwhile, Marni hauled a bucket of cleansers to a downstairs bath and turned on the light. She gazed at the gold-plated fixtures and etched glass shower door, the yards of marble counter tops and acres of tile. Sighing, she set the bucket down, donned rubber gloves, and began to spray the mirror with glass cleaner.

As she was working, the boy they had seen race out of the house, Bobby, came into the bathroom. Marni glanced up, smiling. He was about fifteen and would have been nice looking but for the habitual scowl on his face.

Without ever seeing her, he walked over to the toilet and unzipped his fly. Appalled, Marni backed out of the bathroom to wait until he finished his business. He flushed the toilet and came out as if she were totally invisible. Marni watched him go, then went back in to resume cleaning.

By six o'clock she had knocked only two chores off the list, but she was tired and hungry, so she went to the kitchen to ask the cook, "Excuse me. What time are we supposed to eat?"

"The Family takes their meals at seven o'clock, and you're certainly not eating before them. Any time after they're served, you may come eat," the cook informed her.

"That smells wonderful," Marni said innocently, leaning over the rangetop.

The cook put her long-handled spoon down and turned around with a fist on the general area of her hip. "This is for the *Family*. You and your husband do not eat from the dishes prepared for the Family, unless it's leftovers," she said stridently.

"Of course," Marni murmured.

"Now, haven't you got something you need to be doing?" the cook demanded.

"Yes," Marni admitted, taking the list out of her pocket. Before leaving the kitchen, she looked out the back window at Sammy, in his undershirt, washing one of the cars. He saw her and lifted his chin. She blew him a kiss and turned back to her list with a sigh.

While she was oiling the paneling in the foyer, she observed the Family gathering for dinner. There was Mrs. Threlkeld, Bobby, and the young woman; the elevator beside the staircase opened and a private nurse wheeled out an elderly gentleman in a wheelchair. He stood from the wheelchair, brushing aside help, and seated himself at the dinner table. Just before dinner was served, another man came in through the front door, and Marni reflexively looked up.

He was about forty, with full brown hair and a definite resemblance to Bobby. He wore a handmade silk suit and carried an eelskin portfolio. Meeting Marni's eyes, he stopped in midstride and she quickly looked away. "Are you new?" he asked.

Marni turned guiltily. "Yes, sir. I'm Melody Brandon. My husband and I just started today," she explained.

"Well, Melody," he extended his hand, "My name is Stan Threlkeld."

"Mr. Threlkeld," she murmured in surprise, wiping oil from her hand in order to shake his.

"You're doing a fine job here, Melody," he said, surveying the wood.

"Thank you," she replied, glancing into the dining room where the rest of the Family sat waiting for him.

"Nice to have you aboard," he said, resuming his walk toward the dining room. "Oh—and Melody—" he paused and she looked up attentively. "Hellier is full of hot air. Ignore him. Audrey is a liar. Don't believe a word she says. And Mother is really a harmless old broad—she can't bite because she hasn't got a tooth left in her head." He growled and snapped for emphasis, then went on in to dinner.

two

As soon as the Family was comfortably into dinner, Marni took her cleaning supplies to the laundry room and went out back to get Sammy. He had washed and garaged two cars, and was now sweating over the Maserati. "You can come in and eat now," she said, brushing damp hair back off his forehead.

"Great," he sighed, dropping a sponge into the bucket of wash water at his feet. "The things I do for a living," he muttered.

"Tell me about it," she smiled, offering him a rag for his hands. They went into the house, where Sammy stopped in the laundry room to wash up.

Hellier and the cook were already seated at the long wooden table, eating. Marni paused over them to ask, "Do you mind showing me what we can eat?"

"Any leftovers in the refrigerator," the cook replied haughtily. Marni could not help but notice that they were eating from the dishes on the range.

She opened the enormous refrigerator unit and found the remains of a stroganoff, and vegetables. "Where do the other servants eat?" she asked, having seen several others.

"The other *staff*," replied the cook, "eat at home. We are the only ones who live in with the Family."

At that time Sammy came into the kitchen and hesitated. "Sit down," Marni smiled at him. He plopped down in a chair. She loaded two plates and heated them in the microwave, found silverware and napkins, and filled two glasses with ice water.

As she set Sammy's dinner before him, he looked up and said, "Thanks, baby."

"You're welcome," she replied. He pulled down on the front of her apron to bring her within range for a quick kiss on the lips. The cook stirred, eyes on her plate.

The four of them ate in silence awhile, then Sammy said, "This is excellent. What do I call you besides World's Hottest Cook?" He gifted her with one of his spine-tingling smiles.

"Mrs. Hellier," she replied frostily. Sammy and Marni looked in surprise at her and Hellier. He appeared to be about five years younger, fifty pounds lighter, and light-years more intelligent. Besides which, the two of them hardly looked at each other and said not a word between them. Marni suddenly felt sorry for them, married and disliking each other so much.

"Ah," said Sammy. "Just my luck." No one took him seriously, nor did he intend for them to—it was just a nice icebreaker. Mrs. Hellier glanced at him and almost smiled. "How long have you worked for the Threlkelds?" he asked conversationally.

"About two years," she said, shifting. Hellier stared down his nose at Sammy in a mute demand for silence. When they weren't talking, snatches of conversation from the dining room were quite audible, and, as dinner progressed, increased in volume. The Helliers were apparently discouraging conversation in order to listen.

"Daddy! I don't *want* to go to Radcliffe! I want to go to New York and be an actress! I'm good; I'm really really good and I *know* I can make it!"

"Jess, we've already discussed this."

"Grandma! *You* always said that a woman should be free to pursue her own goals and not be tied down to what a man expects of her!" Jess wailed.

"This is not just any man; it's your father, dear. He wants what's best for you," Mrs. Threlkeld replied.

"Yeah, he dudn't want to see you fall flat on your nose job," Bobby snickered. (Sammy glanced at Marni, observing, "Direct hit.")

"Shut up, pimple king!" Jess shouted. ("Adequate retaliation," Marni countered.)

"Children, are you aware that the staff is tape-recording you from the kitchen?" Stan wondered, and Marni had to clap a hand over her mouth to keep from spewing.

There was a sudden silence in the dining room, then the sound of a chair scraping back. At that, Sammy reached over to take Marni in his arms for a serious kiss. She willingly complied, and that's what Bobby saw when he stuck his head in the kitchen. He went back to report, "Nah, the new guy is just makin' love to the maid at the kitchen table."

Several chairs scraped back. When the eager faces appeared in the doorway, Sammy and Marni looked up innocently from their dinner. "Mr. Threlkeld—?" Marni said, half-rising.

"Nothing, Melody," he said in disgust, punching his snickering son. "Finish your dinner." The Family turned out and Sammy winked at the Helliers. They glanced at each other and then actually cracked smiles.

After dinner, Sammy and Marni were free to retire to their quarters. Marni sat tentatively on the bed, wondering how long it had been since the sheets were last washed. Sammy was examining the doorknob. "No lock," he observed, and she looked at him in disbelief.

He went out to the dining room and brought back a side chair, which he jammed under the doorknob to secure the door shut. Curious, Marni got down on her knees and peered up under the chair to find the manufacturer's label. "Now that's an expensive lock," she nodded, getting up.

"To protect the valuables," he grinned, sitting on the bed and opening his arms. Marni sank into him. He untied her apron, then unzipped her dress. "I love them zippers," he murmured, and she giggled into his lips.

They fell back onto the bed and Marni remembered, "Oh—I've got to tell you what happened before dinner." He drew back with an expression of interest and she quietly related her conversation with Stan Threlkeld.

Sammy's face darkened. He whispered, "He wants to get personal with you, Ma—Melody. You keep your distance and make him do the same."

"Oh. Sure," she said, disappointed. She had been excited over the possibility of finding someone nice in the household. Sammy resumed his husbandly enterprise, and Marni closed her eyes. "Um-hmmm."

Suddenly the doorknob turned and the chair creaked under the pressure from the door. Sammy jerked up and glared back over his shoulder. "Jim!" Jess's voice called impatiently through a quarter-inch crack.

"Just a minute," he said tightly, scrambling for his pants. Marni threw her dress back on over her head.

Zipping his pants and shrugging on his undershirt, Sammy removed the chair and opened the door. Jess looked down at the chair. "Grandma'll have a cow if she sees you using one of her chairs like that," she observed.

"Then perhaps Mrs. Threlkeld will put a lock on the door," he grunted as he bent for his shoes.

"I need you to take me someplace," Jess ordered, tossing her head. Sammy nodded and reached for his coat and hat, meeting Marni's eyes on his way out.

Following Jess out back, Sammy slapped on the hat and strained to button the coat. Glancing back, she observed, "You don't need that," so he left it unbuttoned.

At the garage, Sammy asked, "Which car did you want to take?"

"Tonight, the Rolls," she said meaningfully. He nodded and opened the garage, then assisted her into the back seat.

Sammy sat behind the wheel, started the engine, and carefully backed out of the garage. He drove down the long cobbled drive, then paused at the gate to look for a remote opener. "What's the matter? Go on," she said impatiently.

"Uh, where's the opener?" he asked.

"It's built into the dash, stupid," she said.

He found it, opened the gate, and went on through. Stopping at the street, he looked in the rearview mirror and asked, "Where to?"

"White Rock Lake," she said, smiling. He nodded, reluctantly turning down the street.

As he drove, he heard muffled rustling from the back seat. Guessing what she was doing, he avoided looking in the rearview mirror. *Who would be on duty at White Rock Lake tonight?* he thought. *Man, I hope it's not Shocter. "Shoot-to-kill Shocter."*

He pulled onto the road encompassing the lake. "Anywhere in particular?" he asked without looking in the mirror.

"A nice, quiet, private spot," she said in a low voice.

"I'll try to find one, but this car is going to attract a lot of attention," he warned her. He pulled up to the water in a wide-open space with ample view all the way around. "Here we are," he said cheerfully, cutting the engine.

"Come to the back seat," she purred.

He chewed his lip and turned around. As he had surmised, she sat there without a stitch of clothing on. She smiled seductively and he said, "The water'll be too cold for skinny-dipping tonight. You better wait till May, at least." It was presently mid-March.

"I don't want to go skinny-dipping. Come back here," she said, patting the seat.

He turned to the front and looked at her face in the mirror. "Not a chance, Miss Threlkeld. I'm married, I like being married, and I want to keep my job for more than one day."

Her smile faded. "If you don't, I'll tell Daddy and Grandma that you tried to rape me."

He inhaled. "Well, I guess you'll have to do that, then. I'll deny it, of course, and it would be interesting to see who they believe." She crossed her arms, sullen and humiliated. "If you'll get dressed, we can stay and talk awhile," he offered.

Eyeing him, she reluctantly picked up her jeans from the floor of the car and began putting them on. When she was dressed, he turned back around, took off his hat, and leaned against the car door. "There. I feel more comfortable now," he smiled at her.

She leaned her head on her arms propped on the front seat. "Why are you a chauffeur? You ought to be a doctor, or lawyer, or something," she murmured.

"Oh, I guess I never decided what I wanted to be when I grew up. I always liked cars, though," he said easily.

"Why not a race-car driver?" she asked.

"Takes too much money," he replied.

"I'll fund you!" she said, sitting up.

He laughed. "Your dad and grandma would love that! It's *their* money we're talking about here. I imagine there are other things they'd rather spend it on. Like . . . art."

"Art, schmart," she said in contempt. "Nobody cares anything about art but Uncle Wes, and everybody knows he's a crook."

"That a fact?" he murmured.

"Yeah, he makes these trips to Europe and brings home all this stuff. It's all so shady, so Daddy and Grandma don't want anything to do with him," she said, playing with her hair. Then she reached down and picked up his hand.

"Well, if what he's doing is illegal, why hasn't he been arrested or anything?" Sammy asked, allowing her to hold his hand.

"Are you nuts? Who's going to arrest a Threlkeld? They'd find themselves on the wrong end of a stack of lawyers!" she hooted. Then she leaned very close to peer at his eyes in the dark. "Do you wear mascara?" she demanded.

"No," he smiled tightly. He was up against the door and had no room to maneuver away. She moved in, aiming for his lips.

Suddenly a bright light illumined her face. Jess blinked and put her hand up. Half-turning to the spotlight, Sammy rolled down the window and said, "Good evening, officers. We're fully clothed, sober, and just talking. You can search the car if you like—there's nothing here." He was glad he had just cleaned the Rolls, so he knew that for a fact.

The spotlight swept the interior of the car as the two officers approached. "Let's see an ID, please," one patrolman said.

When Sammy reached into his back pocket for the fake driver's license supplied by the police department, Jess blurted, "You idiots! Back off and leave us alone!"

"Shut up, Jess," Sammy ordered in a low voice.

The patrolman stepped back. "Get out of the car, please" he instructed.

Opening the door, Sammy handed the patrolman his ID. Glancing at his name tag, he said, "Officer Wilson, don't mind Miss Threlkeld. She's had a hard day and she's just letting off steam." He glanced at Wilson's partner, a woman. Sammy did not know either of them.

Jess, however, wanted a fight. She came out of the car swearing a blue streak until Sammy turned and clapped a hand over her mouth. This amused Wilson, who was studying Sammy's driver's license. "Where'd you get this ID?" he snorted.

Sammy loosened his grip on Jess in dismay, and she continued, "You bast—" until Sammy quickly replaced his hand.

"Officer, it's quite genuine. They must've been having trouble with the laminating machine that day," Sammy said, beginning to sweat. On a gamble, he added, "The issuing officer's name was Mike Masterson."

Wilson's eyes shot up, then he exchanged glances with his partner. He handed the ID back to Sammy, saying, "Okay. You'd better take that little girl on home."

"Yes, sir," Sammy said in relief.

Jess, fiercely stung by the policeman's reference to her, spread her feet, threw back her head, and announced, "I'll have you know that I am Jessica Morgan Threlkeld. My grandfather is *the* Morgan Herwald Threlkeld who built half of this city! Who do you little uniforms think you are, to order me around? You're *nothing*. I spend more on makeup than you make in a year! I can have Daddy make *one* phone call and you'll be shoveling crap behind parades for a living!"

She glared supremely, breathing deep, indignant breaths, but the three faces that looked back at her were uniformly stony and unmoved. Then Wilson put his hands on his hips, pursed his lips and said, "Little lady, I don't doubt that at all. But I'd rather be shoveling crap than dishing it out. At least I can hold my head up at the end of the day." He motioned to his partner, and they got back in the patrol car and drove off.

Sammy wordlessly opened the back door for Jess to fling herself onto the seat with disdain. Sammy sat behind the wheel and started the car. As he drove from the lake, he commented, "That was a snotty thing to say, Jess."

"So? It's true," she said defiantly.

"And how much better do you feel for having said it?" he asked. She tossed her head, glaring out the window. He glanced back. "Buckle your seatbelt."

"Stuff it, servant," she sneered.

"Buckle your seatbelt *now,* Jess," he said with authority.

She glared at him. "You can't tell me what to do."

The Rolls lurched to a stop on the shoulder of the road. Sammy got out, opened the back door, and buckled Jess's seatbelt around her hips. Then he reseated himself behind the wheel and turned back onto the street.

Smiling, Jess unbuckled the seatbelt and dangled it so he could see it before she tossed it aside. Sammy stopped the Rolls again, opened the back door and refastened her belt. "If you do that again," he said, "I'm going to spank you."

"Ooh, really?" she breathed in anticipation. But she waited until he had turned the Rolls back into traffic before unfastening the belt again.

Sammy did not do anything right away. He just continued to drive until he found what he was looking for: the entrance to an isolated cul-de-sac of homes under construction. He turned down this deserted street, parked in the cul-de-sac, and turned off the lights.

Opening the back door, he sat and smiled at Jess. She smiled back. The night was dark, the stars were twinkling, and Jess was primed to get what she wanted. He patted his lap, and she willingly draped herself across it. Then he proceeded to spank her with his open hand as hard as he dared. After the first two whacks she was screaming and struggling to get up, but he held her down until he had delivered at least ten smacks.

While she cried in furious disbelief, he sat her up and fastened her seatbelt. "If you unfasten it again, I'll spank you again," he said before closing the door.

When he sat in the front seat, she screamed, "You—idiot! You moron! You're finished! You're fired!"

"When your grandma tells me I'm fired, then I'm fired," he said, starting the car.

"That's assault! I'll have you arrested!" she shouted.

"After what you said to that cop tonight, they'll probably give me a commendation," he noted. *Internal Affairs will crucify me,* he privately reflected.

Jess cried all the way home and Sammy grew miserable over the rash act that would probably end his career. He wasn't her parent and he never should have tried to straighten her out—just do the job he was sent to do. He thought of Marni's humiliation when this would all come out and he almost started to cry himself.

He pulled through the massive iron gates and parked in the garage, then glumly opened the door and offered his hand to Jess. She hesitated, still sniffling, before accepting his help from the car.

He walked her up to the house, where Jess abruptly stopped on the back steps. When he turned toward her, she threw her arms around his middle and pressed her face into his t-shirt. "I love you," she whispered tearily.

Blinking bemusedly, he put his arms around her and laid his cheek on the top of her head. Since he did not know what to say, he felt it unsafe to say anything, so he just held her for a few minutes. Then he drew back and kissed her lightly on the forehead. "See you tomorrow," he whispered.

"Okay, Jim." They went in; she upstairs and he to his quarters.

When he opened the door Marni sat up in bed, drawing the sheet up before seeing that it was Sammy. "What happened?" she asked.

"You won't believe it," he groaned, throwing himself backward onto the bed.

The following morning as they sat at breakfast, Sammy presented Hellier with two requests: spare uniforms for himself and Marni, and a lock for their door. The uniforms were provided immediately; the lock, he said, would have to be approved by Mrs. Threlkeld.

"Fair enough," said Sammy. *I'll just keep using the chair.*

Before Marni took out her never-ending list of chores that morning, she altered Sammy's uniform and cleaned their quarters. That took a while, as the previous tenant(s) had trashed it spitefully. Although she understood why, she wished these people would stop to realize that the bulk of their anger never touched the Threlkelds—it fell on the next unfortunate tenant to clean things up.

Sammy left for a while that morning to pick up some belongings from their apartment and the needed shop manuals. She also bet that he would be visiting with Mike about the incident with the patrol officers last night.

When their quarters were clean enough to be comfortable, Marni turned to the next item on her list: dusting the downstairs study. It was a tedious, time-consuming, sneeze-inducing task that she found particularly irksome. There was also a strong temptation to snoop around the desk and shelves, which Marni wisely resisted. The Threlkelds would certainly leave nothing incriminating lying around for the new maid to find. She remembered a Pink Panther movie in which Inspector Clouseau wreaked havoc snooping around a study, and snickered to herself.

At lunchtime, she looked out back at Sammy bending over the engine of the Jaguar. He couldn't see her from the window, so she went out to get him. When she approached, he straightened and reached for a rag to wipe his hands. "What a car," he muttered.

"Here I am slaving away while you're out here playing with expensive cars," she chided, leaning over to kiss him.

"Umm," he responded. "Yeah, it's fun until I put something in backwards and blow up eighty thousand dollars' worth of import."

"Come eat," she laughed, tugging at his arm. He shut the hood and she added, "Mrs. Hellier is going to let us have the crêpes from breakfast with the cream cheese filling."

He glanced at her. "Marni, could I get you to just make me a sandwich?"

She glanced back. "Melody. Sure, Jim."

He winced and hit his forehead, leaving a black streak. "Melody, Melody, Melody," he whispered.

They went up the steps to the house. "Be sure to wash your face, Jim," she added carefully.

About the time he sat down to the double-decker Marni had fixed for him, Jess, freshly made up, stuck her head in the kitchen. Seeing Sammy, she came up behind him to put her arms around his neck and kiss him on the cheek. Mrs. Hellier's narrow eyes widened. "Good morning, Miss Threlkeld," Sammy said without looking up.

"Good afternoon, Jim, darling," Jess breathed, holding on to his neck. Sammy did not let that prevent him from taking a large bite of sandwich. Marni, unfazed, cut into her crêpe. "I'm in love with your husband," Jess informed Marni.

"Everybody is," Marni smiled with the slightest condescension.

Jess raised up, eyeing her rival. "Do you know that he spanked me last night?"

"Yes. I'll bet it hurt," Marni noted.

Jess looked astonished that he would tell his wife about it, then cracked, "Like hell!"

Marni laughed and Sammy smiled. Pleased with herself, Jess tossed her head and drew back a chair. "I'm eating right here, Mary," she told the cook.

Mrs. Hellier turned hesitantly. "Miss Threlkeld, Mrs. Threlkeld expects you to lunch with her on the north veranda."

"Tough beans," Jess snapped, scooting up next to Sammy.

"Go eat with your grandma, Jess," Sammy said quietly. "I have to go back out in a minute, anyway."

"Oh. . . ." She leaned on his arm in disappointment, then sighed, "Okay. See you later." She kissed him on the temple and turned out of the kitchen.

Mary stared after her with a chopping knife poised over the cutting board. Then she shifted her round body to look at Sammy. "Did you really spank her?" she whispered.

"Hard," Sammy replied wryly.

"Goodness gracious," Mary gasped, turning back to the board. Then in a hard voice: "She needed it."

three

One of Marni's chores that afternoon was delivering freshly laundered clothes to the Family's bedrooms. She knocked and listened carefully at each door before going in. Jess's room was being cleaned by another maid as Marni brought in her laundry. While she put the items up, she glanced at the antiques, the recessed ceiling with its chandelier, the balcony looking toward downtown Dallas. Then she went downstairs for another batch.

As she came to the stairs with Mr. Threlkeld's underwear, the front door opened and in he came with Bobby. Marni tried not to listen, but it was clear that Stan had picked Bobby up from school after some incident in which the boy was a key player. They started up the stairs behind her. Marni self-consciously kept her eyes on her feet, aware that they had stopped talking on the stairs.

She turned off the stairs toward Mr. Threlkeld's room and went on in. It was a cavernous, gorgeously decorated room, but without a hint of a Mrs. Threlkeld. Marni pulled out a bureau drawer and placed underwear in it (red-faced) as Stan entered and shut the door behind him. "Good afternoon, Melody. How are you today?" he said pleasantly, shrugging off his coat.

"Fine, thank you," she murmured, turning to his vast closet to hang up several freshly ironed shirts.

She turned back to find him eyeing her critically. "That uniform looks just awful. I'm going to tell Audrey to get you something more flattering," he said.

Visions of the dreaded French maid outfit flashed across her mind. "Actually, I don't mind it at all. It's comfortable, and I'd hate to get something nicer all dirty," she assured him.

He smiled approvingly at her. "How old are you, Melody?"

"Twenty-one, Mr. Threlkeld," she replied.

"And how long have you been married?" he asked.

"Since last October," she said, glancing down.

"Aw, you're still newlyweds," he teased. Nodding shyly, she prepared to move around him to get to the door beyond. "Come here, Melody," he said suddenly. "I'd like your help with something." Marni stiffened as he disappeared into his dressing area. "Melody?"

Mentally, she shed the maid's uniform and put on riot gear. She went to the door and said, "What is it, Mr. Threlkeld?"

He was pawing through his closet. "What size shirt does your husband wear?"

"Uh—sixteen and a half, thirty-four, I believe," she said, caught by surprise.

"Yeah? How tall is he?" he asked, pulling out shirts.

"Um, five-eleven."

"What size pants?" he asked, looking through some suits.

"I—don't remember, Mr. Threlkeld. He buys his own clothes. Why?" she asked.

"Oh, I just remember what it was like starting out as a newlywed with nothing to my name. I've got a lot of clothes here I never wear, and I'd like your husband to have them," he said, carrying an armload to the bed.

Marni slowly turned. "Mr. Threlkeld, I can hardly imagine you starting out with nothing to your name."

He smiled sideways at her. "You can't, eh? Then you haven't been reading your Threlkeld Family History. Stan Threlkeld, the black sheep of the family, who defied his parents and got kicked off the dole." He took his eyes off her to view something in the past. "Stan the Wimp, who came crawling back busted and broken," he said softly. "Oh, yes. I know what it's like to live on nothing but love. I want your husband to have these—they should fit. If they don't, they're worth getting altered."

Marni didn't doubt it, seeing the $500 shirt sitting on top of the pile. "I—couldn't, Mr. Threlkeld. Thank you, but—"

"Don't worry, I'll make sure the Dragon Lady knows you didn't steal them. Come on—I'll help you carry them down." He scooped up the pile and Marni followed him, picking up the things that he dropped.

He carried them to her room while other staff peeked around corners. Marni opened the door and he laid them on her bed. As he went out, she murmured, "Mr. Threlkeld, I . . . don't know what to say. Thank you."

He stood looking at her, and there was something sharp in his eyes. Then he nodded and turned away.

"Young man!" Sammy raised up so quickly at the barked command that he banged his head on the underside of the Jaguar's hood.

"Yes, Mrs. Threlkeld?" he said, rubbing his head.

"I expect *never* to have to come get you like this again. I am due for tea at three o'clock at Lady Primrose's. You will clean and dress yourself immediately and bring the Rolls around front," she declared, affronted.

"Yes, Mrs. Threlkeld," he said, hastily slamming the hood. She stalked back into the house through the sunroom while he ran to the back door of the kitchen. "Where is Lady Primrose's?" he muttered. "*What* is Lady Primrose's?"

Darting into his quarters, he drew up in surprise at the pile of men's clothes on his bed. He looked over them, scowling. *Expensive* men's clothes, which could have come from only one person. Leaving them for now, he washed his face and hands and donned the rest of the uniform.

Dashing back to the kitchen, he looked around for Mary, or Marni, or Hellier, or anyone who could tell him where the heck Lady Primrose's was. The only person he saw was Bobby, coming sullenly down the stairs. "Hey, pal, can you tell me where Lady Primrose's is?" Sammy asked.

He looked up and smiled. "Sure. It's in the Hotel Inter-continental."

"Right. Thanks," Sammy said, heading out back for the Rolls. On the way, however, he slowed and stopped. Something about Bobby's devilish smile gave him pause. He returned to the house to find out for sure—better to be a few minutes late than to drive Mrs. Threlkeld clear across town from where she was supposed to be.

He saw Mary enter the kitchen, and followed her. "Mrs. Hellier, where is Lady Primrose's?"

Mary looked up at the clock and gasped. "Oh! I forgot to tell you! Mrs. Threlkeld has tea there every Tuesday at three."

"Where is it?" he asked patiently.

"It's in the Crescent. You'd better hurry—she hates to be late."

"Right," Sammy muttered, trotting out again. "Kid, I'm gonna wring your adolescent neck," he warned the unseen Bobby.

Sammy brought the Rolls around front and retrieved a bristling Mrs. Threlkeld from the foyer. He assisted her into the car and headed out the drive. Actually, he was glad for the little excursion to the lake last night, as it gave him the neces-sary practice with the gearshift to drive more smoothly today. That was important—this lady made him sweat.

He pulled into the parking lot of the Crescent at straight-up three o'clock. As he approached the awning-shaded entrance, he glanced in the rearview mirror to ask, "Would you like me to stay with the car or accompany you in, Mrs. Threlkeld?"

Now, had he been a real chauffeur, he would have known better than to ask such a presumptuous question. But Mrs. Threlkeld paused. "You may assist me in," she said stiffly. "I have arthritic knees."

Sammy nodded and tossed the key to the valet. He sprang around the car and stiff-armed the doorman before he could open the car door. Sammy gave his hand to Mrs. Threlkeld, then unconsciously put her hand on his arm as if she were a date. It was inappropriate for a hireling, but Mrs. Threlkeld said nothing. Under her direction, he escorted her up the elevator to the antique shop that housed the little restaurant. Sammy then turned her over to her friends and went outside the shop to wait, watching the door.

He had only been in the restaurant a few moments helping Mrs. Threlkeld get comfortably settled, but it was time enough for everyone there to notice her handsome new chauffeur. Sammy's ears should have been aflame as he leaned against the wall outside, for all the comments about him that were making the rounds inside.

"Dolly, he had his hands all over you!" one plastic-skinned matron exclaimed, patting her for emphasis.

Mrs. Threlkeld pooh-poohed it. "He's young and green. He'll learn not to do that—if he lasts," she said grimly.

"If you fire him, be sure to give him my address," another old dear giggled. Several ladies involuntarily glanced out the door, and Mrs. Threlkeld then determined that none of them should have him.

Sitting on a bench, with his hands clasped and his elbows resting on his spread knees, Sammy idly watched the owner of the restaurant come out with a plate of cake and cup of tea. She spotted him, and came over smiling. "Mrs. Threlkeld wanted you to have some refreshments while you were waiting."

"Me?" he said incredulously. Then he recovered, "Uh, thank her very much for me." He eagerly took the cake and tea, wolfing them down.

The woman returned shortly for the dishes, then Sammy was left to wait some more. To pass the time, he idly calculated how long it would take him to make enough on $375 a week to buy anything showcased in the antique shop's window, assuming his entire gross half of the salary went toward the purchase. His calculations left him to conclude that the rest of his life could be spent earning one feather fan. When he tired of that exercise, he watched aristocrats come and go from the expensive shops. During the next hour and a half he observed one pickpocket and two shoplifters, but could say nothing for fear of blowing his cover.

Shortly before five o'clock, ladies began emerging from the antique shop, so Sammy went to the door to wait. When Mrs. Threlkeld appeared, he offered his arm, smiling.

Supremely conscious of her friends' envious faces, she casually took his arm and bid them goodbye. "Thank you for the cake," he leaned down to whisper to her, and her friends poked each other. Mrs. Threlkeld pursed her lips. On their way to the exit, she could not help but notice—and enjoy—the glances from much younger women.

When the valet brought the car around, Sammy himself seated her. Then he touched his hat to her and started off. She eyed him in slight disapproval—he wore his hat too far back on his head, detracting from the solemnity of his uniform. Little did she know that Officer Kidman had drawn that very criticism countless times.

As he was proceeding through a green light, a speeding car suddenly came barreling through the intersection against the red. Sammy saw it coming out of the corner of his eye and instinctively slammed on the brakes and spun the wheel. He managed to turn the Rolls enough for the speeding car to miss them by inches. A police car pursued with sirens and lights.

Sammy twisted to look at his passenger. "Are you hurt? Mrs. Threlkeld!" Dazed, she shook her head.

Urgently, he pulled the car into a parking lot, jumped out and wrenched open the back door. Placing both hands on her neck, he asked, "Does that hurt? Does your neck hurt?"

"Take your hands off me!" she demanded.

He reseated himself behind the wheel. "I'm going to take you to Baylor to get that x-rayed. Who's your doctor?"

She sputtered, "You will do no such thing! I'm not hurt! Now stop treating me like a china doll!"

He looked back, smiling. "But you *are* a doll."

She was momentarily shocked into speechlessness, then began, "Of all the forward, impudent, brash—! First you put me on your arm like a trollop, then you paw me in the restaurant, and then order me to the hospital—"

"You're wonderful," he grinned over the seat. "You're the only woman alive besides my wife who could make me sweat, and if I were ever in bad trouble, you two are the only women I'd care to know about it."

Mrs. Threlkeld's whole being seemed to melt. She had absolutely nothing to say for thirty seconds, then Sammy added, "If you're sure you're all right, I'll take you on home. But if your neck gets to hurting I'll have to bring you back up to get it x-rayed."

"That will be satisfactory," she said, attempting to reinsert some sternness in her voice.

"It's a deal, then," he replied, starting the car.

He drove home watchfully, then pulled up to the front of the mansion to help her up the massive front steps. She had so much difficulty mounting them that he finally just lifted her over the last three steps. As he opened the door and relinquished her hand, she looked back to say civilly, "Thank you, Jim."

"Any time, Mrs. Threlkeld," he grinned.

He drove on back to the garage and came out whistling. Then he stopped. Bobby was on the back lawn, playing with a model airplane. When he saw Sammy, he threw down the control and ran for the house.

But he wasn't fast enough. Sammy caught him before he got to the back steps and lifted him bodily. "*Aayiah!* What're you doing? Let me go! I'll tell Dad! I'll tell Grandma!" Bobby shouted, kicking and struggling.

Sammy lugged him to the edge of the pool, sparkling in the sunny March afternoon. "Here, pal—cool off in the Hotel Intercontinental!" Sammy grunted. He hoisted him up and threw him six feet over the water.

"*AAYIAH!*" Big splash. Sammy watched him thrash and sputter (to make sure he could swim), and then sauntered toward the house as Bobby pulled himself up on the edge of the pool.

The gardener watched with sidelong glimpses. "He needed me to do that," Sammy explained on his way in, and when he looked back, he saw the gardener's shoulders shaking.

Sammy went to his quarters and threw off his coat and hat, eyeing the clothes on the bed. Then he went back out to see if he could figure out why the Jaguar wasn't purring the way it should.

He worked over the engine until his back hurt and it got too dark to see well. He glanced at his watch: it was 7:20, and Marni had not come out for him. Sammy closed up the car and went in to wash his hands.

When he came into the kitchen freshly washed, Mary looked up from the stove. "I suppose you'll be wanting something to eat," she said grumpily.

"Sure, if you have anything handy," he said, glancing around. No Marni. "Uh, where's Melody?"

"I don't know. I haven't seen her all day," Mary replied.

Hellier, sitting down, said, "I believe she is upstairs with Mr. Threlkeld."

Sammy eyed him. "Isn't he coming down to eat?"

"When he's ready, I assume he will," Hellier said lightly.

Sammy sat with the plate Mary handed him. He put an elbow on the table, rubbed his eyes, and just sat waiting for a few minutes. Then he reluctantly picked up his fork and began to eat.

Marni sat in a lavishly embroidered armchair watching Stan Threlkeld pace the room. "She was much like you—beautiful, of course, with a certain streak of willfulness. She went after what she wanted until she got it. And—for a while—she wanted me." He paused, leaning both hands against the window casing to look out over the flat green terrain.

"She and Mother never got along—they were too much alike. And I suppose there was the mother's reluctance to give up her son's affections to another woman. Anyway, when I told her my intentions to marry Linda, Mother simply informed me that to do so would mean cutting myself out of the Family. I accepted that proviso."

"What did your father say?" Marni asked quietly.

"Dad," he said, smiling wryly, "knows enough not to challenge the power behind the throne. What she says goes. Then and always."

Marni looked down and he continued, "Linda and I were very young and very naïve. We had two babies right away—Jessica and Robert—and I earned barely enough in commissions to feed us. Still, I think we could have made it, but for the little salvos Mother tossed our way—hints about the position I could have in the Threlkeld empire, updates on how very well my older brother Wes was doing—all I needed to do was abandon my wife and bring my children home. Mother had no problems accepting Jess and Bobby, by the way. You would think they were hers.

"Well, I wouldn't consider it, but these little tricks of Mother's drove Linda crazy. She began to doubt my love, and whether we should have ever gotten married. She saw friends of my parents everywhere, and they all treated her like a leper. I realize now that we should have pulled up stakes and moved as far away from Dallas as we could get, but—you know what they say about hindsight.

"Then one day Linda just disappeared. It took me two months to find her, and by that time she had filed for divorce. I should have fought it—done whatever was necessary to keep her—but I guess Mother's manipulations had affected me more than I realized. I caved in, and . . . I haven't seen Linda for almost ten years now." He finished his story and Marni was silent.

"So. . . ." He turned to her with a forced smile. "I guess that's why I wish the best for you and your husband—" There was a knock on the door. "Yes?" he called.

"Mr. Threlkeld, Mrs. Threlkeld wonders when you're coming down for dinner," Hellier said through the door.

"I'll be right down," he sighed. "Capitulating again," he shrugged to her.

"I need to get down as well," she said, rising. "Thank you again for the clothes, Mr. Threlkeld."

"You're welcome, Melody." He opened the door, and Marni made a point to hasten her step so they would not seem to be coming down the stairs together.

When Marni got to the kitchen, Sammy was gone. "Your husband ate and left already," Mary told her. Marni nodded, disturbed, as she pulled out some leftovers and ate them cold.

Mary did not bother to tell her that she had fed Sammy the same *osso buco* that the Family ate that night.

After a hasty dinner, Marni hurried to her quarters and opened the door. Sammy was sitting on the bed, listlessly watching a small television. He looked up with slightly reproachful eyes and her heart sank to think he was angry. But he clicked off the TV and held out his arms. Marni lowered herself down to him and he eased back on the bed. After greeting her with a deep kiss, he nodded toward the clothes piled on the end of the bed: "What gives?"

"Mr. Threlkeld wanted you to have them. He said he knew what it was like to be newlywed, living on love," Marni said, holding her hair back so it would not dangle in his face.

Sammy's chin came up in a knowing appraisal. "He's trying to make you feel indebted to him, to reduce your resistance. Jerk."

"Should I give them back?" she asked.

He thought about that. "No; that would just make him mad. Where were you at dinner?"

She groaned slightly and rolled off him to lie beside him. "In his *room,* hearing the sad story of his divorce," she said dramatically.

"Let me guess: his wife didn't understand him," Sammy said sarcastically. "He's fast, isn't he?"

"I don't know," Marni sighed. "He didn't say or do anything suggestive, except—"

"Except what?" Sammy asked quickly.

"He wanted Audrey to get me a nicer uniform," she mentioned.

"I'll bet," he snorted.

"Oh, I don't know. Now that I think about it, I really don't think he meant anything by it. Oh, I don't know what to think," she admitted.

"Want to know what I think?" he asked, leaning over her. "I think you'd look really hot in a short black skirt and fishnet hose."

"Sam—!" He cut her off before she could blurt out his name and Marni laughed deep in her throat, caressing his muscled shoulders.

"So," he grinned, "ask me how my day went."

"What happened?" she asked, lifting up slightly.

In a whisper, he told her about driving Mrs. Threlkeld to Lady Primrose's. Marni listened quietly until he related the part about Bobby's unscheduled swim, then she gasped, "You didn't! Jim, you're going to get us fired!"

"Nah," he said, "if Jess didn't tell anybody about the spanking, then I don't need to worry—"

There was a pounding on the door. Sammy looked up quickly, having neglected to put the chair in place. "What?" he called.

"Jim, come out here!" Jess called authoritatively, without trying to open the door.

He opened the door in his t-shirt, then glanced up warily at the group of young people clustered around her. "Jim, I want you to meet my friends. This is Taylor, and Jeff, and Heather, Chynna, Kristi, Alex, and Raul. Jim is the chauffeur that spanked me," she said breathlessly.

Sammy looked at her in dismay. "Miss Threlkeld, why do you say things like that? You're going to get me fired."

The kids turned on Jess with cynical faces. "Aw, there you go again," one guy muttered.

"He did! Really hard!" she exclaimed.

"Miss Threlkeld, I need this job. Please don't make trouble for me," Sammy said with convincing humility. Blonde Kristi eyed him with a knowing smile, and he steadfastly kept his eyes off her to avoid giving himself away.

"Let's go," Raul said, and the others accompanied him.

Jess looked at Sammy in disappointment, and he returned the look with stern lips and smiling eyes. Then she turned after her friends, along with the perceptive blonde.

Sammy shut the door and lay back down on the bed. Marni, tired, began to get undressed, but he forestalled her. "Wait awhile," he whispered. So she lay on his shoulder and stroked his solid chest. He seemed to be waiting, listening. He waited so long that Marni drifted to sleep.

Some time later he woke her with a nice firm kiss. "Um-hmm," she murmured.

"Time to get up," he whispered.

"Uh?" she said, looking out the window. It was dark outside.

"We're gonna do some poking around, just to see what we find," he whispered, noiselessly opening the door. "Have you got some soft shoes? Those are good. Okay, come on."

four

Heart hammering, Marni followed Sammy out into the darkened hallway off the kitchen. "Where are we going to look?" she whispered.

"Wherever they would keep anything of a personal or business nature," he murmured. "You're more familiar with the house. Other than the bedrooms, what looks likely?"

"Well, there's a study off the foyer," she mused. "But I can't imagine them keeping anything important in there, can you?"

"Doesn't hurt to look," he shrugged. They went out into the grand, echoing foyer and paused. Marni pressed closer to Sammy. In the darkness and stillness, the foyer was spooky. An inexplicable cold draft moved around their feet.

Sammy was looking up the stairs. "Jess is still entertaining her friends," he noted.

"Shouldn't we go back to our room, then?" she asked a little anxiously.

"No," he said, without bothering to whisper. "So where's the study?"

She pointed it out and they approached its closed door. Sammy looked underneath the door to make sure the room was unoccupied before he cracked open the door and peeked in. They slipped inside and he closed the door behind them. This made the room very dark, but Sammy had come prepared with a couple of pencil flashlights. He handed one to her, whispering, "Check out the bookshelves. Look for papers hidden in books, or hollowed-out books." She nodded, turning to start with a shelf at eye level as Sammy sat at the desk.

Holding the flashlight in his mouth, he opened the top desk drawer and began quietly rummaging. He pulled out a paper, perused it, then turned to whisper, "Bobby's flunking algebra at St. Mark's."

"That figures," she whispered back. They continued looking. Suddenly Marni said, "Oh-oh."

"What?" he turned. She brought him an open book. The middle of the pages had been cut out, and nestled inside was a plastic bag of marijuana and rolling papers. "Yeah," he said despondently. "Well—put it back, and keep looking."

Before replacing the ruined book, Marni looked at the title page. It was a first-edition copy of *The Good Earth* by Pearl S. Buck. "What a waste!" she mourned.

They continued browsing. "Mrs. Threlkeld is a member of First Metropolitan Church," he noted.

"You're kidding," Marni said over her shoulder.

"No, really. And she's been considering making a substantial gift to the church," he said, holding a letter.

Marni paused. "To salve her conscience?"

He stuffed the correspondence back into the desk, smiling slightly. "I think the ol' warhorse has got a good heart under all that armor," he said. Marni glanced over skeptically.

Sammy's penlight was now bouncing under the chair, under the desk, under the edge of the Oriental carpet. He found what he was looking for—the key to a locked drawer—and as he started to open it, he spun and hissed, "Someone's coming!"

They clicked off their lights; Sammy dove under the desk and Marni fell behind a wingback chair. The door to the study opened and the light came on. Jess ran in and went straight for the bookshelves. Sammy scrunched himself under the desk as compactly as possible. Jess pulled down *The Good Earth* and removed its hidden stash, then selected another book and took something out of it. Skipping out, she slapped off the light but did not close the door.

Sammy waited until her footsteps completely died away; Marni remained paralyzed. She heard him shuffle, then whisper, "Marni."

"Melody," she whispered back.

"Whoever," he breathed impatiently. "I'm stuck."

Choking back a laugh, she got up from behind the chair and went over to scrutinize him curled up under the desk. "Shut the door, first," he said.

"Yeah, we don't want anybody to see *this,* Inspector Clouseau," she snickered.

"Ha, ha," he said dryly as she peeked out the door and gently shut it.

She came back over to the desk and leaned on it casually. "What can I do for you, dear?" she asked, shining down the slender light at him.

"Nice legs. Just hold the desk down so it doesn't tip over while I get out," he grunted, shifting.

Marni hopped up and sat on the desk. It raised up slightly as Sammy squirmed out, rubbing his shoulder. "Okay," he said, retrieving the key to the drawer. "Get back to work."

As she turned around to the bookshelves, he added, "By the way, if you ever feel tempted to tell Mike or Pruett about this, just remember: I spank hard."

Chuckling, she began going through the books, and Sammy opened the drawer.

They searched in earnest quiet for a while. Marni found the other book Jess had pulled, but it was now empty. She went over the shelves mechanically, glancing back at Sammy at the desk. His penlight was still, trained on a paper.

"Find something?" she whispered.

"I don't know," he stirred. "Come look at this."

She came to the desk, shading her light from the uncovered floor-to-ceiling window a few feet away. She saw out the window one of the several Dobermans that were let loose to roam the grounds at night. "What is it?" she asked, bending at Sammy's side.

"An invoice for a painting that Stanley bought—*The Elder Sister* by W. Bouguereau," he said, stumbling over the name. "It came from a New York gallery and cost him half a mil."

"Wow," Marni breathed. "He paid a lot, but—is that suspicious?"

"No, not in itself," he murmured, folding it and stuffing it in his pocket. "We'll have Mike check it out, then we'll put the receipt back. I wonder . . ." he mused, "why he just stuck it in a drawer like that."

"Well, it *was* locked," she chided.

"Yeah, with the key taped under the desk," he said scornfully.

They looked around a while longer, but did not find anything else promising. So they left the study and headed back toward their quarters. Sammy paused at the foot of the broad, curving stairway, looking up pensively. "Which is Jess's room?" he asked.

"Third door on your right. Why? What are you thinking?" Marni asked with a touch of apprehension.

"Nothing," he shook his head resolutely, and they went on. "It's none of my business," he argued with himself. "I'm not her father, and I'm not responsible for what goes on in this house." Marni agreed with him wholeheartedly, but he had more trouble convincing himself.

At the door of their room he stopped, and she knew he had lost this particular argument with himself. "You go in, and . . . I'll be back in a minute," he murmured.

"Don't get caught," she said half-seriously. She couldn't help but admire the internal consistency that drove him. He would always be a cop, regardless.

After dropping Marni off, Sammy returned to the foot of the stairs and leaned against the balustrade, thinking. His eye fell on the telephone on the small table beside him. Contemplatively, he picked it up to hear the dial tone. Then he smiled and started up the stairs.

He stopped at Jess's door and knocked. There was a sudden quiet within, then Jess shouted, "Who is it?"

"Jim," he replied softly.

She opened the door with a pleased, curious expression, weaving slightly so that she had to lean on the frame for support. "Whaddya want?"

Sammy did not look at the bodies draped across furniture behind her, or take note of the heavy aroma of marijuana. "I'm sorry, Miss Threlkeld; it was not my intention to eavesdrop, but I was lying awake worrying about the Jaguar, so I thought I'd call a friend of mine who works at this all-night gas station—"

"What *is* it, Jim?" she repeated impatiently, blinking several times.

"I heard somebody on the phone talking to the police. They're sending out a car—" he was cut off as Jess slammed the door in his face and started screaming to her friends. Putting his ear to the door, Sammy heard general bedlam and flushing toilets. Grinning, he turned back down the hall.

On his way down the stairs, he was passed by teenagers flying at a high rate of speed. They zoomed down the stairs and out the front door. Sammy paused, then returned to Jess's door. He gave her twenty seconds before knocking.

"Who is it?" she called fearfully.

"Jim," he said. She opened the door immediately, wearing a modest nightgown. "I hope I haven't caused any trouble—" he began.

She held up her hand in a mature manner. "No, Jim. None at all. Don't worry about it. I'm going to bed now. I'm very tired. Goodnight."

"Goodnight, Jess," he smiled as she shut the door.

Sammy had several errands to run the next morning, *after* checking with Mary to make sure Mrs. Threlkeld had no standing appointments that required his services. First he took the Jaguar to Gordon, the police mechanic, to drool over. "Why doncha see if you can get it tuned up for me?" Sammy asked. "I can't seem to find the problem."

"Sammy, this is a finely balanced piece of engineering which you gotta keep your ignorant, untrained fingers out of," Gordon lectured severely. "Now leave me alone with it for a coupla hours."

"You were made for each other," Sammy grinned.

He then went upstairs to brief Mike. Sticking his head in Mike's office, he greeted him with, "Hello, coward."

"Yeah?" Mike said, looking up from mounds of paperwork in front of him. "How's that?"

"Just wondering when all you brass are going to find the backbone to stand up to these special interests that want to run the department," Sammy said, flopping into a chair beside the desk.

"You're trying my patience, Kidman," Mike said ominously. "Have you got anything *substantial* to report?"

"You can have someone check out this painting," Sammy said, drawing the invoice from his pocket and tossing it on Mike's desk. "But I doubt it'll amount to anything. The receipt was illegally obtained, by the way. I took it from a locked desk."

"Great, Sammy, that helps a lot. Why don't we just send a bunch of Republicans to break into the house?" Mike said sarcastically.

"That would make as much sense as what I'm doing," Sammy grumbled, then sat up. "There's nothing, Mike. The Threlkelds have a lot of money to burn and the usual family secrets, but nothing we could hang an indictment on."

Mike looked up from the invoice. "You're not letting your personal feelings get in the way of an investigation, are you, Sambo?"

"Why shouldn't I?" Sammy asked brazenly. "What if your gut feeling tells you these people ought to be left alone?"

Mike blinked at him. "I never thought I'd hear that from you, Sammy. Any other cop might be tempted by that much money, but you—"

Sammy bolted up in the chair. "That stinks, Mike! I haven't been offered a dime!"

Mike coolly replied, "There's just one way to prove it. You have to follow through with it. If they're clean, you have nothing to worry about."

Sammy got up and went to the door. Looking back resentfully, he said, "I'll be back for the invoice. I have to return it." Tight-lipped, he left.

Mike stroked his creased forehead, muttering, "Sorry I had to do that, Sambo." Then he squinted at the invoice and picked up the telephone.

Audrey, cool and chic, entered the downstairs gameroom where Marni was vacuuming. "Melody," she said, but Marni did not hear her. "Melody! MELODY!"

Marni startled and turned off the vacuum cleaner. "Yes, Mrs. Cox?"

Audrey thrust a black garment at Marni. "Mr. Threlkeld instructed for you to be given a new uniform. I will have—

additional ones for you as soon as I can locate more." She looked none too thrilled about it.

Marni held up the long-sleeved sheath dress. "I can't do housework in this," she observed, glancing at Audrey.

"Mr. Threlkeld," she said tightly, "also decided that you should be given a new set of responsibilities." Audrey handed her a short list.

Marni looked at the list. "'Interface with staff'?" she read, looking up incredulously. "'Facilitate communication'? What does that mean?"

"That means," Audrey said, "that you're to be available to do whatever Mr. Threlkeld wants." Marni eyed her uneasily and Audrey turned with perfect poise to leave.

Audrey then went directly upstairs to confer with Mrs. Threlkeld on plans for a party Friday night. After covering the food list from the caterer and the seating requirements for the orchestra, Audrey casually mentioned, "Mr. Threlkeld seems vastly impressed with the latent abilities of the new maid. He has taken her off housework and given her a much less specific set of duties."

"The new maid? Jim's wife?" Mrs. Threlkeld asked.

"Yes. If you ask *me,* she hardly seems to have merited such a leap after two days," Audrey noted. Mrs. Threlkeld was silent. Desiring to press the point, Audrey added, "It certainly seems that we need her services as a maid more than anything else right now, especially with this function coming up—"

"Adequate staffing is *your* responsibility," Mrs. Threlkeld snapped. "If you have to hire additional help for Friday night, do it and don't bother me about it!"

In her room, Marni shucked off the maid's uniform and slipped on the black dress. It was certainly more form-fitting—nothing like a uniform at all. Marni turned to look at the back in the mirror, then bent to search the small closet for shoes. All she had that remotely matched was a pair of flats, which Marni decided were preferable to heels, anyway.

Carrying her list of new responsibilities, she went to the rear of the house to look for Sammy, but he was not back yet. Mr. Threlkeld was at his office downtown, of course. Marni decided that her sudden elevation gave her the right to free movement in the house, so she began to have a look around.

She stayed away from the bedrooms, which she had already seen, and from areas where other staff were at work. If someone was in a room that she entered, she just asked, "Do you know where Mrs. Cox is?" They usually didn't, so she left.

The house was extremely large and fantastically appointed: Priceless carpets on the floors and museum-quality furnishings in every room. Masterpieces hanging on every wall. But for all that, or maybe because of all that, there was a certain desolate air that pervaded the house. No one looked at the paintings but to dust the frames. No one gave a second thought to the skill and toil that went into the rugs they continually walked over.

But Marni regarded it all. She touched the finely carved wood and opened hundred-and-fifty-year-old books. She caressed the dusty silk draperies and fingered the elaborate needlework covering the seat of a Chippendale chair. There were twenty-three other chairs just like it.

Wandering through the great house, she took particular note of the paintings. They were all originals, of course, and standing so close before such great works made her hold her breath. They were far larger than she imagined, from seeing tiny pictures in art books or encyclopedias. And she was staggered by the range—Monet, Boccioni, Goya, Degas, Matisse, Picasso, Masson, Pollack—nothing was out of the Family's means or interest.

And yet, as little as Marni knew about art, she realized that these acquisitions did not reflect a *serious* collector. They were certainly famous works, but there was no theme, no focus for the collection. It was an expensive hodge-podge.

Staring intently at the surrealist *Divisibility Undefined* by Yves Tanguy, Marni wondered, who bought all these? Jess had told Sammy that nobody in the family had any interest in art but the shady Uncle Wes. But it was Stan's signature on the invoice for *The Elder Sister.*

Marni moved on down the hall, and suddenly stopped at a stunning full-length portrait of a teenaged girl, barefoot, holding a younger girl in her arms. The realistic expression of tenderness, the large, dark eyes of the pair—before she ever looked for a signature, Marni knew that she had encountered *The Elder Sister.* A glance at the bottom right-hand corner of the canvas confirmed it: in large letters was "W. BOVGVEREAV-1879."

Marni hurried downstairs to look for Sammy out back, but he was not there.

Sammy was in the police department garage, receiving the keys to the Jaguar from Gordon. "Somebody's been driving the dog-fool out of this car," Gordon said accusingly.

Sammy nodded. "I'm sure they have, and they'll continue to, until next year when they buy a new one."

Another officer leaned out of a cubicle. "Kidman! Mike wants you in his office," he called, hanging up the telephone.

Sammy went back upstairs and opened Mike's door. "Yeah?"

"It checks out okay," Mike said, holding up the invoice, which Sammy took. "Except: the gallery it came from, Hastings, has also been targeted by Mutual Life."

"Well, that makes sense," Sammy said agreeably. "The Threlkelds are under suspicion because they associate with Hastings. Hastings's under suspicion because they do business with the Threlkelds. Perfectly logical."

Mike eyed Sammy, then got up from behind his desk and shut the door. "Sammy, there's a reason I picked you for this assignment, and that is—I feel the same about it as you. I don't like Foster and I don't agree with his methods. But we're stuck with this job, uncomfortable as it makes us. If anybody could dig out the truth without compromising himself or the department, I knew it would be you."

Sammy looked down at the invoice in his hands. "Okay, Mike," he said quietly, and opened the door to leave.

Driving back to the Threlkelds', Sammy was so gratified by the smooth, powerful purring of the Jaguar's engine that he momentarily considering hiding the keys. He garaged it, then turned his attention to the Maserati.

He had not been back five minutes when Mary leaned her head out of the rear kitchen door and shouted, "Jim! Mrs. Threlkeld wants to see you right away!"

As he trotted up to the kitchen, he caught a movement from the corner of his eye. "Oh, no. That wouldn't be—?" But it was. Bobby came roaring from the garage in the Jaguar amidst the gnashing of gears being stripped. "Wait, kid! *Wait!*" Sammy shouted in pursuit, but Bobby disappeared in a cloud of exhaust. In a fit of disgust, Sammy yanked off his hat and threw it to the ground.

Then he hung his head in resignation and collected his hat. Returning to the kitchen, he asked Mary, "Where was I supposed to meet Mrs. Threlkeld?"

"In her room—second floor, last room to the right," Mary said, eyeing him and his hat.

Sammy retrieved his coat from his room and whipped it on as he trotted up the stairs. On his way up, he met Jess coming down. "Good afternoon, Jim," she said with bloodshot eyes.

"Jess," he nodded, repressing a grin.

"Oh—Jim," she said in studied casualness, "I just wanted you to know that I certainly have no concerns about the police coming to our house or what they would possibly find here—it's just that my father has made some irrational statements about what he would do if I did not conform to certain restrictive rules he has put on me, and—did they ever come last night?" she asked in a whisper.

"Not that I know of. I went back to my room and went to sleep," Sammy said in all honesty.

"Well, anyway—thank you for coming to tell me. I would appreciate it if you would do that whenever you hear anything else that you think may be of interest to me," she said in an artificial voice. Discreetly, she held out a folded hundred-dollar bill.

Sammy looked up from the bill with ice-blue eyes. "I do what I think is right, Jess," he said, bypassing her outstretched hand on his way to Mrs. Threlkeld's room.

five

"Come in," Mrs. Threlkeld said in response to Sammy's knock. When he opened the door, she looked up from an ornate, cluttered dressing table. "Ah, Jim. I need you to run me on an errand."

"Sure, Mrs. Threlkeld," he said, standing at the door. Audrey Cox glanced at him disdainfully on her way out of the room.

"I can't find . . . now where did I leave that?" she muttered to herself, searching through priceless jewelry scattered on the table. "Here it is. Jim, come help me with this." She held up the ends of a pearl necklace.

Sammy stepped into the room and took the necklace from her fingers, fastening it around her neck. "You look lovely, Mrs. Threlkeld," he said sincerely.

She sighed. *Somebody would have to teach this boy what constituted an appropriate distance—someday.* But for now she just took his proffered arm.

He took her down in the elevator and parked her in the foyer. "Sit tight; I'll bring the Rolls right around."

"Don't coddle me!" she protested as he sprinted to the back of the house.

In an alarmingly short time he had appeared out front, and sprang from the Rolls to assist her down the steps. It *was* nice to have a strong arm to lean on going down those steps. *Dang steps.* Of course, she could always use Morgan's wheelchair on the ramp, but she was not ready to submit to that. Besides, it was more fun to curse the steps.

When Sammy had seated her in the car, he asked, "Where to, Mrs. Threlkeld?"

"I am to meet with the senior pastor of First Metropolitan Church downtown," she said.

"Yes, ma'am; I know where that is," he said quietly, turning the car down the long cobbled drive.

Some minutes later he had parked close to the offices in the sprawling conglomerate of church buildings. He assisted Mrs. Threlkeld from the car, then bent down to let her lean on him as much as necessary to make it up the steps to the door. "Dang steps," she muttered.

She announced herself to the secretary, who hustled back and brought out Senior Pastor Ron L. Berger, Ph.D., D.D. He was an athletic, energetic man of forty-four, short of stature but long on ambitions. He shook her hand warmly, without squeezing hard, and gestured her back to his office.

Sammy would have waited in the outer office, but Mrs. Threlkeld suddenly threw an arm back, commanding, "Jim." He came up beside her, nudging Senior Pastor Berger out of the way, and accompanied her into his leathery, book-lined office.

"Mrs. Threlkeld, I can't tell you what an honor it is that you'll be participating in our building program. Purchasing the office complex next door to our property will give us much-needed space to expand programs that will reach more people with the good news. And that's what our church is all about, Mrs. Threlkeld—helping people." As he settled on the corner of his desk in front of her, Dr. Berger glanced up at her chauffeur. Something about his vivid blue eyes distracted the senior pastor.

"That's what I want to be sure of, Dr. Berger—that this gift will be used in the area of most need," Mrs. Threlkeld replied.

"Let me show you something," he said, standing. He picked up a bound report from his desk and handed it to her. "Here are the results of a study made by our Space Utilization Committee. The purchase price of the building is three point five million, which includes the parking lot to the west of the building—and that has been estimated to be three hundred thousand below the current fair market value. The interior can be renovated to meet our needs for as little as four hundred and fifty thousand. With this building, we can add twenty-four classrooms in four departments—that's about two hundred and fifty more people coming to hear the good news of Jesus Christ.

"We have many good programs, Mrs. Threlkeld, and many more ideas for programs to help people in need—to help them cope with the pain and problems and pressures of living in today's fast-paced world. But in order for these programs to be implemented, we must have the space to put the people. *People* are our priority and our mission here at First Metro, Mrs. Threlkeld, and if one person can be saved through this purchase, then we will know it has been all worthwhile," he ended warmly.

The clock on the bookshelves ticked while Mrs. Threlkeld opened the report and read it through. Dr. Berger watched her cordially, leaning forward in anticipation of any questions. He pointedly ignored the cool gaze of her chauffeur, who, as an insignificant nobody, did not merit so much as a nod.

Mrs. Threlkeld suddenly shut the report. "I will take this under advisement," she stated, tucking the folder under her arm. "Jim." She reached up and Sammy was immediately at her side to help her up.

"Thank you very much, Mrs. Threlkeld. I'll be looking forward to hearing from you soon," the pastor said, following her out. He stood at the door, waving warmly, while Sammy practically carried Mrs. Threlkeld down the steep steps.

Sammy seated her in the Rolls, then sat behind the wheel. "Home, Mrs. Threlkeld?" he asked.

"Yes," she said. He started the car and drove toward the parking-lot exit in shrouded silence. Mrs. Threlkeld opened the report as if to read it through again, but when he glanced in the rearview mirror once or twice, he saw her watching his eyes.

"What do you think, Jim?" she said suddenly. "What do you think of this gift?"

Sammy slowed the car to a stop and twisted in the seat to look her in the face. Then he cleared his throat. "Let me show you something," he said, turning the car out of the parking lot.

He drove down to the area around West 15th Street, with its depressing, windowless buildings and mangled signs. The car bounced gently over the potholes he could not avoid. Pointing to a building on the left, he said, "There are ten, fifteen women who are living here at any given time, some of them with children. They sleep on rotted mattresses and eat what they can find in the garbage. Most of them are addicts who prostitute themselves for crack."

He pointed out another building: "This is called 'the morgue' because some new body is found here everyday. The cause of death is usually violent trauma or drug overdose and the coroner can't identify most of them. Here, on the other side, the rats are so bad that 'most everyone who lives here carries scars from the bites. There's no air conditioning, no hot water, and no one day when the plumbing, heat, and electricity all work. The health department keeps shutting it down, but people keep coming back because they have nowhere else to live."

Stopping the car in the middle of the street, he said, "He wants to help *people,* Mrs. Threlkeld? What people? The ones who already have everything money can buy? If you want to make them a gift, fine—subsidize First Metro Country Club. But if you want to help the people who have nothing, there are any number of agencies that fight a losing battle every day trying to do that. The man says, '*people* are our priority,' but you notice that what they're spending the money on is *buildings.*"

Having spoken his mind, Sammy turned back around and took the car on up to the freeway. Mrs. Threlkeld was looking out the window. Then she asked, "Are you a Christian?"

"Yes, ma'am," he said tightly.

"Well then, don't you believe in proclaiming the good news?" she asked.

He glanced in the mirror. "If I read my Bible right, the 'good news' was healing and miracles, not a slogan. The religious establishment built buildings. Jesus raised the dead."

They rode in silence the rest of the way home. As Sammy pulled up to the front of the house, Jess came tearing down the steps, waving her arms hysterically. Sammy rolled down the window and she screamed, "Grandma! Bobby had an accident! He's at the hospital!"

"Get in," Sammy ordered, and as Jess scrambled in, he asked, "Which hospital? Parkland?"

"Oh—yes! Parkland," she gasped, falling into her grandmother's arms.

Sammy turned back down the drive, then stopped. "Fasten your seatbelt, Jess," he said. She did so immediately, and he took off again. On the way he prayed desperately for the life of that bratty, snotty-nosed kid.

In ten minutes they were parked near the emergency entrance to the hospital. Sammy helped Mrs. Threlkeld out; she was less steady than usual, so he put his arm around her. Jess clung to her other arm.

He seated her in the waiting room and strode to the desk. "Bobby Threlkeld's family is here. What's his condition?" he asked.

The admitting clerk looked up. "He was brought in alive—that's all I know. His family's here? Have them fill this out." She shoved an admitting form toward Sammy and then turned to the next person waiting in the long line before the counter.

Jess sat close beside her grandma, looking around the waiting room with glazed eyes. There were a lot of people here—they spilled out of the waiting room into the halls. An orderly had just finished wiping up blood from the floor when someone threw up in the corner. Several people leaned against the wall, seemingly unconscious. It was chaos.

Then she looked up at Jim striding toward a policeman who had his notepad out. Jim didn't look fazed in the least, checking out the situation as if he knew just what to do. She watched him.

"Were you the officer at the scene of the Threlkeld boy's accident?" Sammy asked, glancing at his nametag and badge number.

"Yeah," he replied, his eyes flicking up.

"Jim Brandon. I'm the family's chauffeur. Can you tell me what happened?"

"Well, he was driving east on LBJ at an excessive rate of speed and lost control of his vehicle. He crashed into a concrete embankment—totaled the car," the officer replied. "Here's the bill from the wrecker."

"Was anyone else injured?" Sammy asked, taking the invoice.

"No; he was alone in the car and traffic was successfully diverted around the accident scene," he said, appraising the chauffeur.

"What's his condition?" Sammy asked.

"He was banged up pretty bad, but the paramedics gave him a thumbs-up. By some miracle, he was wearing his seatbelt," the cop said.

Sammy exhaled in relief, then he heard someone say, "Sammy! Hey, Sambo!" He did not respond, but looked off as if contemplating another question.

A second policeman whom Sammy knew vaguely came up, slapping him on the back. Sammy eyed him distantly. "Excuse me?"

The officer saw his chauffeur's uniform and realized his blunder. "Ah, sorry, pal. Thought you were somebody else."

"No problem, officer." Sammy turned and almost caught his breath when he saw Mrs. Threlkeld and Jess watching from across the room. But he assumed the earnestness of a messenger as he went over and sat beside them.

"The cop says that he was speeding and hit an embankment. He's alive, though—he was wearing his seatbelt." He couldn't resist a glance at Jess.

Mrs. Threlkeld put her head in her hand and Jess hugged her. Placing the clipboard with the admittance form in Mrs. Threlkeld's lap, he advised her, "You need to fill this out."

She gazed helplessly over the form. "I can't think to save my life right now. You do it, Jim." She thrust it back on him.

He pushed his hat up. "I'll need your insurance card, ma'am." So Mrs. Threlkeld shoved her clutch purse at him. Sammy opened it and took out her wallet. Seeing the amount of cash she carried, he almost had a heart attack. But he pulled out her proof of insurance and a pen and began writing.

When the form was completed, Sammy took it back up to the desk and asked the clerk, "When can we see Bobby?"

"When they're through with him. We'll call you," she said crisply, taking the form. He knew that, but felt beholden to ask anyway. He went back to Mrs. Threlkeld's side.

Handing her back the small clutch purse, he leaned over to whisper, "I hate to see you carrying around this much money."

"Then you carry it, Jim," she moaned, pushing the purse away. Sammy tucked it in his belt under his jacket.

Then he pulled his hat down lower on his head and sat back, crossing his arms to wait. Jess watched the keen, observant manner in which his eyes covered the room. He glanced at her, then looked down.

As they waited, a man in a nicely tailored suit burst in. Seeing Mrs. Threlkeld, he practically flung himself beside her, attempting to dislodge Sammy from his seat. The presumptuous chauffeur wouldn't budge, so he knelt before her. "I'm here now, Mrs. Threlkeld. Don't you worry about a thing—everything will be taken care of. We'll see that whoever's responsible pays for this!"

"I'm afraid Bobby is responsible," she said weakly.

"Well, we'll let them know that any deficiency in his care will be very costly," he said, rising to do battle with the harried admissions clerk.

Sammy's eyes coolly swept the room again. Mrs. Threlkeld turned to him with a wan smile. "I assume you don't have much use for lawyers, either," she observed.

He shrugged, "It's just interesting that the paramedics who saved Bobby's life probably make one-tenth of what that leech does."

Blinking tearfully, she reached over to pat his arm, and he gently took her hand. Jess looked on in amazement at the open demonstration of affection between them.

An emergency-room doctor leaned into the waiting room and called, "Threlkeld?"

Sammy supported Mrs. Threlkeld as she stood, and they followed the doctor to a treatment room. He pulled back a curtain to show them a groggy, bandaged Bobby. "Grandma," he moaned, reaching out one hand. She quickly moved to his bedside to clasp his hand against her tear-stained cheek.

"Okay," said the doctor, flipping open a chart. "He's got contusions and lacerations, a broken right clavicle and fractures of the eighth and ninth costae—overall, I'd say his condition is fair."

"May we take him home?" Mrs. Threlkeld asked with dignity.

"I'd recommend he stay under observation," the doctor countered politely.

"Thank you for your opinion," she said, then turned to Sammy. "Jim, please take care of the paperwork to get us out of here."

"Sure, Mrs. Threlkeld," he said, turning back to the admissions desk. On the way, he muttered under his breath, "Why can't your hotshot attorney earn his retainer by filling out a few of these forms?"

Twenty minutes later he was back with a wheelchair. "Okay, pal, you've been sprung," he said. He set the brakes on the wheelchair, leaned over the bed, and carefully lifted one-hundred-and-sixty-pound Bobby into the chair.

Sammy wheeled Bobby out to the curb while Jess and Grandma walked on either side. Then he brought up the car and loaded the groaning patient in the back seat. Mrs. Threlkeld sat in back with him; Jess took the front seat beside Sammy.

And he carted them all home. As he pulled up to the front of the house and opened the car door, Marni came out. "How is he?" she asked anxiously, coming up to place a hand on Sammy's arm and look down in the car.

Sammy did a double-take at her slinky new uniform. "Cracked ribs and contusions, but he'll be okay," he murmured. "Nice dress."

She shook her head at him slightly as Sammy bent to unload the center of attention. He lifted Bobby from the back seat and carried him up the steps to the house. Marni ran ahead to open the front door. Sammy brought him in, paused at the foot of the steps with his fidgety burden, then turned aside to take him upstairs in the elevator. Marni rode up with them, and disembarked first to open Bobby's door.

She turned down the bedcovers and propped up the pillow while Sammy laid the moaning patient in bed. Mrs. Threlkeld, behind him, said, "That will be all, Jim." Sammy touched his hat to her and started to leave the room, then remembered something. He withdrew Mrs. Threlkeld's clutch purse from his waistband and stretched it out toward her at Bobby's bedside.

She glanced up. "Put it on my vanity, Jim." He nodded and went down the hall, catching Marni's hand on the way out.

He led her to Mrs. Threlkeld's room, where he put the purse on her dressing table. He took her back out, looked up and down the empty hallway, then threw Marni up against the wall for a lusty kiss. She struggled just a little, for form's sake.

"So," he said, "what gives with the dress?"

"Audrey brought it to me. It's the new uniform Mr. Threlkeld wanted me to wear. And there's a new set of chores to go with it." She pulled out the list to show him.

He read it, and looked up with raised brows. "Well, well. Just let me know when your duties get more personal."

"That's not what he wants—I think," she said with a worried expression. "But never mind that," she waved it off. In a whisper: "I found *The Elder Sister.* It's hanging in the hall on the third floor."

He nodded. "Mike checked it out. It's clean. Only thing is, Mutual Life is investigating the gallery it came from, as well. Oh—" he reached into his pocket and gave her the receipt.

"Why don't you put this back? It came from the locked drawer on the right. Key's under the desk."

"It'll cost you." She reached up for another kiss and he paid one out, moving his hands over her contours.

While they were thus engaged, there was the sound of someone clearing a throat. Sammy and Marni quickly looked up at Mrs. Threlkeld standing outside Bobby's door. "If you are not *too* busy, I want you to see about Bobby's car," she said caustically.

"Yes, Mrs. Threlkeld," Sammy said, smiling as he began escorting his blushing bride down the hall.

"Jim," Mrs. Threlkeld said, and he turned. ". . . thank you." He winked in response and she rolled her eyes in horror.

That evening at dinner, the staff in the kitchen quietly listened to Stan Threlkeld in the next room vent his wrath over Bobby's accident. "A brand-new Jaguar, totaled! And him with a suspended license! It's a miracle he didn't break his neck. I'll have you kids know that some things are changing in this house as of today!"

"Daddy, you need to be upstairs telling Bobby all this! *I* didn't do anything!" Jess whined.

"Oh, you don't think I know about all *your* escapades, young lady? I'm putting a stop to that! From now on, wherever you need to go, Jim will drive you," her father declared. Sammy crossed his eyes in repulsion.

Before Jess could react, Mrs. Threlkeld quietly asserted, "I'm afraid that won't do, Stanley. I need Jim here. And you mustn't punish Jess for what Bobby does."

"Mother, I wish you would stop correcting me with the children," Stan said.

"When it involves *my* staff, I'm afraid I have to," she replied.

"Since when did you give a hoot about the staff?" Stan returned.

"You should talk. Look at what Melody is wearing. And Mary said she doesn't *do* housework anymore," Jess taunted. Mary studied her plate. Marni smiled at her reassuringly.

"That will be quite enough from you, young lady!" Stan threatened. "And Mother—"

Suddenly he was interrupted by a voice that could only have come from the patriarch at the head of the table, the elder Mr. Threlkeld. It was a raspy, broken voice, not strong enough for anyone in the kitchen to discern what he said. But it was enough to silence conversation in the dining room for the duration of the meal.

After dinner, Sammy and Marni went back to their room to get comfortable. "I've got a job for you," he whispered. "Did you get the invoice back in the desk?"

"Yes," she said.

"Good. Well, since you've got free run of the house now, you can do some looking around for me." He pulled a paper from his shirt. "I went to see Mike after paying my last respects to the Jag. Mike gave me Interpol's list of recent art thefts. I want you to see if you can match up anything in the house to what's on this list. If you find anything, we get a warrant, and—boom. We're done."

"Okay," she said, looking down the list.

"You need to memorize it and leave it here in the room. Don't carry it around with you," he cautioned.

"Right," she said.

There was a knock on the door. "Yeah?" Sammy called as Marni stuffed the list under the mattress.

Mary's voice said, "Mr. Threlkeld wants to see Melody."

Sammy and Marni exchanged wary glances, and she opened the door. "Here I am," she said with a forced smile. As she followed Mary out into the hall, she asked, "Where is he?"

"In his room, of course," Mary replied as if she should have known that. Then she stopped to add: "I'm talking about Mr. Morgan Threlkeld."

"The elder Mr. Threlkeld?" Marni asked in astonishment, and Mary nodded. "Where—uh—where is his room?"

"Right across the hall from Mrs. Threlkeld's," Mary said, turning out of the hall into the kitchen.

Marni slowly ascended the stairs and went to the patriarch's door. She knocked, and it was opened by the private nurse Marni had seen before. The nurse nodded toward the center of the room, where there was a hospital bed covered by an oxygen tent. Tentatively, Marni went to the bedside and pulled back the tent. The old man looked to be asleep. She glanced inquiringly at the nurse, who nodded at him again.

"Mr. Threlkeld?" she said softly, and he opened cloudy eyes. "I'm Melody Brandon. Did you want to see me?"

He reached over for the control to raise the head of the bed to a sitting position. Marni straightened the pillow behind his back as he cleared his throat loudly. Then he said, "They're nincompoops."

"Pardon?" she asked weakly.

"My sons are nincompoops. Bobby, too. Only one with a shred of sense is Jess, and that's only because she had the great good sense to inherit some of her grandmother's backbone. Stan's wife was a trollop and I wouldn't have her in this house," he declared.

"Wes is an idiot—him and his harebrained schemes. He never would listen—you couldn't beat sense into him with a board. And Stan is too weak to stand up to him. They're worthless. Wes's boy—a bad seed. And Bobby is just like Stan, but without any brains at all. Spaghetti. That's all the family I've got left. Do you know how it makes an old man feel to leave his life's work to a family like this?

"Dolly, now—ah, she was beautiful. So young. A spitfire, too. Told me just where to get off first time I tried to walk her home. They don't make 'em like that anymore. A real lady. She could take anything that came her way and still hold her head high. But she's not young anymore, and something's got to be done before those boys ruin everything. Wes'll be home for this party of Dolly's. Stan'll be here, too. That's when I want it done."

"What, Mr. Threlkeld?" she asked.

"You and your husband—that young man Dolly's taken a fancy to—I want you to kill those nincompoops."

six

Marni gaped at the elder Mr. Threlkeld, then turned to look for the nurse, who had apparently left the room. Looking back at the sharp-eyed old man, she saw his mouth twitching. "What, got no stomach for murder?" he asked derisively.

On a gamble, she leaned down on the bed and said languidly, "Oh, it's just so much hassle. If they're such pea-brains, why don't you just fire them? Or don't you have the stomach for it?"

He leaned his head back on the pillow and laughed as hard as he could in a hollow, weak voice. "You know," he said, wiping his watery eyes, "I once had a girl take me up on it right off the bat. Most of 'em at least ask how much I'm willing to pay. Couple just walked out and quit that very day. But so far ain't nobody accused me of not having the stomach to fire 'em." He patted her hand approvingly.

"Oh, they're not such a rotten lot," she said, holding his gnarled hand. "They just haven't had your experience."

"I wish that was all they lacked," he moaned, rubbing his crinkly face. "But there's that factor of trustworthiness—of being worth an honest day's work. I don't think either of those boys knows what it means to work so hard through the day that you fall asleep afore you can take your boots off at night." He paused, and Marni said nothing. "That was a good feeling," he murmured. "To be young and strong and able to work hard. It was good to sweat for a living. It made me a man."

Marni smiled at him, still holding his hand. He turned to look at her. "You're such a pretty young thing. You wouldn't know it to look at me now, but when I was young I was considered a pretty fair catch—and that before I had made a dime. The girls used to gather on the corner and giggle as I walked by, trying to catch my eye." He closed his eyes, smiling in remembrance.

Slowly, he opened them again. "I hate my life. I hate this useless old body. I hate that I sweat and toiled all those years to build a fortune, and then have to lie here and watch those idiot boys of mine run it all to the ground. What's the use in that?"

He looked at her as if he really wanted an answer, so she asked softly, "Have you talked about this with Mrs. Threlkeld?"

He jerked his head in hurt defiance. "She says I'm being an old fool."

That, Marni understood. "She's afraid, Mr. Threlkeld. She's afraid of losing you and winding up alone. I know that fear," she admitted. "My husband almost died a few months ago. It was the most horrible thing I'd ever experienced. Your wife can't be expected to *want* to look at that possibility. You have to talk her through it—gently, you know."

"Eh," he grunted, shifting. "Maybe. But I still want you to waste them boys."

Marni burst out laughing. He looked gratified, continuing to insist, "I mean it. Both of 'em. Linda, too."

Marni stopped laughing. "I thought—that your daughter-in-law was gone."

"Never for very long," he snorted. "Oh, she divorced Stanley all right—only 'cause she found Wes more to her liking."

Marni considered this. Apparently Stan had been less than forthright in his version of the Threlkeld Family History. She carefully asked, "Will Linda be here Friday?"

"Eh, if Wes comes, she'll come. They're a pair, and they deserve each other," he said spitefully.

The nurse came up behind Marni. "Time for your bath, Mr. Threlkeld."

He clutched Marni's hand. "Save me from this woman. She's full of Ol' Nick."

"Stop whining," Marni said severely, standing to kiss him on his forehead. "I'll check on you tomorrow to see what kind of damage she's done."

"Traitor," he muttered, and she turned out of the room smiling.

Jess was coming out of Bobby's room, so Marni stopped at his door. There were several young men clustered around his bed commiserating with him. Marni decided that the investment of a few minutes might pay off here.

She went in, leaned over his bed, and sweetly asked, "How're you feeling, Bobby? Can I get you anything?"

Suffering under the weight of his oh-so-serious injuries, Bobby uttered, "I didn't call a maid. Get out of here." The other boys snickered as Marni nodded and left.

She came downstairs to find Sammy cornered in the foyer by Jess and one of her girlfriends—apparently. One glance at his demeanor told her he had been watching the stairs. As Marni came off the stairs, Sammy pulled her into his side with one arm. She leaned her head on his chest and he covered her with his other arm.

Jess and her friend looked on silently. Then Jess observed, "That would bore me to tears—get married, get a job, have children. . . . Be stuck with one person all the time. What a drag."

Sammy, smiling, reached out to touch her face in spontaneous affection. "When you get through rebelling, Jess—when you've been beaten up and bloodied enough—you'll fall on your knees to find one person who cares enough to stick around. I'm talking from around the bend of that particular road."

Jess's eyes began watering. She jerked her head at her friend: "Come on, Sudie," and they went upstairs.

Sammy looked after them, then led his essential other back to their quarters. That drab little room which housed the married help then became the scene of the most intense, exciting and satisfying activity that had taken place in this house in years.

A half-hour later Sammy sighed and murmured, "So. What did Stanley want?"

Brushing tousled hair from her face, Marni laughed, "It wasn't Stanley, it was Morgan! The elder Mr. Threlkeld."

"Yeah?" he said, reaching behind him to pull the pillow up under his head. She stroked the five o'clock shadow that gave his fine features that dangerous air.

"Yeah. He just wanted to see what the new maid was made of. Right off the bat, he said he wanted you and me to kill his sons."

"No kidding?" he said, brow furrowing.

"No, he was kidding. He's unhappy with the way Stanley is running the business, and he thinks Wes is lame-brained, but I can tell when somebody says something just to get a reaction from me," she said, digging into his ribs.

"Watch it!" he squirmed, grabbing her fingers to put them in his mouth.

"Wes has a son, too. And get this," she whispered, retracting her fingers, "Linda divorced Stanley all right, but only because she liked Wes better. Those two are still hooked up, and will probably be here Friday."

"Ah," he breathed, enlightened. "Well, sure. Wes *and Linda* and stolen art. You always need a woman accomplice for the high-class jobs." He stuck her fingers back in his mouth.

"That's unsanitary," she protested, withdrawing them again.

"Ooh, yes, let's be unsanitary!" he growled, and they rolled over in a heap, laughing.

The next morning, temporaries were out in force to help with preparations for Mrs. Threlkeld's event the following night. Audrey summoned Marni long enough to give her two additional uniforms similar to the black sheath—that was all. Marni was given no additional duties, and the housework that she had first been assigned was now divided among three temporary maids. So Marni sat in her room until she had memorized Interpol's list of stolen works, then went out to wander the house.

Sammy was out back cleaning the interior of the Maserati—something that had not been done since the car was first bought. From the trash that had accumulated, he deduced this was Jess's car. (Stanley drove a Lamborghini that would have to wait till the weekend for maintenance, though Sammy was itching to get his hands on it.) Some of the stuff Sammy found in the Maserati made him want to turn Jess over his knee again, but he resolved to just shut his eyes and throw it all away.

There was a grounds crew out back, erecting tents and tables for the party. With the balmy March weather they were experiencing right now, it made sense to utilize the sculptured grounds. Audrey, with her clipboard, was hither and yon, directing the work. Sammy observed that despite her outward appearance of serenity, she was one of those people who thrived on chaos, and if there was none present, created it.

Right now the workers were doing a dismal job with the poolside decorations. Despite her exhortations, their efforts to satisfactorily place the heavy cement flower urns around the pool failed. Audrey looked around and saw one person not embroiled in the turmoil, so she called, "You! Jim! Come here—I need you!"

Sammy hesitated, then went over. "What is it, Mrs. Cox?"

She regarded his posture in a glance: hands on his hips, feet spread assertively, and she wondered where a chauffeur ever got the nerve to assume such a provocative stance in front of a higher-class woman. Assuming that his attitude was the result of frequent liaisons with previous employers, Mrs. Cox fluttered briefly under his blue eyes. "Jim, I need you to move these cement urns to the other side of the pool and—"

"Excuse me, Mrs. Cox. If I stop what I'm doing to help these guys do their job, then who is going to do my job?" he asked.

Mrs. Cox was flabbergasted. "Are you refusing orders?"

"I'm doing what I was ordered. I'll do differently when Mrs. Threlkeld tells me to," he replied, turning back to the car.

Seething, Audrey turned to vent her wrath on one of the hapless workers. "It's the little things that make a job interesting, Jess," Sammy said to no one as he shook out car mats.

During a whole morning spent combing the house, Marni saw many beautiful things, but nothing from Interpol's list. So at lunchtime she went down to the kitchen to fix a large double-decker sandwich, then went out to where Sammy was standing over a gleaming Maserati. Since Audrey was watching, Sammy made a point to greet his wife with a leisurely kiss. "My, haven't we been working hard," she teased.

"That's a fact. As trashed out as this car was, it could've inspired Stephen King to write *Christine*," he avowed.

"Well, I've been doing my job," she said, glancing around. Audrey turned her back on them. "There's nothing in the house," Marni whispered. "I looked all morning. Zip."

He nodded, taking her into the garage to put up supplies. "We're not going to find anything unless we figure out a way to target Wes and Linda. I'm thinking that Mutual Life needs to take it from here," he whispered.

Marni felt strangely disappointed, as if she would be leaving something undone. "Well—come on in. I made you a sandwich," she said, and they headed for the house.

"Gee, you didn't have to do that, with all the other work you've got on you," he teased, opening the back door.

"Look who's talking. Bobby wrecked the Jag and cut your work load in half," she threw back, and he grinned.

"Yeah, well, Madame Cox—" he began, but as they entered the kitchen they were faced with Mary Hellier leaning her round little body on the counter and crying her heart out. Sammy informed Marni with a glance that he was not about to touch this situation and unobtrusively sat down to his sandwich.

"Mrs. Hellier! What's wrong?" Marni asked.

"That woman!" Mary jerked up and pointed out the back door. "As if I didn't have enough to do already, and then she puts all this cooking on *me* and does she hire one single soul to help me in the kitchen? No! Why, I—"

"I can help you, Mrs. Hellier," Marni offered.

First Mary looked dumbstruck, then dubious, then slightly mollified. "Well, fine, if you're sure it won't interfere with your *other* duties," she said.

As seriously as possible, Marni replied, "I'll try to do both jobs, as long as you understand that I'll have to drop whatever I'm doing if Mr. Threlkeld calls."

"All right," Mrs. Hellier sniffed, dabbing at her puffy eyes. First Marni sat to eat a bite of lunch with Sammy, who had to work very hard to keep a smirk off his face.

Afterward, Sammy went back out to the garage and Marni stood beside Mary. "Now. What can I do to help you?" Marni asked brightly.

"Well. . . ." Mary looked at the clutter scattered across the work island and countertops. "Here. You can grind the meats for the pâté. Have you ever used a meat grinder?"

"No," said Marni, gazing at the multi-bladed machine.

"Forget that, then. Here—you know how to use a blender, don't you?" asked Mary.

"Of course," Marni said in relief.

"Well then, you just purée half the chicken livers with the eggs, the cognac, and the cream," Mary instructed.

"This?" Marni said, beginning to pour.

"No! Not that much at once!" exclaimed Mary. "Oh—never mind that. You can slice the foie gras."

"The what?" Marni said, picking up a thin strip of meat. It slithered from her fingers onto the floor.

"Oh, no!" Fussily, Mary bent to pick it up and place it in the sink. Marni reached for more and Mary said a little desperately, "Don't touch that. Here—slice the meats for the galantine." She opened the refrigerator, took out a bundle wrapped in white paper, and slapped it on the counter in front of Marni.

"Okay," Marni said, tentatively picking up a huge butcher knife. Mary turned to another counter as Marni unwrapped the bundle and then gasped in horror.

"What is it?" Mary said, quickly looking over.

"It's—oh my word, it's a great big *tongue,*" Marni moaned.

"You need to slice it," Mary said impatiently.

"Slice it *up?*" Marni repeated, holding her stomach.

"Get out!" Mary shouted, taking the butcher knife to wave her away. "You're worse than no help at all!"

"I'm sorry!" Marni shuddered on her way out. "I wonder if all those rich people know what they're *eating,*" she groaned.

Just then Mary stuck her head out of the kitchen. "One thing you *can* do is go tell your husband that Mrs. Threlkeld needs him!"

"Sure, Mrs. Hellier," Marni said sheepishly as Mary clicked off the intercom and went back to work with a martyr's sigh.

Minutes later, Sammy, in coat and hat, was knocking on Mrs. Threlkeld's door. "It's Jim, ma'am," he called.

She opened the door, adjusting her suit jacket. "Jim, I need you to drive me to several places," she announced, handing him a list.

"Okay," he said amiably, scanning the list. Then he looked up quickly. "The Salvation Army? Wings of Mercy Shelter?"

"I wish to tour these facilities before I just hand them money," she said stiffly. Sammy reached out and grabbed her around the waist. "Jim!" she gasped.

"I like you, Mrs. Threlkeld," he said, grinning.

"Let go of me!" she demanded.

"I'm going to kiss you," he warned solemnly.

"Jim Brandon, I'll fire you!" she threatened.

But he tightened his grip on her and slowly lowered his face. She held her breath. Then he kissed her very tenderly on her taut pink cheek. "I'm sorry, Mrs. Threlkeld; I couldn't help myself. You'll just have to fire me when we get back," he said in resignation, releasing her.

"Hmmph!" She smoothed her ruffled jacket and strode to the elevator, looking back for her chauffeur's strong arm.

Sammy took her around to four places on her list that afternoon, sticking close to her side while she walked through the various missions. Agency heads fell over themselves to present their needs to her, and she actually met several beneficiaries of the charities. A roving newspaper reporter who got wind of her tour came up with a camera; Sammy ducked his head and pulled his hat down low.

He worried for a while that he might be recognized, as his police duties had frequently brought him in contact with a number of these people. But he soon discovered that with everyone's attention focused on Mrs. Threlkeld, his uniform made him invisible. She was correct in what she had first said—he was quite literally an accessory to her.

Until . . . they were touring one of the homeless shelters in the southwest sector, where Sammy had been a patrol officer, when a bag lady turned from her corner to look them over. Sammy recognized her at once: her name was Sally, and she lived in an endless dream world. She had rotting teeth, incontinence, and generally poor health, but she imagined herself to be young and beautiful.

Seeing him, she smiled flirtatiously. "Hello, Sammy," she creaked in an old lady's voice, throwing a wisp of stringy gray hair over her shoulder. Of course, no one except Sammy paid any attention to her.

He went on over and sat on the floor next to her. "Hi, Sally. How's my girl?"

"I haven't seen you around," she chastised, cutting her cloudy eyes toward him.

"I've been doing other work," he said, glancing up at Mrs. Threlkeld, who watched sympathetically from twenty feet away.

Sally looked up at her also, and giggled, "Who's the old broad?"

"Have a heart, Sal, not everybody can look like you. That's Mrs. Threlkeld, my new employer," he told her.

"It's not the same anymore as when you were around. The cop on your beat is mean and ugly," Sally pouted.

"What's his name?" Sammy asked.

"It's ugly. Hatcher," she said.

"I'll see that he gets transferred. Who would you like instead?" Sammy asked.

"I don't know any of 'em any more. They're all new to me. It's not like it used to be when you were here," she said sadly.

"I had to move on, Sal. But I can get somebody nice in. Would you like that?" he asked.

"Jesus came by to see me today," she said suddenly. "He came by to talk to just me."

Sammy slowly opened his mouth, but then Mrs. Threlkeld started off, shaking her head in pity, so he had to get up. "There goes my boss. See you later, doll."

She held out her ragged arms. "I'm supposed to tell you goodbye, Sammy."

Bemusedly, he hugged her. "Where're you goin', Sally?"

"I'm goin' to live in a big, beautiful house. I'm goin' to wear beautiful dresses and eat at a big table with all my friends. It will be lovely," she sighed. "So I have to tell you goodbye."

"Well, you have a good time, doll. I'll miss you," he said fondly.

"Oh, you'll be there by and by," she noted. He glanced at her as he ran after Mrs. Threlkeld.

They walked through one more wing of that building, then as they were leaving, an ambulance pulled up to the curb screeching. Attendants ran inside with a gurney. Sammy left Mrs. Threlkeld locked in the Rolls and ran back into the building to see if he could assist. "What happened?" he caught a volunteer worker.

"Oh, it's Sally. She just keeled over dead," the woman said. "I guess she's better off, poor thing."

Shaken, Sammy stood back as the gurney came out with its sheeted load. "Goodbye, Sally," he whispered. After pausing to wipe his face, he returned to Mrs. Threlkeld in the car.

Back at the house, Marni was doing what she could to stay out of everyone else's way. She went in and visited with the elder Mr. Threlkeld for a little while, but steered clear of Bobby's room. And she explored some far reaches of the house that she had not gotten to yesterday. As before, she found nothing. It occurred to her that any stolen works would probably not be hanging out in the open anyway; but nonetheless, she agreed with Sammy that nothing even smelled suspicious here. They would have to look elsewhere.

She was on the front steps when Sammy brought Mrs. Threlkeld home that afternoon. Marni went out back to wait while he parked the Rolls, then, shucking off his coat and hat, he stood with her on a rear balcony to watch preparations for the party come together. Sammy had charmed some hors d'oeuvres out of a vulnerable, distracted Mary, which they now ate on the balcony with conspiratorial delight, and Marni gave not a thought as to what they were made of.

The party was to be a monumental affair: tents, lights, flowers, music, food, drinks, servers—everything in abundance, all the best. "Oh—I finally found out why Mrs. Threlkeld is having it," Marni said as she watched the work crews construct the stage for the band.

"Yeah?" muttered Sammy, popping a stuffed shrimp in his mouth.

"To show up another society lady who hosted a party for the new director of the Dallas Symphony Orchestra," Marni relayed, then added in an excited whisper, "It's a big secret, but *Van Cliburn's* supposed to be here tonight!"

"If it's a big secret, then how do you know it?" Sammy asked with a half-smile.

Marni tossed her head aloofly. "I listen."

He chortled softly, looking down at the cement urns sitting crookedly around the pool. "Those guys never did get the urns placed where Audrey wanted them, poor girl." His eyes went glassy as he thought of another girl who went to a party today. "You can have it now, or have it forever," he murmured.

"What?" asked Marni, leaning into his shoulder.

He pressed his cheek to her head. "A bag lady I knew when I walked a beat died today."

"Sammy, I'm sorry," she whispered, raising her face.

"It was one of those good things," he said. "She waited to leave until she could tell me goodbye. She . . . finally got to be the girl she was on the inside," he struggled to explain. Marni eyed him and he shook his head, turning to walk with her into the house.

seven

The next day Sammy and Marni found themselves in a maelstrom of activity centering on the party that night. Jess required him to run numerous errands to pick up shoes, return shoes, pick up a dress, return the same dress, until Sammy was threatening to add her and all her selections to the existing in-pool decorations. This pleased Jess, but not enough to settle her mind about what to wear until late that afternoon. Part of her dilemma was due to her fears that the unseasonably warm weather would turn nasty as soon as she decided on the strapless dress. But it didn't.

Bobby felt he was sufficiently healed to attend the party, though he was forced to reapply the bandages that the doctor had deemed unnecessary at his last house call. Stan came home from work early to get ready, and the elder Mr. Threlkeld was being freshly bathed for the occasion.

Sammy was instructed to wear some of Stan's hand-me-downs, which he graciously accepted with the impeccable logic, "They're better than anything I've got hanging in my closet."

Marni had to settle for one of the black sheath dresses. This caused her some anguish until Sammy came back from one of his many errands with a string of pearls and a pair of black satin heels for her. Marni kissed him and promised him ample rewards to come. Neither of them was given any specific responsibilities for the evening—they were just supposed to "be there."

As the hour approached, the waiters arrived in their smooth tuxedos and Mary collapsed from nervous exhaustion. Mrs. Threlkeld emerged from the elevator in a glittering gold brocade ensemble, and the party was on.

The orchestra played inside the house and a contemporary band was outside on the lawn, which was lit from the pool to the gazebo in the formal gardens with thousands of stringed lights. Marni walked beside Mr. Threlkeld and his nurse, watching the guests arrive and mingle. There were some faces she recognized from the society pages of the newspaper, but besides them and the family, Marni knew no one. The celebrated Mr. Cliburn had yet to show up.

Standing beside the pool glittering with the reflections of countless tiny lights, she watched Sammy talking with Mrs. Threlkeld and one of her girlfriends. As always, Marni marveled at his ability to glide from one situation to the next, to project an air appropriate for whatever his surroundings. He looked better in Stan's clothes than Stan did, but he never gave the impression of conceit. Like any good actor, he had the ability to immerse himself in the present moment. Smiling at something the lady said, Sammy glanced up at Marni and winked. Even while listening to another woman, he was aware of Marni's eyes on him.

Sighing, she turned to one of the buffet tables with its fabulous ice sculpture and array of food. Marni bypassed the pâté and the foie gras, and was dubiously eyeing the caviar when she detected a sudden silence behind her. Then the elder Mr. Threlkeld spat to his nurse, "I just lost my appetite. Take me up to my room."

Marni turned and laid eyes on the most exotic woman she had ever seen. She had auburn hair wrapped in a sleek French twist, languid eyes heavy with eyeliner, and a svelte body packed into a tight leopard-print dress. Sammy took one look and started to sweat.

"Hello, Dolly." The woman leaned forward and puckered her bright red lips beside Mrs. Threlkeld's cheek. "Morgan," she purred, turning. "So good to see you again." She bent to leave a set of lip prints on top of his head.

"Get me out of here," Mr. Threlkeld ordered his nurse, who wheeled him away from the group.

The woman laughed deep in her throat. She never saw Marni and pointedly ignored Sammy. "Dolly, it's been ages. You look wonderful. That plastic surgeon in New York is worth every penny, isn't he?" The other lady with Mrs. Threlkeld hurriedly moved away.

"What have you brought to pawn off on Stanley now, Linda?" Mrs. Threlkeld asked tiredly. Before the other could respond she added, "Has Wesley come tonight?"

"Certainly, dear; I'm sure he's at your bar. You—do have a bar tonight, don't you, Dolly?" she asked dubiously.

"Of course," Mrs. Threlkeld bristled. Sammy cleared his throat softly, but the woman kept her smiling green eyes on her hostess. Reluctantly, Mrs. Threlkeld added, "Linda, I would like you to meet my chauffeur, Jim Brandon. Jim, Linda Threlkeld-Rains—which is the name I believe you're using now."

Then Linda turned her sultry eyes on Sammy. In her spike heels, she was almost eye-to-eye with him. She breathed, "I am so happy to meet you—" drawing closer to his face with each word, until the last was lost in his lips as she kissed him.

Sammy looked as though he'd been hit by lightning when she finally drew back; she evaluated with satisfaction the lipstick smeared over his mouth. After the moment he required to start breathing again, he brought up a napkin to wipe his mouth, mumbling, "Nice to meet you, Mrs.—Ms.—"

"Do call me Linda," she invited, stroking lipstick from his face with one gloved hand.

As Marni stared at Sammy, Jess came up. "Oh, hi, Mom," she said listlessly.

"Shhh!" Linda smiled, putting a finger to her puckered lips. "We don't want to spill family secrets."

"I'm doing great, Mom," Jess said sarcastically, in answer to a question that was not asked.

"Well, hidy, baby girl!" A man came up behind Linda with a glass of bourbon. He had a trim mustache, full, prematurely gray hair, and wrists full of jewelry. "How's my FA-vor-ITE little niece?"

"Great, Uncle Wes," Jess answered in a sneer. Turning to her mother: "D'you want to see Daddy?"

"Daddy?" Linda's expressive face momentarily went blank. "Oh, Stan. No. Wes, darling," Linda turned to finger his collar, gaining his full attention. "I want you to meet my new secretary, Jim Brandon." The fingers of her other hand curled around Sammy's lapel, and he watched her without blinking.

"Linda, you may not have Jim," Mrs. Threlkeld said firmly.

"Since I know what Dolly must be paying you," she purred in Sammy's face, "I know that I can afford to offer you three times that much."

"He'll never go with you," Jess said spitefully.

Sammy cleared his throat. "I'd . . . like to bring my wife."

Linda laughed in his face. "I only need *one* person, darling. The offer stands for the next thirty seconds," she added in a harder tone.

"Taken," he said.

Mrs. Threlkeld looked steely-eyed and Jess breathed, "I don't believe it."

Smiling like a big cat after a kill, Linda said, "Come pack your things, Jim. You do have a passport, don't you?" When he nodded, she continued, "Good. We're leaving tonight—I have an important soirée to attend"—as if this one were not.

Sammy looked at Marni. Everyone looked at Marni, but she saw only him. In an instant, he conveyed his thoughts to her: *You understand why I have to go, don't you? Please understand, Marni. Please.*

She blinked at him. Linda glanced back at her and took his arm. "Come along, Jim." He went with her into the house. Wes paused, glancing at Marni as well, then hurried after them.

"I don't believe it," Jess muttered tightly, tears coming to her eyes. She turned and flounced away.

Marni looked down at the remains of a ham roll in her hand, which she had unconsciously crushed to a pulp. *It's an act. It's all an act, right, Sammy? Dear God, let it be all an act.*

Mrs. Threlkeld slowly turned toward her. "We make a mistake to think we know them," she whispered. "In the end, we have only ourselves to rely on. Wanting more is wishful thinking." She lifted her chin with dignity and turned to greet her other guests.

Sammy discovered that when Linda had said "tonight," she meant "right now." Grudgingly appreciative of Stan's generosity, Sammy filled a suitcase with his employer's nice clothes.

As soon as he was packed, the three of them climbed into a limousine and headed for the Dallas/Fort Worth Airport. Wes eyed Sammy as he sat beside Linda in the dark back seat of the limo. "What's your name again, boy?"

"Jim Brandon."

"Where're you from?" Wes asked.

"Dallas," Sammy answered. "Lived here all my life."

"We're willing to overlook that, darling," Linda said, placing a hand on his thigh.

Wes, seeing that, fumed, "Linda, sweetie, I wisht you'd'a tole me you needed a secretary. I coulda got you one." Sammy evaluated his heavy Texas accent with a knowledgeable ear. It was a tad thick, especially for an international jet-setter. But it was a good cover if he wished to appear stupider than he really was.

Linda laughed, "I wouldn't dream of burdening you with such insignificant decisions, dear Wes." She stroked Sammy's thigh, and he shifted, looking out the window.

Drawing his legs together, Sammy looked back at her to ask, "Where are we going?"

"New York, of course," Linda said. "Then on to Paris."

"You're not takin' that boy with us to Paris, Linda," Wes said irately.

"Don't be silly, Wes. Can't you see that he would be perfect for helping us put Leslie at ease?" Linda said, dropping a hint of a scheme.

Wes narrowed his eyes to evaluate Sammy from that viewpoint. "Well, shore. As long as he's *just* for Leslie," he said in a subtle threat.

"Of course, darling," Linda said soothingly. Turning to Sammy, she murmured, "Just never forget that *I* am the one who pays you, Jim." And she discreetly dug her fingernails into the inside of his thigh. He eyed her without flinching.

At the airport, they boarded a private charter for New York City. Without so much as a glance around the plush interior of the jet, Sammy threw himself into a seat and looked out the window.

"Don't slouch, Jim," Linda reproved smilingly as she took a seat across from him. "Your bearing is very important." He looked at her and sat up an inch.

The flight attendant came around to take their drink orders. He looked inquiringly at Sammy, who mumbled, "Beer," and looked out the window again.

Linda fixed Sammy with green spikes for eyes. "He will have the Bordeaux," she corrected. Sammy glanced at her before returning his gaze to the runway lights.

"Cheer up, there, young fella. It hurts for jest a little while, but by the time Linda's done with you, why, you'll fit into any of them high-falutin' crowds. Jest look at me," Wes offered. Sammy did, and smiled.

"Don't let dear Wes mislead you, Jim. You are to play an entirely different role," Linda said with a quiet smile.

After they were in the air, they received their drinks from the flight attendant. Sammy regarded his half-full glass of wine, tossed his head back and downed it in one gulp. Wes looked at Linda and chortled, "You got your work cut out for you, sweetie pie!"

"Jim," she said through clenched teeth, "do not hold the glass by the bowl; hold it by the stem. Do not gulp—sip. We are not going to a beach party."

Sammy looked mildly interested. "What kind of party are we going to?"

Linda set her glass on the small table between them. "We are going to a very important showing at a gallery. Many of my associates will be there. Your job will simply be to make your first public appearance as my secretary. You will not attempt to converse with anyone about anything of import—you will simply smile and listen. That is especially crucial if Matthew Constantin attempts to talk to you. He is my enemy. Do make a point to flatter Emily Bohr—attractive men make her babble, and she'll tell you many useful things. Where is that little voice-activated tape recorder?" she turned on Wes.

"Darlin', you musta left that at home, 'cause I sure as heck don't have it," he said defensively.

"Drat. Well, just listen to her carefully so that you can repeat everything back to me. Especially *names,* Jim," she instructed.

"Who is Leslie?" Sammy asked, resting his elbows on his knees.

"Leslie is the daughter of a Parisian dealer who has something I want," she answered chillingly. "I'll tell you more about her when the time comes. Do you speak any French?" she asked.

"Not a word," he said truthfully.

"Pity," she muttered. "That would have been too much to hope for, I expect. We'll simply have to make do. A little ignorance can be charming. Let me think about the best way to work it." Sammy sat back, regarding her with a reluctant admiration.

In less than two hours they landed at La Guardia. It was much colder here than in Dallas, and as soon as Sammy stepped into the chilly air, his chest squeezed painfully. Linda had her fur and Wes an overcoat, but Sammy had nothing to cover the silk suit he wore.

Fortunately, it was a short walk to a waiting limo, which took them straight to Hastings, a swank Manhattan gallery. Linda swept inside on Wes's arm, leaving Sammy to follow.

The importance of this gallery could be determined by the bare white walls and industrial carpet on the floor. Set at strategic locations were all of three works on display. After receiving a drink thrust on him by a waiter, Sammy paused in front of a slashed canvas. It was a plain white canvas, slashed.

"It makes such a statement, don't you think?" Sammy looked down at the speaker: a pale brunette woman with round glasses and deep red lips. "You can almost feel the force, the violence, thrusting out from plainness of the everyday world—the voice demanding to be heard through the white noise of life," she intently observed.

"Is that why it's hanging upside down?" Sammy wondered, sipping his drink.

"Upside down . . . ?" the woman scrutinized the canvas.

"Unless the artist slashed up with his left hand, it's upside down," he maintained.

The woman giggled. "Niels is a genius, except when it comes to displaying other artists."

Sammy stuck out his hand. "Jim Brandon."

"Emily Bohr," she said, shaking his hand with a bright smile. "I've never seen you here before."

"I'm Ms. Threlkeld-Rains's new secretary," Sammy said, successfully getting the words out without gagging. He could feel the scrutiny directed at him from around the room.

"Really?" Emily breathed, sliding her arm through his. "Wherever did she find you?"

"I used to work for her mother-in-law in Dallas," Sammy replied.

"Really? Oh my, I bet Dolly just had a fit when Linda hired you away. Dolly is a dear, but she is terribly possessive of her staff. I heard she's a monster to work for," Emily said in her breathy voice. Linda looked over, smiling in approval.

"Actually, once we reached an understanding, we got along fine. I like Mrs. Threlkeld," Sammy said softly.

"Really?" Emily giggled. "You must be some prize." She walked him over to look at a freestanding sculpture. Nearby, Linda was casually relating how she stole him from Dolly. Sammy glanced up at the faces turned his way, and felt like maybe he should just sit on a pedestal for a grade from this group.

A tall man entered the room and instantly became its focal point. He was dressed solely in black, with his black hair slicked back in a short, curled ponytail. His every move telegraphed his importance, and everyone got the message. Even Emily abandoned Sammy to fawn over the new arrival.

Sammy moved to Linda's side, questioning with his eyes. "That," she said tightly into her drink, "is Matthew Constantin."

Then Sammy watched the curious Dance of Social Standing. Linda conversed with a man at her other side while Constantin went around the room, bestowing attention on his flatterers like a benevolent monarch. Linda and Constantin ignored each other while he drew closer and closer. Then, at an invisible signal, they looked up in utter surprise to see the other at the exact same moment. "Matthew, darling!" Linda exclaimed, throwing open her luscious arms.

"My beautiful Linda." He took her in his arms as if she were a porcupine. He had a vaguely European accent that Sammy immediately doubted was genuine. "Whatever have you been doing, my darling? Not purchasing more Nankin porcelain out from under me?"

"Now, Matthew, you must allow me my little coups. You, being so important, and I just a nobody," she pouted.

He laughed. "Never for a moment, darling, would I under-estimate you so." He glanced at Sammy beside her and asked, "Where did you get the cop, dear Linda?"

Her cheeks flushed in anger but she smiled as she said, "Matthew, darling, that's not the slightest bit amusing. Jim is my secretary, and it cost me dreadfully to separate him from Dolly."

"Ah. Then I am certain he will perform to your expecta-tions, no?" He condescended to inform Sammy: "Ms. Threlkeld-Rains prefers leather to metal."

Linda was apoplectic with rage, but masked it under a radiant smile. Sammy watched with keen interest as Constan-tin kissed her cheek and moved on. Only a hardened felon had that kind of sixth sense for cops.

As if in defiance of Constantin, Linda took Sammy around the room and introduced him to a number of people who were in some way useful to her. In between introductions, she gave him murmured instructions as to how he should manipulate each one: "He fancies himself an expert on Dresden china. Ask his opinion on any piece, and he'll consider you his friend." "She's terribly vain about her hair. The best comment is to apologize for staring at it." Sammy absorbed the names, faces, and weaknesses with ease.

In the course of talking with one woman, Linda turned to Sammy and instructed, "Do make a note that I'm to meet with Regina on the thirtieth, Jim. Oh, say, four?" she inquired of her associate, who nodded.

"Sure," Sammy muttered, digging in his pockets for a pen and paper. He had neither, so he borrowed a pen from a gallery assistant and wrote the note on a napkin. He stuffed it in his pocket and looked up to see the women smiling.

"Their training is somewhat deficient nowadays, isn't it?" Regina murmured knowingly.

"Jim has other strengths," Linda purred, and they eyed him lasciviously.

Sammy decided he was fed up. "Ms. Threlkeld-Rains, I'm quite competent. Don't be sexist," he protested sardonically.

Completely missing his sarcasm, the women burst into shrill laughter. "Oh, Jim, you're so cute!" Linda exclaimed, pinching his chin and kissing him. Sammy bridled a strong desire to knock her across the room.

Wes, who had been circulating with his good ol' boy routine, came over and said through clenched teeth, "Linda honey, you got such a nasty habit of kissin' stray dogs and hired help. You got to curb some of that natcheral affection, sweetie pie."

"Don't tell me what to do, Wes dear," Linda returned in a smiling murmur.

Grinning back at her, he said, "It's my money that got you here, darlin'. Don't forget who brung you to the dance."

Linda looked straight in his eyes and whispered, "Without me, you'd still be kicking cow patties in Texas. At any time I could see that you go back wearing stainless-steel bracelets. Don't forget *that,* darling Wes." He became quiet and sullen.

The party dragged on with ample liquor, skimpy hors d'oeuvres, pretentious conversation and ingenious backstabbing. By two A.M., Sammy was ready to go begging for some aspirin. But then Constantin left and the party began to sputter. Not wishing to be caught at a dying affair, Linda quickly decided it was time to leave and they piled into the limousine.

Seated in the closed car, Linda lit a cigarette. Sammy looked over at her and she held the pack toward him. Although Sammy had quit smoking once before, the strain of this evening and the aroma of her cigarette brought back the craving as strong as ever. He took one gratefully, placing a hand over hers as she lit it with her gold lighter. Sitting back, he took a long drag and closed his eyes to embrace the soothing rush of nicotine.

Immediately he felt a searing pain in his chest, in the area of his wound. Coughing violently, he tossed the cigarette out the window and held his chest until the pain subsided enough for him to draw shaky breaths. In the back of his mind was the humorous picture of one tough guardian angel making sure he didn't relapse into nasty habits.

Linda eyed him in a superior way. "Such an innocent," she murmured. Sammy kept the window rolled down a crack to suck in some fresh, stinging air.

The limo delivered them to Linda and Wes's Park Avenue apartment, where Sammy had to be reminded to let the doorman take their luggage up to their fortieth-floor suite.

As they opened the door and turned on the light, he stared dumbly into the room. It was rather small and very sparsely furnished—not what one would expect of a couple living in such high style. *Big deal*, Sammy thought; all he was interested in was a bed. And that's what he saw, looking into the next room—one very large bed.

After tipping the doorman, Wes turned to see Sammy eyeing the bedroom. "You don't sleep in there, boy," he said in a low voice that had lost some of its twang. "They's another bed in that little room past the john," he pointed.

"That's all I want," Sammy uttered, rubbing his achy chest. He dragged himself and his suitcase into the next room and flopped onto the bed. As he pulled off his shoes and socks, a hollow feeling welled up in his stomach. He missed his partner. He needed her. Without her to watch his back, he felt vulnerable and exposed.

Miserably, he tossed his coat, shirt and tie onto a chair. He unzipped his pants and sat on the bed to pull them off. "Oh, baby, how I wish you were here," he whispered. He fell back onto the still-covered bed and was instantly asleep.

He dreamed about Marni. He saw her face with those foxy eyes close to his. He felt her soft hands caressing his body, and he moaned. Then he felt her lips pressed to his, and he seized her.

Something was wrong. Sammy's eyes cracked open in the dark room. The lips were not Marni's, nor was the hair. He bolted upright as Linda breathed, "There, now, you were doing so well."

"Uh—Wes—" he stammered.

"—has gone down to the bar, and I imagine he won't be back for *quite* a while," she said in a low, throaty voice.

He began seriously, "Linda, I don't want to make any trouble between—"

"Shut up," she said. "It's time for you to start earning your pay." She pushed him back down, kissing him forcefully.

God, I don't want to do this. You gotta help me out here. He did his part by holding her hands firmly away from his underwear.

Suddenly the door banged open, the light came on, and a red-faced Wes appeared. "I knew it! I knew the minute I turned my back you'd be in here!" he shouted.

"How *dare* you! Who do you think you are?" Linda screamed back at him.

Sammy, beneath her, laid his head back on the bed and shut his eyes. *I'm dead. Lord Jesus, receive my spirit.*

But as Linda jumped up from the bed screaming and Wes hollered back at her, neither of them paid any more attention to him at all. They took their screamfest to the next room.

Sammy quietly got up, locked the door, and sank back onto the bed. "Marni, save me," he groaned, then rolled over and went back to sleep.

eight

The following morning Sammy awakened to soft hands on his shoulders, but after last night, he was not fooled. He opened one eye to look back over his shoulder at Linda. "Good morning, Jim," she purred. With her hair hanging limp around her face and her makeup worn off, she looked less the enchantress and more the witch. Sammy groaned and put the pillow over his head.

"Now, don't worry about last night," she assured him, rubbing his shoulders. "What fine muscle tone," she murmured, and he warily looked out from under the pillow. "Everything's fine. Dear Wes just had a little too much to drink."

"Where is he?" Sammy asked, looking behind her toward the bathroom.

"He said he had to go to the airport to claim some cargo," she said, a slight frown wrinkling her brow. "Never mind. You need to shave and dress—we fly out this afternoon."

Nodding, Sammy started to get up, then stopped and cocked a brow at her as she watched him. "You're not modest, are you, Jim dear?" she smirked.

He slowly opened his mouth and replied, "With you around, I'll never get dressed in time." Pleased, she swept out in her silk kimono and Sammy let out his breath.

Linda attended to some business while he showered, shaved and dressed, then they went downstairs so that he could get a bagel and coffee. She did not offer to pay for it, however, and Sammy had no money on him.

So while she was receiving a message from the doorman, Sammy helped himself from her purse to a large cash advance on his next theoretical paycheck. He also removed a business card with her and Wes's New York address and phone number.

Linda returned to inform him that Wes would meet them at the airport, so they climbed in the limousine and set off. Sammy couldn't help but notice how much less demonstrative she was now than when Wes was around—apparently, tormenting "dear Wes" gave her the most pleasure. In spite of himself, Sammy felt a trifle chafed.

They arrived at the airport, checked their luggage, and waited to board the flight to Paris. The way Linda kept glancing around for Wes, Sammy surmised that she needed him a lot more than she cared to admit.

The minutes passed, and no Wes. Linda began to get edgy as she scanned the terminal. Then she exhaled, "Finally! Here he comes. Who—?" She caught herself, and Sammy turned to look.

There was a young woman walking beside Wes. When Sammy glimpsed her easy swing, his heart bounced right up to his throat and he had to bite his tongue to keep quiet. "Mm—!"

With his arm around her, Wes and companion drew up to Sammy and Linda. "Wes, darling, what is this?" Linda uttered.

"Wall, sweetheart, you needed a secretary, and so did I," Wes answered in great satisfaction. Sammy gazed at his companion, who eyed him coolly before looking away. "Jim should reckanize her. This here's Melody Brandon, *my* new secretary."

"I'm so pleased to meet you, Ms. Threlkeld-Rains," Marni said, extending her hand. Linda stared at her as if she could choke her, ignoring her hand. "Actually, I hope to be of use to you, as well. I'm afraid *your* secretary couldn't tell a Gauguin from a Cézanne if his life depended on it." Marni spoke with the bitter superiority of a betrayed wife, which gratified Wes to no end. Sammy stared at her. *This is an act, Marni, right? Tell me this is an act.*

The thunderstruck expression that Sammy and Linda shared made Wes throw back his head and chortle at his unparalleled cleverness. Marni returned Sammy's gaze with clenched teeth, and he broke out in a cold sweat.

In barely restrained fury, Linda grabbed Wes's elbow to drag him aside a few feet. "We are not taking her to Paris!" she hissed.

"Why not?" he flared back. "You got *you* a nice young secretary. Wall, wot's good fer the goose is good fer the gander!"

"I won't have it!" she screamed. "You're ruining everything! I won't let you do this to me!" She carried on so loudly that she attracted the attention of almost the whole terminal.

Marni watched her serenely while Sammy gazed sickly at Marni. When Linda was at the height of her histrionics, Marni turned only her eyes to him and winked slyly. Relief flooded his soul. He had his partner back.

"Linda," he said calmly.

She turned to him in extreme aggravation, snapping, "What?"

"Do you think Constantin would be interested in her?" Sammy posed callously.

Contemplating the possibilities brought Linda to abrupt silence. Suddenly her whole demeanor changed. She took Marni's arm with a silky smile. "What an interesting suggestion. Dear—Melody, is that it?—*of course* you'll be useful. Wes just can't resist throwing little surprises into my day—that's one of the things I love about him. We mustn't leave for Paris yet, Wes. Jim, please see that our luggage comes off the plane." As she walked off with her arm in Marni's, Wes looked crestfallen and Sammy had to scramble to reclaim their luggage before it took off for Paris without them.

First, Linda determined that Marni required a makeover. Linda called the limo service from the airport about sending out another car. Because she had planned to be in Paris, however, she had not bothered to pay them for the last month of service, and they refused to accommodate her until she did. Linda hung up on them and hailed a cab.

The cab first took them to the Park Avenue apartment where they dropped off their suitcases. Then the men were left to cool their heels in an upscale Manhattan bar while Linda took Marni to her very own salon and favorite Fifth Avenue dress shops.

During the time the women were gone, Wes and Sammy talked. Wes had a taste for strong liquor, particularly bourbon, so after a few highballs he was leaning on Sammy like an old friend. "She's an eyeful, ain't she?" he said mournfully. "Most beautiful woman I ever laid eyes on. I was jest eaten up with envy when Stan brought her home. Sure, I was married at the time, with a boy, but that didn't matter to me. I jest wanted Linda. So I worked like a dog to win her. An' fer a while there, oncet I did, I was king of the world. Then she got hard on me, Jimbo. I got to see that all she really wanted was the money. Ever'body tole me that afore, but I didn't want to hear it.

"I know, I know," he groaned in response to something Sammy had not said. "I know I oughta drop her right on her cute little fanny. But I love 'er, Jim. I cain't hep it. I see ever' blessed thing she does and I still love 'er. Someday, though, she's gonna need me again. Someday she's gonna go bust, and I'll be there to pick up the pieces," he vowed. Sammy turned up his beer, watching him, and reevaluated whether the hick Texan routine was really just a routine after all.

Linda's makeover experts did such a thorough job that when she brought Marni to this bar four hours later, male eyes followed them from every corner. Sammy looked up to see his partner so heavily primped and made up as to be almost unrecognizable. He bristled at the tampering, even while noting the general envy when she slid into his booth. Linda, of course, sat between them.

"Wes, darling, go check on the action this evening, and *especially* where dear Matthew will be," Linda instructed. After four hours of elbow-bending, Wes wobbled a little in rising from the bar. Sammy was still nursing his second beer—the one thing he could drink socially with the lowest alcoholic content next to a Shirley Temple.

"Jim, you *must* stop ordering that nasty stuff," Linda declared, removing the mug from in front of him. "Now, Melody, dear, the way to arouse Matthew's interest is to be as rude as possible to him. When he demands an explanation, you will simply inform him that you are Jim's wife and have no intention of sleeping with anyone else."

"I can do that," Marni nodded.

But this did not suit Sammy. Constantin knew he was a cop, so to tell him that "Melody" was his wife would render her useless in uncovering anything about him. "That may not be the best idea, Linda," he spoke up. "Constantin expressed his opinion of me pretty succinctly last night. Letting on that Melody and I are married is not going to enhance her to him. Better that she should be someone else—a woman with a shady past, or something."

Linda blinked at him. "Why, that's very good, Jim. You're learning very nicely. Yessss," she scrutinized Marni thoughtfully. "Your name is Ann Blythe. You're from—oh, Oklahoma, with that accent—I don't have time to teach you to talk properly. You're Wes's secretary and Matthew doesn't need to know anything more about you. When the time comes to tell him more, I'll tell you what to say."

She turned excitedly as Wes approached the booth. "We have it all worked out, dear. Melody's name is Ann Blythe—

she's from Oklahoma and she is *not* married to Jim. Please keep her new name straight."

"Sure thing, sweetie. Uh, Harbour House is havin' an estate auction at six. Constantin is s'pposed ta be there," he said, face flushed.

"Excellent," Linda said, consulting her diamond-studded watch. "We just have time to make it there." They got up from the booth to leave. As Wes had spent his last dollar on drinks, he walked away from the table without a backward glance. Sammy dug in his own pocket for the tip.

At the street, Linda thrust out an arm (and a leg) and a taxi screeched up to the curb. They piled into the cramped, stuffy back seat; Linda was too distracted with plans to notice that Marni was practically sitting on Sammy's lap. It was a very pleasant ride to the auction house, as the driver drove like a lunatic and Sammy had to keep clutching "Ann."

They disembarked at the West 57th address, where Linda signed in and received a catalog and a numbered paddle. She worked her way to a row near the front while her retinue followed, waiting while she greeted all her friends with air kisses. Sammy was able to walk with his wife until they reached a suitable row, where Linda made sure to seat him on her left and Marni on Wes's right.

Just before the bidding was to begin, Constantin entered in his trademark black. Linda looked irritated at being upstaged, then informed Marni with a glance that her target had just walked in. Marni made a point to ignore him and hitched up her skirt an inch or two. Sammy crossed his arms to sit back and watch.

This auction consisted of the art and antiques from the estate of a private collector. Since Linda had not planned to be here, she was not particularly interested in buying anything, and Marni got the definite impression that she did not buy spontaneously. The gentleman who died had a very fine collection of late nineteenth-century French paintings. One by one they came under the hammer, and sold for a hundred thousand and up.

The bidding was quick and silent. The bidders raised their paddles to indicate their acceptance of a figure the auctioneer called out, and anyone who blinked missed something crucial. Marni watched with keen interest, but Sammy stifled a yawn.

So he almost missed the significance of the next painting that came up on the block. Marni gaped, then leaned over to whisper to Linda, "May I see the catalog, please?" She handed it across to her and Sammy looked over.

Marni nodded toward the auctioneer, who announced, "This fine painting is number fifteen in your catalog: *The Elder Sister* by William Adolphe Bouguereau. The bidding will begin at seventy thousand." Sammy woke up.

Marni studied the text in the catalog under the picture: "Painted in 1879; Recorded and illustrated in Vachon, Baschet and Art Treasures of America. Ex collections of M. L. O'Bower, Jas. S. Cornell. Size without frame: approximately 171 x 101 cm." This was purported to be the original. But if this was the original, then what had Stanley bought for half a million dollars?

Sammy and Marni watched the bidding rise to $220,000 before it was claimed by paddle number 206. They looked at each other; Sammy leaned forward and Marni combed the rest of the catalog. She did not find anything else that she recognized from the Threlkelds' house.

The auction continued. Matthew Constantin bought a Bernard Palissy dish for a sum that made Marni's head swim; watching him, she had little doubt that he would recoup his investment easily. He happened to glance toward Linda and his eye landed on Marni. She delivered the sidelong glance she had perfected on Sammy and then looked away in disinterest.

Sammy restrained himself from watching Constantin's reaction.

When the bidding was done and the dealers settled up with the auctioneer, Constantin came over to Linda. "Darling! I thought you would be in Paris by now." He gave her that peculiar embrace. Marni gazed in boredom at the wall past his shoulder.

"Last-minute change in plans, dear Matthew. And I am so glad, else I might have missed the unique pleasure of watching you buy the Palissy dish. Have you a buyer for it?" she asked incredulously.

He smiled cunningly. "My dear, I have *two* buyers for it. Ah, that I had another Palissy to offer!" he sighed. "But some works of art are unique . . . perfect, and extraordinary." He looked at Marni as he said this.

She turned her heavily blackened almond eyes up at him. "And some are fakes," she noted.

He turned toward her, folding his hands loosely in front of him. "Linda, my sweet, you must introduce me to this charming creature."

Linda smiled like a crocodile. "Matthew, this is Wes' secretary Ann Blythe. I'm afraid Ann already knows you well, Matthew dearest."

He laughed and bent to kiss Marni's hand. "*Enchanté, ma chère.*" Marni smiled indulgently and removed her hand. "You must all come dine with me at Le Joker," he declared. "But Linda—may we leave the cop at home?"

Marni startled imperceptibly but Linda smiled thinly. "Your little joke is wearing on me, Matthew dear. I wouldn't *dream* of leaving such a useful man behind." Pointedly, she stroked Sammy's chest.

"As you wish, darling," he smiled ironically. "To my car," he gestured.

They went out to Constantin's limousine, which seated the five of them quite comfortably. Marni wound up in between Wes and Constantin. As she crossed her legs and looked languidly out the heavily tinted window, Matthew murmured, "Ann Blythe. Is that your real name, my love?"

"Of course not." She glanced over at the ridiculous question.

Constantin started on a hearty laugh and Sammy asked him, "Is 'Matthew Constantin' yours?"

The presumption caught Constantin in midlaugh, and he had to think a moment as to whether he should ignore this upstart or cut him down to size right away. He decided on the latter: "I have people," he said, "who can find out anything about anyone."

Sammy leaned forward in great interest. "People who know a lot tell a lot."

Constantin studied him through eyelids so narrowed that he looked like a lizard with hair. They rode in a silent standoff until arriving at the restaurant.

Constantin led them sweeping inside past the line of hopefuls waiting to get in, and procured one of the best tables—a large round one that sat conspicuously in the middle of the room.

Then the dynamics of seating kicked in. Constantin quickly pulled out a chair for Marni and sat beside her. Sammy had to make the instantaneous choice of grabbing the seat on Marni's other side or more properly seating Linda first. He chose to forgo formalities and took the seat beside Marni. The maître d' was left to seat Linda next to Constantin. Wes, more or less sloshed, claimed the last seat between her and Sammy.

The restaurant was one of those intimidating, wildly expensive places that served nouvelle French cuisine and the daily gossip columns. Marni masked her interest in the Art

Deco glass lights above the gilded mirrors by appearing to stare off into space.

The process of ordering was a mystery that defied explanation, but she found that sniffing, "You seem to know what's edible here," to Matthew both pleased him and got her past that hurdle. Sammy ordered competently for himself, and only the sotted Wes made a fool of himself. Linda quietly rescued him.

"Dear Linda," Matthew began, "it's time for us to put our differences behind us and join forces. We can make much more working together than butting heads, no?"

"Why, Matthew, how perfectly sweet," Linda cooed. "What did you have in mind?"

"An American actor has found himself deeply in cash after his last film—some dreadful action picture—and has decided to acquire 'culture,'" he said with a sneer. "He is looking for someone *trustworthy* to guide him through his acquisitions."

"I can't imagine anyone better qualified than you, dear Matthew," she murmured into her wine glass with irony so thick it almost overflowed.

He laughed. "Nor can I, my love, but this man has the reputation of being one—how you say—'stud.' He should be putty in your lovely hands."

"What terms?" she asked succinctly.

"We split all profits fifty-fifty," he proposed.

"Matthew, I can hardly believe my ears. That sounds almost fair," she marveled.

"*Accompli,*" he declared, raising his glass.

"*Tout accompli,*" she confirmed, raising hers.

"One stipulation, my dear," he added. "We must streamline. The actor is willing to spend millions to achieve his notion of culture, and that means he desires to surround himself only with people of culture. Ms. Blythe possesses the aura I require, but you must drop your quaint Texas sidekick and your gigolo."

Wes, deep in his wine glass, was too far gone to know what was said, but Sammy glanced up shrewdly. Linda evaluated her male companions against several million dollars, and the green won. Wes she could drop and pick up again at will, but Jim— she turned to Sammy and said, "I regret that I no longer require your services. You may pick up your things and leave tonight."

He smiled. "Oh, Linda, you do need me. You don't know how much. Why, I'm an authority on certain types of artists. Like Bouguereau. I was *extremely* interested to see *The Elder Sister* come up for auction tonight."

Linda froze, then turned to look at Marni, who wore a quizzical frown. Matthew was silent, smelling blackmail. "They say a little knowledge is a dangerous thing," Linda purred to Sammy.

Sammy's smile was all deviousness. "A little is dangerous, but a lot is powerful. Maybe I aimed to be your secretary before you offered me the job."

Linda actually paled. Marni did too, under her thick makeup. Sammy was piling risk on top of risk with a wild guess that would either hurl the case forward or get him killed.

Constantin looked at Sammy with new regard. "My friend, I misjudged you completely. Linda dearest, *mon erreur*. Your young man will fit nicely into the picture." He was almost frothing in his desire to know what Sammy had on Linda.

The dinner progressed with the lighthearted banter of jackals circling each other, looking for weaknesses. Marni maintained a quiet, aloof air, well aware that she was in over her head. To sustain the mystery of what he had on Linda and how he might use it, Sammy smiled and kept his mouth shut. So the bulk of the conversation fell to Constantin and Linda.

"What in the world would you be after in Paris this time of the year, darling?" Constantin asked. "Cold and rainy—so unpleasant. Like a nagging woman."

In an unguarded moment Linda admitted, "A dear friend of mine has two damascened suits of armor—"

Constantin threw back his head and laughed hilariously. "Oh, darling, old Previn called you, too? He's been trying to unload those suits forever. *Everyone* knows the damascening on those suits isn't inlaid, only gilt! They aren't worth one-tenth of what he's asking for them!"

Linda merely arched an eyebrow, and he continued seriously, "How providential that I was able to warn you before you bought them, my dear. Partners must watch out for each other, no?" She smiled tightly in response.

After a moment he added, "I hear that Leslie has taken up residence with an Italian count on the Riviera. Poor dear—someone should tell her that he means only to gain access to her father's contacts."

"Pity," Linda murmured, glancing up, and Sammy could see her attempting to weigh how much truth there was in all that Constantin said.

Marni had no idea what she ate that night, but it was wonderful. As the party rose to leave, she hoped that she and Sammy could come back sometime—alone. She looked in pity at Wes, unconscious on the table.

Constantin pointed at the pathetic figure. "Garçon, this man is not with our party and I will not pay for his dinner."

"Certainly, sir," the waiter replied, looking malevolently toward the blissfully sleeping Wes. Marni cringed for him.

"I wish you to repair with me to my humble home," Constantin said pretentiously, "where I might offer you some stimulating refreshments." So saying, he leered at Marni.

"Why, Matthew, how delightful," Linda replied, having no intention of being left out.

"Yeah, thanks," Sammy added ironically.

As the four of them headed out, Sammy looked down at his loosely dangling French cuff. He roughly grabbed Marni's arm and jerked her around. Matthew and Linda quickly looked. "Okay, baby," he snarled, "where's my gold cufflink?"

In character, Marni sputtered, "You—moron! I don't have your stupid cufflinks! Let go of me!"

"Perhaps you dropped it at the table, Jim," Linda suggested mildly.

"You better hope I did," he growled to Marni, then went back to look.

He got to the table in time to catch two burly busboys removing the leaden Wes. "How much is his bill?" Sammy whispered. They presented it to him; he paid it, with a nice tip, then handed over another fifty. "He lives at, uh, the Cloisters on Park Avenue. See that he gets home all right—*after* we leave."

He paused to scribble this note and stuff it in Wes's coat pocket: "You passed out at the restaurant and I paid to get you home. Linda, Melody and I have gone with Constantin—I will call you later as I know more. Jim."

As he went back to the exit, he dug the missing cufflink from his coat pocket, where he had placed it earlier. He was refastening it when he joined the others waiting in Constantin's limo. "I'm so glad you found your cufflink, Jim, dear," Linda said.

"Yeah, you better be," he replied to Marni. She tossed her head, and the driver started for Constantin's Manhattan apartment. Marni sat uneasily beside Constantin, who rested a hand on her knee. Sammy and Linda sat across from them, watching.

They arrived at the Park Avenue address, and Sammy's jaw dropped to find it the same as Linda and Wes's. It was a luxurious apartment building with old, ornate stone and gutter work. As they rode the elevator up to the second floor (out of sixty), Sammy uneasily kept an eye out for any Le Joker employees who might be carting Wes up to the fortieth floor.

Constantin showed them into his apartment, which was larger than Linda's but almost as spartan. Though he had no interest in interior design, Sammy did note the general value of things from a professional point of view. Either minimalism was *de rigueur* in New York decorating circles these days, or neither Linda nor Constantin had the money they pretended to have.

"Welcome, my friends," Constantin effused as Linda dropped her coat onto the sofa. He put on a CD of something barely recognizable as music, then brought out an assortment of drug paraphernalia. "How you say—time to party!" He waved toward a large bed in the next room.

Scared stiff, Marni bit her lip and looked at the floor. But Sammy coolly surveyed the chemicals and the master bedroom. Oh, how she loved him! If anybody could get them out of this, he could. She nudged him along with a little prayer, not knowing that he was mentally on his knees himself.

He walked over to another room, which had a bare mattress on the floor and a window facing the street. Then he turned back to Constantin and Linda with a look of cool contempt that could rattle stone. "Great," he leered, "I'll take *Ann.*" He seized her hand and yanked her toward him.

His manner clued her to the appropriate response. "You will *not!*" she shouted, jerking away her hand and drawing back to slap him.

He grabbed her wrist and twisted so hard that tears came to her eyes. "Oh, yes I will," he breathed, then flung her into the second bedroom.

"No!" Marni screamed. "Linda!" She and Constantin were watching with interest.

Sammy pointed at them. "*Don't* disturb me. I might get riled."

Constantin paused, but his lust for Ann was not strong enough to challenge this blackmailer with a hair-trigger temper. "Do leave her alive, dear boy," Constantin murmured as Linda turned with greater interest to his toys.

"Maybe," Sammy grunted, slamming and locking the door. Marni gleefully greeted him. He kissed her soulfully, then tickled her, whispering, "Scream."

Marni opened her mouth and began to let out a good one, which he promptly muffled. They jumped on the mattress to make it groan nice and loud, and Sammy smacked his fist into his palm a few times. He instructed Marni on various other noises to make, which she did as well as she could for the spasms of silent laughter.

Finally, he had her quiet down and they listened at the door for a while. "Okay," he whispered, then went to the window and opened it, looking out at the narrow concrete ledge and fancy grillwork. The cold night air rushed in.

"What are you going to do?" she asked anxiously.

"Finish the day's work, baby. I'll be back as soon as I can," he said, sitting on the windowsill and throwing a leg over.

She caught his arm. "Sammy, I'm scared at the way you're pushing Linda. She's liable to push back."

"Don't worry; I'm stringing a safety net. And I'll deal with *you* when I get back," he winked. Then he was out on the ledge.

nine

Marni leaned worriedly out of the window, shivering, to watch Sammy step tentatively onto the ten-inch-wide window ledge. With his back pressed against the stone façade, he slid along the ledge about four feet until he was able to reach out and grab the gutter pipe. Then he swung over and climbed down it to the sidewalk below. "Watch for me," he called quietly, and trotted off.

She shut the window, fretting about his being out in the cold without an overcoat. The doctor had warned them that Sammy's injury would leave him susceptible to bronchitis and pneumonia. Turning, she renewed her attacks on the mattress, in case Linda and Constantin were listening, then went over to the window to watch for Sammy to return.

He found a public phone not too far away—a relic in the land of the cell phone—and pressed against the wall on which it was mounted. Checking his watch, he muttered, "Gee, it's only midnight in Dallas. Maybe I should wait awhile to make sure he's asleep." Nonetheless, he picked up the phone and called Mike Masterson at home, collect.

"Hello, gramps," Sammy said when Mike grumpily gave the operator the go-ahead. "I didn't wake you, did I? Tell Charisse to roll back over—it's just me."

"I hope you've got something important to tell me, Kidman," Mike groaned.

"That depends on how well you do your follow-up, flatfoot. Two things: you need to send an art expert out to the

Threlkelds' to check out that painting I showed you the receipt on—*The Elder Sister* by Bouguereau. Marni and I watched that painting being auctioned at the Harbour House tonight for just under a quarter million."

"Wait a minute—the Threlkelds sold the painting?" Mike asked groggily.

"No, it couldn't'a been the same one—one of the two is a fake. I need you to find out whether the Threlkelds' is the fake. Stanley bought it for twice what it sold for tonight."

"Gotcha," Mike said grimly.

"Whatever you find out, you gotta keep it tight. The Threlkelds can't press charges yet or it will blow my cover and I will be in deep doo-doo," Sammy said solemnly.

"I'll keep that in mind," Mike said, deliberately casual.

"You're a sweetheart. Oh yeah, I also need to know how Linda Threlkeld-Rains—Stanley's ex—was involved in that sale. I'm blackmailing her with that information, so I can't go asking what it is that I know," Sammy added.

"I didn't hear that," Mike said in disavowal.

"Second item: You got a pencil? Matthew Constantin, Caucasian, black-brown, six-two, two hundred thirty pounds, late twenties, light two-inch scar under his chin. He usually wears his hair slicked back in a ponytail and dresses in black—a real arty type. He's a known felon to someone somewhere, and I need to know the details," Sammy stated.

"You got a locality to get me started?" Mike groused.

"No. He pretends to be Continental, but I wouldn't be surprised to hear he's from Cleveland," Sammy snorted, then sneezed.

"Okay, Sambo, we'll get on it. You say—Marni's up there with you?" Mike asked.

"Yeah. She's great, Mike," he sighed. "She's goin' under two aliases—Melody Brandon to the Threlkelds and Ann Blythe to Constantin."

"Yeah? Well, keep an eye on her, Sammy," Mike said uneasily.

"Like a hawk," Sammy said assuredly, and hung up.

He hurried back to the Cloisters, suppressing a cough. When he got below Marni's window he whistled softly, but she did not appear. He found a spent shell casing and tossed it up against the window, but still did not see her.

The blinds of the first-floor apartment windows began to move, so he flattened himself against the stone between two windows for a few minutes. When he cautiously stepped away from the building, the blinds were still again. He looked up then and saw Marni at the window. Relieved, he waved to her and began climbing the drainpipe.

It was old guttering attached to an old building, and the screws began to pull out of the masonry at several points. But Sammy continued up to the second-story ledge, thanking goodness he didn't have to climb up to Linda's apartment on the fortieth floor.

He stepped onto the ledge and backed up against the wall while Marni threw open the window and leaned out. Taking a deep breath, he slid along the ledge until he could grasp her outstretched hand. She pulled him inside with surprising strength. As she shut the window, she whispered, "Constantin has been banging on the door. I didn't know how long I could keep him out."

Sammy nodded, coughed, and croaked, "Undress."

Blue-lipped, they both stripped down to their underwear. Then he scrutinized the bare, dirty mattress with disgust. The room was cold, and a light snow began falling outside. Marni's teeth were chattering as she sat gingerly on the mattress. He gestured for her to lie down, whispering, "You're unconscious." Reluctantly, she stretched out and shut her eyes.

Sammy opened the door and went out in his underwear. Constantin and Linda looked up from the floor, where they sat on an expensive Oriental rug. They were weaving and giggling, far away on a chemical trip. Linda pointed at Sammy and laughed until she was almost convulsed. Constantin curled up on the rug, announcing that he was a pebble.

"Are we having fun?" Sammy asked, bypassing them to look into Constantin's bedroom.

Linda exploded in fresh laughter and Constantin insisted, "I am a SMOOTH, GRAY pebble."

"Sure you are, guy," Sammy muttered, surveying Constantin's king-sized waterbed covered with quilts. "Say," he turned, "mind if we use your bed for the night?"

Linda rolled in circles on the floor, breathless with laughter. Constantin replied, "The water is flowing over me."

"Thanks," Sammy said. He went to the other room to retrieve Marni and their clothes and move to the master bedroom. Sammy locked the door, then curled up with his baby under warm covers while the snow swirled outside.

The next morning, the first official day of spring, white, lacy snowflakes still drifted down between the skyscrapers to be transformed into piles of ugly gray slush along the streets. Sammy was up and dressed long before his hosts, who lay snoring on the floor where they had passed out. While Marni got ready, he searched the apartment, concentrating on Constantin's cluttered desk.

"Find anything?" Marni murmured, coming up behind him to slip her arms around his neck.

He turned to study her, and smiled. She had mostly abandoned the look as Linda's younger clone except for the slinky dress. Sammy approved. Only problem was, she had no bruises to match last night's charade—but then, Linda and Matthew would be the last to notice any such discrepancies. "Just this," he said, holding a letter over his shoulder for her to read. "Remember that armor they were talking about yesterday?"

Marni took the letter. "Constantin's going to buy it!" she exclaimed in a whisper.

Sammy smiled wryly. "He just knocked out one bidder, sly dog." She handed the letter back to him and he held it, thinking, "Now, the question is, how would this information be most useful to us?"

"You're so devious," she whispered in admiration, kissing his cheek.

"Thank you," he said, pocketing the letter. "Ready to go to breakfast?"

"Sure," she murmured. "But what if they wake up while we're gone?"

"Not likely. Just remember that you loathe me, and don't make those sweet eyes at me, Marni."

"I'll try not to," she sighed. Stepping over the other two on their way out, Marni observed, "They're supposed to be so cool and hip. What's so cool about turning yourself into a vegetable?"

Sammy smiled ironically. "You gotta understand the culture of self-destruction."

"I don't want to understand it—not if I have to be part of it," she declared.

Sammy smiled at her innocence, hugging her. "Baby, you're missing less than nothing."

They found a delicatessen on the first floor of this building where they were served a delightful breakfast of brioche with marmalade and butter, glasses of orange juice set in ice, and strong, steaming coffee. Marni tried not to let on how much she was enjoying herself, in case one of Constantin's or Linda's acquaintances should see them. But even Sammy couldn't resist squeezing her knee under the table.

They went back upstairs to find the others still out cold. While Marni looked through Constantin's art books, Sammy sat at his desk to do some long-distance calling to various police departments, trying to pin down something on Constantin's background.

He came up empty. "I feel like I'm asking the wrong questions," he muttered, "in the wrong place." After some time Sammy grew impatient and attempted to nudge Constantin awake. He groaned and rolled over.

About an hour later Linda sat up, moaning, and headed for the bathroom. While she was occupied therein, Constantin woke and also attempted to get into the bathroom—the only one in the apartment. When he couldn't get in, he logically decided to batter the door down with a bronze bust that had been sitting on a pedestal. Sammy restrained him, and a moment later Linda coolly emerged.

Tired with the waiting, Marni curled up on an old Victorian-type sofa while those two pulled themselves together. She thought, *These are the emptiest people I've ever been around, except maybe for Derek Montblanc. . . .* The next thing she knew, she was jolted awake by a rude slap on the rear end. She bolted up to find Sammy standing over her smiling callously, with Linda and Constantin watching in amusement. "We can't wait all day for you, darling," Constantin chided.

"Keep your filthy hands off me," she growled at Sammy.

In reply, he planted one knee on the sofa, grabbed her hands and was preparing to throw her down when Constantin said, "This is all so entertaining, but we do have a plane to catch." So Sammy yanked her to her feet in a proprietary manner.

Freshly made up so as to look human again, Linda checked inside her suitcase before the bellhop took it. "You say Wes was in bed when you went in for the suitcases?" she asked Sammy. Marni blinked in some confusion, then reasoned that while she was asleep, Linda had sent Sammy up to her apartment to get their bags.

"Yeah," Sammy said, knowing that she would eventually find out that Wes was there.

Linda nodded, looking almost relieved. "Wonder how the old dear made it home."

Sammy shrugged indifferently, jerking Marni along by the wrist. His violent possessiveness of her was meant to encourage Constantin to keep his distance, which it did: when they piled into the limo with their suitcases, Constantin sat beside Linda and left Sammy to his wife. Keeping in character, Marni stared out the window, contemptuously refusing to look at him. Meanwhile, Sammy studied Linda, contemplating various uses for the letter in his coat pocket.

They arrived at the airport and boarded a charter jet for Los Angeles. When the flight attendant came around taking drink orders, Sammy stared Linda down and ordered a beer. She said nothing.

Once Constantin had loosened up with a good stiff drink, he began to tell Linda about their new client: "His name is Jock Walker. He has just purchased a large house in Malibu and wishes to showcase his collection there. If you can get him interested in pre-Columbian art, that would be preferable, because I have a supplier right there in California who can get us all the 'artifacts' we want. I have the feeling, though, that he expects something Old World—in that case, steer him toward Etruscan terra cotta."

Linda raised a stiffly penciled brow. "I thought your little hoard was confiscated and destroyed."

"Only a fraction of it, my dear. Just enough to put *La Sûreté* off the scent," Constantin smiled.

Linda pursed her lips. "I'm afraid you're in for a disappointment, Matthew dear. A novice collector always prefers paintings."

Matthew inclined his head. "Perhaps, darling. But we still split profits fifty-fifty."

"Certainly, Matthew," she purred, sipping her drink.

Their conversation turned to a verbal annihilation of other New York dealers, and Sammy got up to go to the restroom. As soon as he was out of earshot, Linda muttered darkly, "We should dump him. I don't see what good he'll be with Jock."

"My dear Linda, what if Jock is gay?" Constantin asked in surprise at her lack of foresight. Linda did not reply, as everyone knew that was not the main reason Constantin wanted to keep Jim around.

Constantin got up to chat with the pilots. Linda glanced at him out of the corner of her eye, then with lightning quickness took a pill box from her purse and dropped something from it into Sammy's beer. "You won't miss him, will you, dear?" Linda smiled. Marni grinned back at her while her heart hammered against her ribs. Then she looked out the window, searching for an angel.

A moment later Sammy came back, plopped into his seat, and picked up his beer. Marni turned to him in gleeful, malicious anticipation. He saw her look. "What're you smilin' at?" he muttered.

"Nothing," she said airily, looking away, but as he brought the glass to his lips she turned back, watching eagerly. Linda lifted a magazine to cover her face and Marni's eyes focused intently on Sammy's glass. He paused, regarding her.

At that moment they hit some mild turbulence which bounced them a little. Sammy lurched forward, spilling the contents of his glass in Linda's lap. She leapt up, sputtering in rage, and Sammy earnestly apologized, "Linda, I'm so sorry. Gee, your beautiful dress. I'm really sorry." He tried to blot it with one tiny cocktail napkin, but she slapped his hand away and stormed to the restroom. Marni leaned back and closed her eyes in silent relief.

Constantin came over. "What happened?"

"Aw, I spilled a little beer on her dress," Sammy said sullenly.

Constantin laughed. "Don't worry; it's a knockoff, like everything else she has." He threw himself into his seat, regarding Sammy shrewdly. "I am terribly interested in what you know about the Bouguereau that was auctioned last night."

Sammy shrugged, "I don't know anything about *that* one."

"Oh?" Constantin's brows shot up. "You mean there is *another* one?"

"I'm sure he did a lot of paintings," Sammy replied cagily, studying the white residue in the bottom of his glass. "When it suits me to tell you something, I will." He glanced up matter-of-factly, and Constantin appraised him like a potential buy.

They arrived in Los Angeles without further incident and took an airport limo straight to the Beverly Hills Wilshire so that Linda could change clothes. From there, Constantin called their movie-star client and arranged to meet him at Le Joker in Beverly Hills in an hour. Before they left the Wilshire, Sammy attempted to make a clandestine collect call to Wes in New York. The woman who answered the phone told the operator that he had left for Dallas.

So they went on to the restaurant. It was every bit as elegant and intimidating as its New York cousin, but its clientele was far more casual, feeling that they were too famous to have to bother with neckties. Sammy looked around and loosened his own tie.

They were given a table overlooking the palms along the boulevard, where they sat to wait for their prospective client. The scenery along the Wilshire was gorgeous, but Marni passed the time watching for celebrities inside the restaurant. She actually saw a few, and if she hadn't been on assignment, she would probably have embarrassed Sammy by asking for autographs.

After thirty minutes of waiting Linda was steamed, but Constantin cooed, "Just add it to the bill, darling."

In walked the sacrificial goat. Jock Walker was the only man Marni had ever seen who rivaled Sammy in looks, except Jock was bigger, with more muscles. He also had blond hair, a square jaw, and a bronze tan. Upon being introduced to him, Marni offered her hand along with her highly effective chin-down look. But he shook her hand with disinterest and then turned to meet Sammy.

Constantin's rationale for bringing Sammy proved to be prescient. From the moment Jock looked at him he never saw anyone else, and drew up the chair beside him to sit. After the initial shock of discomfort, Sammy looked at him and smiled.

"Well, Jock," Constantin said, eyeing the two with satisfaction, "I can already envision a most profitable relationship. I must tell you of a spectacular horde of Etruscan pottery just discovered in a previously unknown tomb."

"Actually," Jock tore his eyes from Sammy, "I'm interested in Paul Klee oils."

"Wonderful!" exclaimed Linda. "I will have no trouble procuring first-rate works for you."

"The one I want most is *Jung Wald Täfel*. I'll pay any amount for it," Jock declared.

Linda ignored his garbled pronunciation and her eyes glistened. "A connoisseur! It is so *nice* dealing with a knowledgeable buyer! There's no ridiculous haggling when one knows the *true* value of the art he wishes to possess."

"Yeah, well. . . ." Jock's eyes went back to Sammy, who was fidgeting with a napkin. "You have beautiful eyes."

"Thanks," Sammy muttered. Constantin nudged him under the table and Sammy smiled thinly at Jock.

The waiter came to take their orders, and Jock said, "Listen, I can't stay. Jim, I have a very interesting collection of Mapplethorpe. Would you like to come see it?"

"Sure," Sammy said weakly. Linda beamed at him. Marni watched, wide-eyed and expressionless.

"Great!" Jock said, standing. "I'll wait to hear from you about the Klee," he told Linda. "Uh, nice to meet you—Nan." Marni nodded blankly.

Then Jock held out his hand to Sammy, who hesitated an instant before taking it. They walked out of the restaurant hand in hand. Linda and Matthew congratulated each other, and Marni sat in total shock.

Jock retrieved his Alfa Romeo from the parking attendant and held the door for Sammy. As they drove away from the restaurant, Jock said earnestly, "Listen, I want you to know that I was tested just last week and I'm clean."

"Good for you," Sammy said absently, watching the road. When they were about five blocks from the restaurant, he pointed to an office building's parking lot: "Pull in here."

"What is it?" Jock asked anxiously as he parked.

With his hand on the door handle, Sammy said, "You poor schmuck. Linda and Constantin are out to fleece you royally. Whatever they sell you is going to be faked or stolen."

"What? I don't understand," Jock protested.

Sammy opened the door. "I'm a cop with the Dallas Police Department, on special assignment to reel in these jokers. Go ahead and buy whatever they offer you, then call the authorities. I may not be around by the time you actually make the purchase. Don't spend too much, though, 'cause it'll be a while before you see your money again." He got out of the car.

"Wait!" Jock leaned toward him. "What about us?"

"Look, pal, I'm married," Sammy said.

"That doesn't matter," Jock argued.

"It does to me." Sammy shut the door and walked away, shuddering.

He entered the building and went to a lobby phone to make a collect call to Mike at his office. As soon as the operator put him through, Sammy greeted him, "Hello, pruneface."

"Sammy, I'm glad you called," Mike said gravely. "An expert went to look at the Threlkelds' painting this morning. It's genuine."

"Genuine?" Sammy repeated in surprise.

"Yes. And Linda Threlkeld-Rains was the agent who sold Stan Threlkeld the painting."

"Linda sold Stanley a genuine painting?" Sammy repeated, still incredulous.

"Yes, so they've begun tracing the one you saw auctioned," Mike said.

Sammy silently absorbed this. "Mike, I asked you not to do that," he said quietly.

"It's out of my hands, Sammy. I have to forward all information to Foster, but he assured me your cover would be protected," Mike said with some anxiety.

Sammy shook his head. "This is very bad news. Have you learned anything about Constantin?"

"You have to give us more time on that, Sammy. We're looking," Mike said.

"All right. I'll . . . check back in with you," Sammy said distantly.

"Frequently, Sammy. You must call back every two hours, if possible," Mike instructed.

"Sure, guy," Sammy muttered, pensively hanging up. He leaned back against the wall to think. It didn't make sense. Why would Linda react so strongly over selling Stanley a genuine painting? She did not have anything to do with the one auctioned at Harbour House . . . did she? She hadn't even planned to be there that night. She had to have known it was a fake, but she showed no surprise at all. "I wish I knew what she thinks I know," he mused, moving off the wall.

Then he stopped, a cold lead weight dropping in his stomach. Wes had gone back to Dallas. Wes had been at the auction. Wes would make the connection between him, Marni and the painting, and there was no way Foster could forestall that.

ten

Sammy hustled back to the Beverly Hills Wilshire and found that the others had not yet returned. So he got himself something to eat, then sat in the lobby to wait and think. Foster had assured Mike that their cover would be protected. Could Sammy afford to count on that?

Then again, if the Threlkelds' painting *was* genuine, what did he have to worry about Wes saying? Besides, Wes was already so drunk by the time they reached the auction, he probably never saw the questionable painting.

Sammy turned his speculations to a related question: If Linda had sold a good painting to Stanley, then what if she were to sell a good one to Jock? Sammy shook his head. No—on the plane they were clearly discussing a scam.

As he sat thinking this through, he grew vaguely troubled. Was he forgetting something? Was there something he was neglecting? He glanced down at a magazine lying face down on the table beside him, and saw on the back cover the quotation, "The earth is the Lord's, and everything in it."

Sammy looked up. When was the last time he had prayed? Marni prayed all the time, he knew, so—wasn't that sufficient? There could have been something in his masculine pride that said, "Okay, God, thanks for your help; I can handle it from here."

He stared at the quotation—*The earth is the Lord's. That covers a lot of territory,* he thought. *Territory.* . . . Sammy mused. Any operator has his territory. And Constantin had mentioned something on the plane about a supplier he had here in California for fake artifacts.

Abruptly, Sammy got up and left the hotel. He took a cab to the central bureau of the Los Angeles Police Department, where he introduced himself, explained what he wanted, and was referred to Detective Larry Statler of the fraud division.

They shook hands and Larry invited him to sit beside a deeply cluttered desk. "Dallas, huh?" Larry twitted him. "Where's your boots?"

"At home in the closet, with my horse," Sammy returned, and Larry nodded vaguely, studying the Armani suit Sammy wore. "Oh, the suit isn't mine. I'm undercover," Sammy explained.

"Your department must have a heck of a budget," Larry muttered. "Now who were you looking for?"

"Okay. Say I want to get my hands on some pre-Columbian artifacts. Who do I call?" Sammy posed.

"'Art and Antiques,'" Larry noted, rolling his chair back to select a large black binder from the credenza behind him. He hefted the book to Sammy and invited, "Take your pick."

Sammy opened the notebook and began leafing through pages of mug shots. Names were neatly printed beneath the photos. As he looked, he tried to remember any names Constantin might have mentioned, but came up blank. Without a face or a name, picking out a suspect was hardly possible. But he kept looking while Larry filled out one of the neverending reports.

Suddenly Sammy stopped dead over a photo. "Well, well, well. What do you know." Then he looked up and asked Larry, "What do you have on Matthew Constantin Threlkeld?"

Larry leaned over to look at the listing, then called it up on his computer. A lengthy arrest record was printed out. "Forgery, extortion, fraud. . . . What's he involved in now?" Larry asked as Sammy skimmed the printout.

"Who'd'a believed it?" Sammy muttered. "This ID's him as Wes Threlkeld's *son*. Guess Constantin didn't want anyone to know that the 'quaint Texas sidekick' is really 'dear old dad.' Poor ol' Wes isn't the crook—his son and his brother's ex-wife are. They're about to pick Jock Walker's pocket."

"Jock Walker? Of *The Annihilator?*" Larry asked eagerly.

"Yep," Sammy said.

"Have you met him?" Larry asked.

"Yeah," Sammy said.

"Wow. He was great in *The Annihilator.* Have you seen it? Great film. He's got to be my favorite actor," Larry said enthusiastically.

"Yeah, well, he's—" Sammy began, then stopped.

"He's what?" asked Larry.

"He's . . . about to purchase a 'Paul Klee oil' from the Threlkelds. I told Jock to go ahead and make the buy, then contact you guys," Sammy said, mentally noting, *And if it's legit then my name is Vincent van Gogh.*

"Great! Then I'll get to meet him," Larry said.

"Yeah. Uh, mind if I use your phone?" Sammy asked. Larry moved some papers off it and Sammy dialed Mike's office. "Hello, you slimy double-crosser," he said when Mike answered, and Larry glanced up.

"Sammy! Listen—"

"No, you listen. Constantin's real name is *Threlkeld*, and I'm sittin' here in the LAPD's fraud division looking at his rap sheet. Another conviction and he'll be down for the count, buddy. He's targeted—"

"Sammy, we know about Matthew. We've been talking to the Threlkelds," Mike said hurriedly. He gave Sammy a rapid rundown of what they had uncovered about him, then asked, "Is Marni with you?"

"No. Why?" Sammy asked uneasily.

Mike took a deep breath. "Mrs. Threlkeld got suspicious when the first art expert came to her house—apparently he's one who had worked with Linda Threlkeld before. So Mrs. Threlkeld called in another expert to evaluate the painting, and he said it's a fake."

"I knew it!" Sammy said. "Linda—"

"Shut up and listen! Foster ran a check on the *other* painting and it's a fake as well! No one knows for sure who has the real painting. You've blown open a widespread counterfeiting operation, and there have been several unexplained disappearances among these dealers in the past several years—"

"Of paintings?" Sammy asked.

"People, Kidman! People have been disappearing. And the cat's out of the bag. I don't know how, but the Threlkelds know who you and Marni are. You gotta get her and get out, Sammy . . . Sammy?"

Sammy was outside on the parking lot, commandeering a police cruiser to take him to the Beverly Hills Wilshire.

When he and two uniformed officers arrived at the hotel, he ran to the desk to breathlessly ask if Constantin had returned yet. The clerk informed him, "Mr. Constantin and his party came in and left again about an hour ago."

"Where did they go?" Sammy shouted.

She shouted back, "I don't know! Okay?"

Matthew, Linda, and Marni arrived by taxi at the gallery of a dealer whom Matthew knew. The dealer, a smarmy "Mr. Jones," took them to a back room to show off his latest acquisitions of ancient pottery while cheerfully describing how they were manufactured just a few weeks ago.

"These are wonderful," Linda said, examining one cracked jar closely. "If Jock isn't interested, some of my New York clientele will be. Regina certainly will be. And since it's not my specialty, she's sure to take it to darling Matthew for his appraisal. Let me call Hastings right away." Linda turned to the telephone while Matthew and Mr. Jones discussed the order.

"Emily, dear, I'm calling from LA, where we found the most—what? Wes called? What—?" Linda turned her back to the others as she listened. Marni paid little attention at first, but the longer Linda listened in uncharacteristic silence, the uneasier Marni grew.

"Well, that's very interesting. Thank you, Emily. We'll attend to it," Linda said, and hung up.

She took her time checking her French twist in a rococo wall mirror, then turned to say lightly, "There has been a change in plans, Matthew dear. It seems that two insurance investigators were posing as hired help in Dolly's house. They found the forgeries and traced them to Hastings. And some-how—" her cool green eyes settled on Marni, whose breathing came hard—"they managed to tag along with us clear out here."

Matthew clenched his fists in rage. "I knew it! I knew he was a cop the first time I saw him! And you, darling—" He grabbed Marni's arm, and she did not resist.

Jones, the art dealer, went purple in the face. "You've ruined me!" he shouted at Constantin.

"No one's ruined," Matthew said calmly. "She's not talk-ing. Go get your packing tape," he jerked his head at Jones, who ran to fetch it off a work table and hand it over.

While Jones held her, Constantin taped Marni's hands and feet together, then put a piece over her mouth. He nodded toward a large wooden crate, stenciled, "FRAGILE: Pottery," which was half-full of wood shavings. Jones moved the lid aside, and Constantin picked up Marni and placed her in the box. Then they fitted the lid and nailed it shut.

Meanwhile, Linda was pacing. "We must do something about Jim. He can't be allowed to continue this charade."

"He'll be at Jock's," Constantin said.

"Then so will we," Linda said. "Matthew, go find us a taxi while I make one more call to New York."

"What about Ann?" he asked darkly.

"I'll take care of her," Linda replied. "Go get us a car."

After Constantin had gone out as instructed, Linda turned to Jones. "Dear Matthew is such an optimist that I'm afraid he misled you. She *will* talk, of course, as soon as she gets the opportunity. Your inventory is ruined and so are you . . . unless. . . ."

"Unless what?" Jones asked guardedly.

Linda stood over the wooden crate, then bent to pick up a handful of shavings which she dropped lightly atop the box. "Your only recourse is a lighted match. Then at least you can collect insurance," she offered.

Jones looked down at the box, caught her hint and paled. "But . . . that's murder," he protested, weighing the word.

Linda calmly dug her cigarettes out of her purse. "I will corroborate your testimony that Matthew overpowered you and then set the fire himself. Use these, and do try to knock yourself on the head, so you'll have something to show when dear Matthew is arrested," Linda explained coolly as she handed him the pack.

Jones glanced miserably around his shop. "I can't let them put me away again. I'll lose everything. You'll back me?" he asked suspiciously, taking the cigarettes.

"With pleasure," Linda smoothly assured him, so he nodded nervously. Linda left without a backward glance at the crate. Jones peeked out the door after her, then scattered paper and wood shavings around on the floor. He shakily drew a cigarette from the pack, lit it, smoked it down, then dropped it to the paper on the floor.

The taxi delivered Linda and Constantin to the front gate of Jock's sprawling Malibu home, where they were announced and granted entrance. A maid showed them to a room decorated with nude statuettes and animal skins. Jock came in from a side room, buttoning his shirt. "Hi," he said uncomfortably. "I didn't expect to hear from you this soon."

"We thought to give you a report on our progress—" Linda began, then Sammy came out from the same room, shirtless, lighting a cigarette.

"Yeah," he said, blowing a stream of smoke (which he had not inhaled). "Give us a progress report." His eyes flicked beyond her. "Where's Ann?"

"The poor dear developed a headache and stayed at the hotel," Linda explained.

Sammy looked from Linda to Constantin, whose face was hard and cold. A wave of nausea washed over Sammy so violently that he dropped the cigarette. In the last few hours he had fully made up any lack in prayer, but now he wondered if it was too late.

There was one gamble he might take, based on what he had just learned from Mike—one chance of finding Marni in time. *God, make it good,* he pleaded, and said, "Linda, I want to talk to you alone."

"It's a stupid cop trick," Constantin sneered.

"Let me tell you what I know, then you're free to leave," Sammy said calmly.

Linda's curiosity got the best of her, and she consented. Sammy opened the door to the side room and gestured her in. "You may leave the door open," she said, following him.

Sammy bent to pick up his shirt and suit jacket from beside the rumpled bed. "You know who I am," he hazarded, glancing out the door to make sure they were out of Constantin's hearing.

Linda regarded him, then accepted the challenge to play along. "Yes, I do," she smiled.

"And you also know who Matthew is," said Sammy.

"What do you mean?" she said apprehensively.

"He's Wes's son," Sammy said.

She dropped her shoulders. "Of course I know that. Get to the point," she said impatiently.

Sammy drew Constantin's letter about the armor from his jacket pocket and handed it to her. "Then you also know that Wes is the one who has been financing Matthew, and tipping him off about your purchases. Wes loves you, Linda, but he got tired of being played for the fool all the time. He's also the one who dropped your name to the insurance company for investigation. He and Matthew had teamed up to drive you out of business. That way, Wes thought, you'd need him again."

As Linda read the letter, she blinked rapidly and her hands began to shake. Suddenly nothing was more urgent than burying Matthew Constantin. "I want immunity from prosecution in exchange for my testimony," she said through gritted teeth.

Sammy's blood ran cold. "No deals."

"At least I want leniency," she insisted.

"You better spill what you know quick!" he hissed.

"Last I saw her, she was with Matthew. He set the fire," she said crisply, folding the letter.

"Where?" Sammy whispered, his eyes watering.

"Jones' Antiquities, on West 22nd," she replied.

"Let's go!" Sammy shouted, throwing on his shirt. Running footsteps answered him, and two uniformed officers sprang from another room. Linda startled.

As Sammy shot past Matthew in the outer room, Constantin yelled at Linda, "What did you tell him? I *told* you it was a trick, you stupid broad!"

Linda gazed at him in dull hatred. "We'll see who gets burned," she whispered.

Jock wistfully watched Sammy bolt out of the house. "When he came to the door, I thought that he had changed his mind . . . but no. . . . He just knew you'd be back," he finished with a cool gaze at Linda.

While the officers handcuffed Linda and Constantin inside the house and began reading them their rights, Sammy ran out to a patrol car that had careened up into the drive. "Jones' Antiquities—West 22nd," he gasped, throwing himself into the car.

"Got a unit already there, responding to a suspicious fire," the sergeant behind the wheel noted, turning on the sirens.

Sammy clutched the dash with white knuckles as they raced up the boulevard. Soon they saw a column of white smoke rising in the distance. "She's not dead. She's not," he muttered. *But what if she is?*

"No—she's not dead," Sammy insisted, and the sergeant looked over sympathetically. *But what if she is?*

"I'm not gonna hear that from you, Satan. She's not dead!"

But Sammy—what if she is? At once Sammy realized this was not a question from the devil, but from the Father, asking him to consider a very real possibility. What if he had indeed lost his partner, his treasure?

Staring at the possibility of life without her caused him to recoil violently. "No! She's so young!" Then came the wordless reminder that no one had a guaranteed allotment of years— each was given whatever the Giver chose to bestow. And Sammy remembered Meredith, who had completed her time on earth after only six hours. What if Marni's sojourn was also complete?

Sammy hung his head on his arms to hide the tears streaming down his face. "Then I'll have two girls in heaven," he whispered. "Marni, meet Meredith."

They pulled up on screeching tires to the building, where the firefighters were cleaning up debris. Sammy stumbled from the car and approached the officer in charge, who was getting a report from the fire captain: "Started from a dropped cigarette. Not much structural damage, but a lot of smoke. The owner's tryin' to tell us that some guy hit him over the head and set it."

"Have you found . . . f-found. . . ." Sammy stammered.

"Ah, you got any casualties?" the sergeant intervened, coming up behind him.

"No, we found no one in the building but the owner," replied the fire captain.

Barefoot, with his silk shirt buttoned crookedly, Sammy stumbled inside the building. He walked over soggy ashes, some still smoldering, while he peered through the thick haze. "Marni?" he called weakly. "Marni?" His voice was hopeless. Several paramedics and policemen followed him in.

"Marni." After stumbling around empty crates, broken pottery, and ashes, he made it to a large crate and sat, burying his face in his hands while the paramedics and firefighters renewed their search of the building.

As Sammy sat on the crate, he heard a faint scratching. He looked up, but there was no one nearby. Nauseous with grief, he bent his head between his knees. And he heard the scratching again, louder.

Suddenly he sprang three feet into the air and spun to look at the crate. When he couldn't pry up the lid with his fingers, he ran out to the firetruck, seized a crowbar, and ran back inside yelling. He applied the crowbar to the lid with such force that the whole crate almost tipped. The paramedics appeared beside him, and with their help, the lid came up on the second try. He gazed down at a barely conscious Marni, nestled in wood shavings.

The paramedics took the tape off her face and applied oxygen before even attempting to lift her out. A few moments under the mask and she came fully awake, smiling at Sammy.

"I'm okay," she murmured, holding up her taped wrists to be freed.

Sammy stood back gazing while they cut the tape off her hands and feet and helped her out of the box. As she turned her eyes up to him, he staggered forward and wrapped his arms tightly around her, clutching her for dear life. He could smell the smoke in her hair and clothes. "Baby," he gasped.

Then he let go and shouted, "Never again! You are *never* coming on a job with me again!"

"Sammy—" she began, shocked.

"Don't talk to me," he insisted, turning away. "You're never gonna do that to me again!" He strode outside.

Marni looked in disbelief at one of the paramedics, who shrugged, "He's had a bad scare. He'll be okay in a minute. We see it all the time."

She went outside, where a detective approached with a badge. "Mrs. Kidman? We'd like to get a statement from you—"

"Just a minute, please." She held up a forefinger, then went over to where Sammy was leaning against the squad car. "Sammy?"

"I mean it, Marni," he said, turning. "I couldn't go through that again. I'm sending you on the first plane back to Dallas, and you're going to stay there."

"Oh yeah?" she countered. "What if the plane crashes? What if I get hit by a car coming home? What if I fall in the tub and break my neck?"

"Don't do this to me, Marni. You're staying put," he decreed.

"No, I'm not," she huffed. "I'm not some servant that you can just fire at will. If you don't want me around, fine. I'll file for divorce and go home. Mom always said I was welcome back any time." She turned on her heel and strode toward another squad car while the emergency team watched in amusement.

"Marni," he said sullenly.

Ignoring him, she asked an officer, "Take me to the airport, please."

"Uh, miss, I think they need to ask you some questions," he began.

"Take me *now*, please," she said louder, surreptitiously winking.

He lowered his head and opened the door for her. "Marni," said Sammy. She got in and slammed the door. The officer sat and started the car.

"Marni!" Sammy shouted as the car started off. He ran up to grab the door handle and wrench it open, tackling her on the seat. "You win," he groaned. "You always win. You don't play fair." The officer behind the wheel looked away, smiling, then slowly backed up the car.

Over the next hour Sammy and Marni gave a thorough statement to Detective Statler. Then he turned off his tape recorder and said, "Okay, that'll do for now. Hang around for a few days. Where're you staying?"

"Not at the Wilshire, that's for sure," Sammy mumbled. "Mike will never approve that expenditure. I'll call you when we find a cheaper hotel."

"For now," said Marni, brushing back her smoky hair, "you can drop us off at Le Joker. *You're* taking me to dinner," she informed Sammy.

"Le Joker? C'mon, Marni, eating there costs more than a new suit! . . . You win," he sighed, after one of her chin-down looks. "You sure know how to play your advantage," he grumbled, and she smiled triumphantly.

After Sammy picked up the rest of his clothes from Jock's, they were taken via squad car straight to Le Joker and seated at a decent table. While Marni happily scrutinized the menu, a waiter came up with a cordless phone. "Mr. Kidman?" he inquired.

Sammy looked up in surprise. "Yes?"

"Telephone, sir." The waiter handed the phone to Sammy.

He and Marni exchanged wide-eyed looks, then he cautiously answered, "Hello?"

"Hello—Sammy, is it? I suppose I can get used to that."

"Mrs. Threlkeld!" Sammy exclaimed joyfully. "Where are you?"

"Dallas, of course. You don't think I'm coming all the way out *there* to thank you, do you? I'm not that grateful," she said.

"Grateful, ma'am?" he asked.

"I understand it was your work that exposed all the forgeries that—that woman sold to Stanley. Several million dollars' worth. Whatever we recoup from the insurance company, I'll donate to charity," she said.

"You're wonderful," he grinned, and Marni glanced up. "But, would you mind telling me how you found out who I was?" he asked.

"After we determined that *The Elder Sister* was a forgery, I called the insurance company, and a Mr. Foster came out and explained the whole situation to us," she said.

"Just like that," Sammy muttered.

"Yes. I was quite surprised to hear that you are an undercover policeman, but Jess said she knew it all along," Mrs. Threlkeld said. The waiter came up, and Marni ordered with quiet confidence.

"I see. And what did Wes say?" Sammy asked casually, pointing to what he wanted on the menu.

"I don't recall that he said much of anything. He's not taking this very well," she murmured. Then: "Enough of that. I had another reason for calling. If you will come back to work for me—not as chauffeur, as head of security, of course—I'll pay you twice what you're making with the police department."

Sammy laughed, "That would be about what you were paying me before! That's a tempting offer, Mrs. Threlkeld. Tell you what—got a pencil, doll? I'm going to give you three phone numbers. Write them down. Ready?" He gave her the numbers, then said, "The first is my office number, the second is my beeper number, and the third—which I don't give to *anybody*—is my home phone number. If you need me, you call me, and I'll come. How's that?"

Mrs. Threlkeld paused. "I underestimated you, young man. Where . . . is your wife?"

"Right across the table from me," Sammy said, looking up and winking.

"Give her my best," Mrs. Threlkeld said quietly.

"Will do," Sammy replied warmly, and put the phone down with a contemplative smile.

"Well?" Marni asked as the waiter brought their drinks and took the phone.

"You won't believe it. She wanted me to come back to work for her at twice what I'm making now with the department. Remind me to be sure to tell Mike that," he said in satisfaction. He looked up and saw Jock Walker enter with a friend. Sammy casually waved.

Jock hesitated, then came over to their table. "Hi, uh, what's your name again? Your real name?"

"Sammy Kidman. This is my wife, Marni," Sammy said, nodding.

"Pleased to meet you, Marni." Jock earnestly shook her hand as if he'd never seen her before. She just smiled. Then he said, "The cops, uh, carted off Matthew and Linda. I hear they're up on a string of charges."

"That is exactly correct," Sammy said humorously. "By the way, I know someone in Dallas who can refer you to a legitimate dealer for that painting you wanted."

"Thanks," Jock muttered. "Listen, I'm sorry about . . . uh, well. . . ." He glanced uneasily at Marni.

"No problem," Sammy said quickly, then added, "I'd appreciate a favor. A friend of mine's a big fan of yours. Could I get your autograph for him?" He took out a pen and Marni found a scrap of paper.

"Sure," Jock said hastily.

"Write, 'To Larry,'" Sammy instructed, and Jock did. "Thanks," said Sammy, pocketing the autograph.

"Sure," said Jock, relaxing. "See ya 'round." He moved off with his friend.

"I've got a prayer job for you—a big one," Sammy murmured and Marni nodded.

The waiter came around again. "Telephone, Mr. Kidman," he said, extending the phone to him.

"Again?" exclaimed Sammy, and Marni looked up in wonder.

"Everybody thinks you're a producer!" she giggled, glancing around in gratification.

Sammy took the phone. "Hello?" he asked bemusedly.

"Hello, horse breath!"

"Mike!" he said gleefully. "And I thought you didn't care."

"Enough to send the very best. Statler briefed me on your status there. Is Marni okay?" Mike asked.

"Yes, thank God," Sammy said seriously, glancing up at her.

"Good. Good job, Kidman."

"Thanks. Foster still there, by any chance?" Sammy asked.

"No, I think he headed back to New York. Why?" Mike asked.

"I had something I wanted to tell him. Can you take a message?" Sammy said studiously.

"Sure. Shoot."

"Here it is," Sammy said. "Foster: If I ever see your lily-livered, prune-sucking face again, I'm going to beat it to a bloody pulp. Love, Sammy."

"'. . . to a bloody pulp. Love, Sammy,'" quoted Mike. "Okay, I think I've got that down."

"Hey, did he ever turn up anything on those heists? We never found any stolen paintings," Sammy remarked.

"Ah, all I know was that he said something about several paintings being 'misplaced,'" Mike replied.

"Misplaced?" Sammy hooted.

"By the way," Mike said, "I thought I'd let you know that you've been the subject of an Internal Affairs investigation."

"What was that?" Sammy asked, his stomach sinking as his dinner arrived at the table.

"Don't worry; you were cleared. Seems one Robert Threlkeld accused you of 'spanking' his sister Jessica. But she told the investigating officers that he was lying to get you in trouble, and they closed it," Mike said confidently.

Sammy was silent for ten seconds. Then he cleared his throat and said, "Bobby was telling the truth, Mike. I did spank her." Marni looked up in horror.

Mike did not respond at once, then Sammy heard a clicking and crackling. "What? What's that?" Mike said over the noise. "I didn't hear you, Kidman." The noise suddenly stopped and Mike said, "Don't *ever* do that to me again." Then he hung up.

eleven

"Hello? Oh, hi, Kerry," Marni answered the telephone in the apartment, reaching down to stroke her gray cat Smoky. "No, Sammy's not here. He left this morning to take Dolly Threlkeld over to meet Mavis Masterson. What? No, we were all done with the assignment at the Threlkelds' when we got back from Los Angeles over a week ago. You see, Mavis is Mike's sister—she keeps several foster children in her house in Oak Cliff. Mike and Sammy are always over there mowing the lawn or fixing something around the house—anyway, Mavis spends every cent she's got on those kids, and Sammy felt sure Dolly would want to do something to help her out. Yeah. I don't know—he should have been back hours ago. I can't imagine what's keeping him." She listened for a moment.

"No, I don't know what's going on with this Targeted Activity Section. What I understand is, while they're trying to work out the kinks in the new section, Sammy's been detailed to auto theft, although he's still working from his desk in the TAS office. Isn't that crazy? Is Dave still in Targeted Activity? He is? Well, maybe Dave can help Mike get it structured right. Sammy wouldn't want to work it unless Dave were there, too—he says the department doesn't know what to do with such an experimental section. Yeah; he said there's no clear-cut method for assigning cases or logging results—makes you wonder how it got approved, doesn't it? The worst part is, Sammy hasn't figured out how to justify overtime."

Marni laughed. "Dave, too? Oh, I'm kinda ambivalent about it. I'd rather have Sammy home, but we really need the overtime pay. You know what they say: 'No crime will be solved before overtime.'" She paused at the sound of the doorbell. "Oh, Kerry, there's someone at the door. Talk to you later. Okay. Bye."

She hung up and Smoky jumped up to sniff the telephone while Marni went to open the door. "Yes?" she said to the stranger on her doorstep. Today was April Fool's Day, and Sammy had warned her to be on the alert for practical jokes by someone from the department—particularly Kerry's husband.

The stranger just looked at her a moment, and she looked back. He had gray hair that hung in his eyes, mingled with a few strands of black. He was dressed in an old, shabby work-shirt and jeans. He would have been a handsome man but for the overwhelming sorrow and weariness in his face. Just looking at him made Marni's eyes water—until the familiarity of his form sent a shock wave through her.

"You must be Marni," he finally said.

"You—" she gasped, "are you—?"

"I'm Sammy's father," he replied. "My name is Sam Watterson. Not the actor." Marni blinked. Sammy's father? Yes. His eyes were the dead giveaway. Faded with grief, they were no longer the vivid blue that stopped hearts, but they were definitely the pattern for Sammy's.

Marni opened the door. "Come in," she said. Hesitantly, he stepped in and glanced around the apartment. It was a nice studio apartment, with a tiled kitchen and upstairs fireplace. "Sit down." She gestured to the leather sofa. "Can I get you something to drink?"

"I would appreciate a glass of water," he said, sitting on the edge of the couch. Smoky ran up the stairs to hide in the bedroom.

Marni filled a glass with ice water and handed it to him as she sat beside him. "Thank you," he mumbled, taking a token sip before placing it on the coffee table. "I . . . read about Sammy in the papers," he said, drawing a crumpled newspaper article from his pocket. It was the article that had appeared after Sammy had recovered the baby taken from Presbyterian Hospital. There were no pictures of Sammy with the article, of course, but it carried his name and the fact that he would be recommended for a lifesaving award for the act. That award was presented last December.

"Then I saw him, coupla weeks ago, stopped at a red light up here on the corner of Forest Lane. He was in this old convertible, just like one I use' ta have. I'd never seen him before—never seen him once—but I knew that was Sammy. It was like lookin' in the mirror at myself twenty years ago. I followed him here on foot. Saw him turn in here. He didn't see me," he added. Marni watched him quietly.

"I hafta talk to him," Sam said, stroking his lined brow. "It took me a coupla weeks to screw up the guts to come over here—I know he won't want to see me. But I got to tell him the truth about what happened. Do you know about me?" he asked suddenly.

She cleared her throat. "Sammy told me you raped his mother and went to jail for it."

"Yeah, I went to jail all right. But I didn't rape Carla. We were in love. We were goin' to get married. But her parents found out about us and hit the roof. They had me arrested, and they made Carla tell the police that I had raped her. She was young, and scared—heck, I was only nineteen myself. But I pled guilty so as not to put her through a trial. I figured they'd go easy on a first offense—I didn't even have a traffic ticket.

"The judge sentenced me to *twenty years.* I served ten years before I got out on parole. Carla's family wouldn't let her have anything to do with me. They wouldn't let her come see me or even answer my letters. They hid my own child from me so I'd never be able to see him and they wouldn't tell me anything about him, not even that it was a boy.

"But I found out this and that, after I got out. I found out she'd had a boy, and she named him after me. Not Watterson, of course—her family's name is Kidman. But Samuel. She named him Samuel, after me." He stopped talking and looked at her. Marni blinked back tears. "I want to know my son. Will you talk to him for me?" he asked.

Marni opened her mouth just as the apartment door opened. Sammy came in, looking haggard. "Man, I thought we'd *never*—" he began, then looked up in alarm as Sam and Marni stood from the couch. "Who are you?" he asked in a low voice.

"Sammy," Marni said quietly, "this is your father."

Sammy stared at him and Sam looked at the floor. "Get out," Sammy said, opening the door.

Marni began, "Sammy—"

"Get out!" Sammy shouted. The elder Sam walked around the couch and quickly left. Sammy slammed the door behind him, then turned on Marni. "Have you lost your mind? Why did you let him in while I wasn't here?"

"He wanted to talk to you, Sammy," she said, coming over to place a calming hand on his chest.

"Marni, I've *told* you about him! That man is a convicted rapist!" Sammy exclaimed, shrugging off her hand.

"That's what he wanted to talk about. He said it wasn't a rape—that they were in love, and were going to get married," Marni told him.

"I can't believe—!" he muttered tightly, grabbing his hair in frustration. "Marni, you have got to grow up! Stop believing everything everybody tells you! *Of course* he'd say that; he's a con man and he's playing you for a sucker! Can't I leave you alone for a minute without worrying about who you're going to let in the house?"

"You owe it to him to at least find out if he's telling the truth," Marni insisted.

"*Owe it to him?*" Sammy gasped. "I *owe it to him?* Marni, you get it through your head right now that I don't owe him a damn thing!"

Marni turned coolly to get her purse. "We'll talk later, after you calm down."

"You're not walking out on me!" he snapped, grabbing her arm. It hurt, and Marni flinched.

Her flinch stabbed him through the heart. Crumpling, he gathered her tightly in his arms. "I'm sorry, baby. I'm sorry, I'm sorry," he whispered into her hair.

Stinging, Marni hung woodenly in his arms. He continued to squeeze her. "Dear Lord, I'm so sorry. I can't believe I did that," he whispered brokenly.

Sighing, Marni reached up to his neck. He rocked her, kissing her hair and her face. She gave him a few minutes to pull himself together before she drew back slightly and said, "Will you listen to me now?"

Sammy opened his mouth, then gently took her hands and led her to sit on the couch. "Marni," he said calmly, "the guy is a liar and a loser. Here I am thirty-two years old, and *not once* in all those years has he bothered to look me up. Now all of a sudden he shows up at our door, trying to weasel his way in. The cold facts are, he raped my mother and went to prison for it. That's all I care to know."

"Then why did she name you after him?" Marni asked. Sammy blinked. "She wouldn't have named you after a rapist." Sammy stared at her. "You don't have to talk to him. Just find out if he's telling the truth," Marni said.

Sammy sagged, stroking his forehead just as his father had done some moments before. "All right," he sighed. "Let's go do some digging."

They went in Sammy's car to the Dallas County Records Building, as Sammy's father had been tried in this city. Sammy asked to see the court records, and was directed to the archives in the basement. There, he and Marni spent the next several hours sifting through old docket books looking for his case number.

"Here it is," Marni said, her voice echoing between the tall metal shelves. "'The People versus Watterson: Case No. 7056486.'" With the case number, they were able to locate the court records. It was a surprisingly slim packet. Sammy had them photocopied, then they took them home to read.

As he was unlocking their apartment door, he paused. "Marni, I can't believe I did that to you. Please forgive me."

"It's okay, Sammy. Really. I know it came as quite a shock," Marni assured him, squeezing his arm.

"It's still no excuse for treating you like that," he muttered. They went in and he threw the photocopied pages on the table.

Marni sensed that he was still shaken by the breach in the wall around his past, so she asked, "What took you so long this morning?" She took a pitcher of tea from the refrigerator.

"Oh, man," he muttered, sinking into a kitchen chair. "Try getting two strong-willed women from different worlds to see eye-to-eye on something—anything. In the first place, Dolly was late because her new chauffeur quit—she had to take a cab and was she steamed. Once she got there, she was horrified at the condition of the house and Mavis got offended. Dolly saw Mavis as too proud to accept help and Mavis saw Dolly as a rich white woman trying to make herself feel good with a little charity. I finally just had to lock them in the same room and stay out of the way while they duked it out."

"Did they get anything worked out?" she asked anxiously.

"Oh, sure, they came out of there lovin' on each other like long-lost sisters. It only took about four hours," he moaned, accepting a glass of iced tea. "Thanks."

"'Blessed are the peacemakers,'" she murmured, smiling at him. He glanced up at her wryly, then they both looked at the pages on the table.

With a heavy heart, he pulled the pages toward him and began reading. Marni stayed back, quietly puttering in the kitchen. Smoky jumped up in his lap and he brushed her off. Marni filled her food dish early, then sat across from Sammy at the table while Smoky investigated her bonanza.

He finished reading and stacked the pages thoughtfully. "Her parents filed the complaint. He waived his right to a trial and entered a guilty plea. He was sentenced to twenty years at Huntsville. After serving about half of that sentence, he was paroled," Sammy summarized.

"That's exactly what he told me," she noted, sipping her tea. "He wanted to spare her from a trial."

Sammy looked up at her, then pulled out a page close to the end to scrutinize again. "When he was released, they got a restraining order against him, and kept it in force for the next eight years. He never violated it."

"He told me they hid you from him and wouldn't tell him anything about you. He also said they wouldn't let Carla answer his letters from prison," Marni said.

Sammy lifted his eyes to gaze out the window. The redbud trees in the apartment courtyard were in full bloom. "I hardly ever saw her," he murmured. "I didn't know for the longest time that she was my mother. Whenever I asked Aunt Patsy why I didn't have a mom and a dad, she'd just say, 'You have an aunt and an uncle.'

"Then one day when my grandparents came to visit—I was about ten—my grandmother looked at me and said, 'Why did he have to look so much like that man?'—like I was deformed, or something. I wanted to know what they were talking about, and that's when they told me that my father had raped my mother and gone to prison for it. I didn't even know what 'rape' meant. All I knew was that I looked just like a man who did a terrible thing—and that I should never have been born." He fell silent, deeply absorbed.

"What kind of people blame a child for being born?" he wondered. "They always let me know—in such subtle ways that I never realized it—that I was the product of what a bad man had done to an innocent girl. Maybe that's why I zeroed in on police work so early . . . to redeem myself."

He stared down at the papers, though he wasn't seeing them. For long minutes he sat thinking, then slowly got up and went to the telephone. He picked it up, toyed with the receiver, then dialed a number. While waiting, he looked at Marni and mouthed, "I love you."

She started to reply when he quickly dropped his head and said, "Hey, Patsy! Sammy here. How're you doing?" He stopped to listen awhile, every now and then remarking, "You don't say," "Yeah?" or, "Well, how's Ralph?"

After receiving ten minutes of news, he finally said, "Patsy, let me tell you why I called. I need my mother's address, to get her verification on something. Nothing major, just some old paperwork that needs clearing up. Would you . . . ? Thanks." He lifted his chin, waiting, and Marni held her breath.

Suddenly Sammy bent and picked up the pen by the telephone to write on a pad. "Thanks, Patsy. Tell Uncle Ralph hello for me. Will do. Bye." He laid the receiver gently on the cradle and Marni came to his side. "She lives about five miles from here," he said, tearing the top sheet from the pad. "So . . . let's go see dear ol' Mom." Marni snatched up her purse and they left.

On the way, Sammy glanced at the address once or twice. "Her name is Bowers now, Patsy said."

"Is Patsy her sister? The one who raised you?" Marni asked.

"Yep," said Sammy, glancing over his shoulder and turning a corner. He began to say something else, but the comment was lost in the echoes from the past.

Shortly, they pulled up to a modest brick house on a quiet, tree-lined street. Sammy double-checked the address on the mailbox against what he had written down, then turned off the engine and got out. He and Marni went up the walk together and paused at the front door. They could hear children's voices inside.

As if his hand were hung with lead weights, Sammy lifted his finger to the doorbell and pushed. There was some scuffling and arguing: "I got it!" "Nuh uh! I did!" "Leggo!" A few moments later one of them got the door open, and Sammy and Marni looked down on two young children, a boy and a girl.

"Hi there," Sammy smiled, removing his sunglasses. "We're here to see Mrs. Carla Bowers."

"I *think* that's Grammy," the boy, an authoritative six, answered. The little girl, about two years younger, studied them with round blue eyes. Marni smiled at her. "Grammy!" the boy shouted, running out of the room.

"I have a niece and a nephew," Sammy noted to Marni. He entered the front room with Marni behind him, and she closed the door while he knelt in front of the little girl. "My name is Sammy," he said with that inimitable charm that melted females. "What's your name?"

She put her fingers in her mouth and began rocking shyly. "Let me guess," said Sammy, looking to the ceiling. "Is it— Lisa?" The girl shook her head. "Is it . . . Megan?" She shook her head again, grinning. "Is it Rachel?"

"No!" she cackled. "It's Britt'ny!"

"Brittany?" he exclaimed. "That was my next guess!"

The boy reappeared in the room with a woman behind him and Sammy stood. She was slender and still lovely, with doelike eyes and short, dark hair. As she gazed at Sammy, she slowly removed a bandanna from her neck. "My word," she breathed. "It's . . . Sammy, isn't it?"

"Hi, Mom," he said, expressionless.

She sat weakly on the couch, mopping her face with the bandanna. Then she clenched it in her hand. "Why did you come here?" she asked in a hard voice.

"Oh," he said, sitting on the couch uninvited, "people get curious about their past, sometimes. Children want to know where they came from. And I want to know if my father really raped you."

She cringed. "Children, go—go play in the back room for a while. You may get down Grammy's Chinese checkers, if you like."

"Oh, boy!" They raced each other to the back room.

She turned back to Sammy with watery eyes. "I was only seventeen."

"Old enough to consent, so they couldn't nail him for statutory rape. Did you love him?" Sammy asked.

"What does a girl that young know about love? Oh, he was so handsome!—but my family, you know—my father was just—just livid. I was so frightened!" she pleaded.

Sammy inhaled. "Did you and he talk about getting married?"

"Oh, we talked about everything. That Christmas was so—wonderful. He gave me a glass angel, and said it was me. Daddy broke it in little pieces," she recalled, her face clouding. "But we kept seeing each other. Sam would hold me close, and talk about what we would do after the holidays, the job he would get and the house we would have someday. . . ." She closed her eyes in remembrance and Marni quietly shed tears.

"Mom," Sammy said, leaning toward her, "why did you let them put him away for rape?"

She looked frightened. "It was—everyone was around me, yelling at me. I was so confused, and they wouldn't let me see him—I didn't know what to do!" she cried pitifully.

"He served *ten years* in prison, Mom," Sammy said, and there may have been a touch of sarcasm in the last word. "Didn't you get his letters?"

"Oh, yes!" she cried, jumping up. "Wait here!" She ran out of the room while Sammy and Marni exchanged glances. In a moment she returned with a bundle tied up with a ribbon. "I kept them all," she said softly. "He wrote many at first, but then, they stopped coming. . . ."

Sammy stared at the bundle she held out to him, then he took it. "Why didn't you answer any of them?" he asked.

"Daddy wouldn't let me," she whispered. "He would have burned them if he knew I was getting them, but the postman knew Sam and always rang the doorbell to give them to me in person," she recalled. Sammy stared hard at her. She was unable to meet his convicting blue eyes—the eyes of his father. "I did love him," she said in the barest whisper.

Sammy stood up as if unable to hear more. "You ruined his life."

"I named you after him!" she said, lifting her head in defiance. "They couldn't change that! I named you Samuel James, after your father!" Her lip quivered as the tears streamed down her cheeks.

Sammy couldn't stand any more of this. He firmly took Marni's arm and escorted her out to the car, tossing the bundle of letters in her lap as she sat. She put them in her purse. With the deliberate precision that signaled how very upset he was, he drove back to their apartment.

As he opened the courtyard gate and approached their door, another couple was just about to enter their first-floor apartment a few doors down. The woman spotted them and stopped the man: "Wait, Kevin, here they are!"

Sammy hastened to unlock the door and go inside, but she managed to catch Marni just in the doorway. "Hi! I'm Cookie Payne, and this is my husband Kevin!" she exclaimed, waving him over. She was a perky blonde in a nice business suit, and Kevin was a very correctly dressed executive with a correct conservative haircut. They were both in their twenties.

"Hello," Marni smiled wanly. "I'm Marni Kidman, and this is my—"

"Boyfriend," Sammy replied from the couch, where he sat pinching the bridge of his nose. He looked up with slightly bloodshot eyes. "I'm her boyfriend Sammy."

"I'm so glad to meet you!" Cookie said, shaking Marni's hand. Then she came in to extend her hand to Sammy. He looked at her a moment, then reached up and took her hand. Her husband did the same. They were both in the apartment now. Marni looked around in some distress, then shut the door.

"I can't believe we finally caught you!" Cookie said, sitting pertly on the edge of the couch. "We saw all your stuff being moved in a few months ago, and I kept looking for whoever was going to live here, 'cause I just love getting to know people, but you two are just never home! What kind of work do you do?"

Sammy stared mutely at her, and Marni cleared her throat. "Um, Cookie, I'd love to sit down and visit with you, but right now—"

"Oh, I understand," Cookie breathed, eyes widening. "Me and my big mouth. Kevin says I have to learn to stop talking and listen more. Did somebody get laid off? No, you don't have to talk about it if you don't want to. But don't feel bad— it's happening all over. Why, Kevin and I feel lucky to have jobs, even though he didn't get the promotion he was promised, and I was *furious* because of all the long hours he's been working—"

"Cookie—" interrupted Kevin.

"It's true!" she exclaimed, turning on him. "You worked sixty hours this week and I don't know how we're going to work a baby into our schedules with you working that long!" She turned back to Marni with a radiant smile. "We've decided to have a baby. Do you have any children?"

"No," Marni whispered, glancing at stony-faced Sammy.

"Listen, it's something you really need to talk about, before you get so caught up in a career that it's too late. I mean, look at me. Sure, I have a great job as a fashion consultant, but I'm already *twenty-five* and that biological clock is ticking away! So we decided to just start planning for a baby right away! First thing we did was get on a waiting list for Nannies Unlimited," she said.

"You're—not even pregnant yet?" Marni asked weakly.

"We have the fertility kit right by the bed!" she giggled, looking at her husband who was looking at his shoes. Marni was mystified as to how the fertility kit was used, but dared not ask.

Sammy suddenly smiled. "Cookie," he said, standing, "I'm so glad to meet you. You just made me feel a lot better. If you'll excuse us, Marni and I need to talk through some things, but I'm really glad you came by." He opened the door with a genuine expression of goodwill.

"Great!" she said, moving toward the door. "I'm always so happy to brighten someone's day. Come *on,* Kevin; they need to talk!" she winked. On his way out, Kevin stuck his hand out and Sammy shook it warmly.

As he shut the door and turned, Marni gazed at him in wonder. "It's true what they say," he observed, "that hearing other people's problems gives you some perspective on your own. So I've been without a dad all my life because he was sent up the river on a false rape charge. Is that so bad? I mean, I could be married to *her.* "

twelve

The following Sunday, Sammy and Marni were returning from morning church when they met up again with Kevin and Cookie outside their doors. "Hi, Sammy and Marni!" she squealed, waving, then came over. She and Kevin were in suits. Marni felt they probably slept in suits. "Have you been to church?" Cookie asked eagerly. "Where do you go?"

"Grace Bible Church," Marni replied. Sammy glanced at her with a corner of his mouth turned up, and, recalling their last conversation about Cookie, Marni squelched a laugh.

"How nice," said Cookie, and she was actually silent for a moment as she regarded Sammy. He looked delicious, as always, with his glistening black hair and long eyelashes; but today he was wearing one of Stan Threlkeld's suits which cost more than a six-month lease on one of these apartments. He hardly ever wore them—certainly never to work—and wound up giving half the stuff to Goodwill. "My goodness, you must have done real well before you were laid off," she noted.

"You can earn a lot in sales," he remarked. Cookie watched him take his key from his pocket to open the door. A yellow warning flag went up in Marni's mind.

"Cookie!" Kevin called from the parking lot. "Come on, or we'll be late to your parents'!"

"Gotta run!" She threw on an extra-bright smile and hurried out to the car.

159

Marni entered the apartment thoughtfully. "Sammy, you'd better let me tell Cookie something more about us. I'm afraid she's picking up clues and putting them together wrong."

Sammy glanced at her as he pulled off his tie. "Baby, you tell her I'm in police work, and pretty soon the whole complex will know. Besides, I don't care what she thinks."

"It's not that I care, either," she began uneasily, "it's just that. . . ."

"That what?" he asked, shucking off his coat. "Come up to the bedroom." She followed him upstairs, where he hung up his suit in the closet. Smoky jumped up on the blue chintz bedspread, and Marni absently stroked her. "That what?" Sammy repeated.

"I don't know," she sighed. "I just feel that she may be jumping to conclusions about us. Please tell me what I can tell her."

"Well," he inhaled, "you can tell her I'm in between jobs. That's true enough. Tell her we have some money in the bank to live on. That's true, too. Actually, Marni, I'd prefer you not talk to her at all. Be friends with Kerry, or anybody else from the department. Talking to them isn't as likely to get me killed."

"Don't worry," she said hastily. "I won't let that happen."

"Why, would you miss me?" he said, flopping back on the bed in his underwear. He held out his arms. Smoky sniffed his face and he brushed her away.

"Maybe a little," Marni conceded, sitting beside him. He pulled her down on top of him, sliding his hand up her dress. His other hand held her head for an aggressive kiss, and a few seconds later she forgot whatever it was that she had been worried about.

The following morning Sammy went down to the Big Building downtown to process paperwork ("If all those cop shows were really true to life, three-fourths of each episode would show the poor stiff drinking coffee at a crummy desk and pushing paper," he swore.) Meanwhile, Marni went to visit her mother, Pam. A beautiful, quick-witted woman whom Marni and Sammy trusted implicitly, Pam lived in a comfortable suburban home in north Dallas with Marni's father Clayton.

"Hi, sweetie," Pam leaned forward for a kiss on the cheek from her daughter at the front door. Marni obliged her, then paused to brush a spot of oil paint from her mother's cheek. "Oh dear—do I have paint on my face again?" she asked, wiping her cheek.

"You usually do," Marni smiled. "How's it going?"

"Oh, pretty well," Pam said casually, dangling a yellow ribbon in front of her face.

Marni grabbed it. "A purchase award! Mom, that's fantastic! When did you—*Mother!* This is for *Purple Sky!*" Marni cried.

"Is that bad?" her mother asked, perplexed. This painting was a desert scene at twilight, with a cowboy in the foreground who looked suspiciously like Sammy.

"Mom, *I* wanted that painting!" Marni whined.

"I didn't know that, dear," Pam said stiffly. "But I told you I was going to enter it in competition."

"Oh, I'm sorry, Mom; I'm being selfish. I just loved the way you put Sammy in chaps in it," Marni sighed.

"Sweetie, if you'll get Sammy to let me, I'll do a full-length portrait of him," Pam said. There were already a number of portraits of Marni around the house.

"I don't know, Mom; he's pretty edgy about showing his face. He won't let anybody take pictures of him, and made me hide our wedding photos," Marni said dubiously.

"Well, work on him. Oh, that reminds me—here's the painting Sammy wanted." Pam pulled out a portrait of Marni done when she was five years old.

Marni looked at it, smiling and shaking her head. "Why did he want that one?" Pam wondered. "I'm happy to give it to him, but I've done others of you that are better."

"Oh, Mom, Sammy has this thing for kids," Marni said dreamily, looking at the portrait.

"Then it won't be long before I'll be painting babies," Pam said happily, and Marni dropped her head. "*All* my friends have grandbabies, and *I* don't have any grandbabies, but that's not going to make me start—"

"Mom," Marni said suddenly, "Sammy took me to see his urologist shortly after we were married. He's . . . we can't have children, Mother."

Pam looked at her and tears came to her eyes. "Marni, I'm so sorry. I was only trying to be funny. I'll never say another word about it." Marni nodded silently, and Pam reached out to let Marni lean into her. She rocked her daughter quietly for a while, then Marni raised up and wiped her eyes.

"It's okay, Mom. We . . . checked into adoption, but the agencies won't place a child with us because of his . . . background. And Sammy just hit the roof when the doctor started talking about artificial insemination and all that—he said there was no way he was going to put me through that; and, well, Sammy has accepted it beautifully, and we don't talk about it at all anymore."

Marni began to drop new tears, and Pam said, "Well, then, we won't talk about it either. Tell me what else is going on."

"Well," Marni murmured, and then laughed, "We met the neighbors a few doors down. This girl's name is Cookie—she's a beauty consultant, or something, and she talks a mile a minute. She's also real curious about Sammy. I can't tell her anything, of course, and I'm afraid she's getting some wild ideas."

Pam looked uncomfortable. "Really," she mused.

Marni studied her. "What is it?"

"Oh, nothing," Pam shifted. "Just—do try to avoid her, Marni. These busybodies can make your life miserable. And in Sammy's case, that could be more than an inconvenience."

Marni nodded. "Yeah, I felt that way, too. But I don't know what to do about it."

"Protect Sammy," Pam said suddenly.

Marni met her eyes. "I hear you," she said softly. Then she looked down at her watch. "Uh oh! I've got another errand to run and I'm supposed to meet Sammy back at the apartment for lunch." She stood, taking up the portrait. "Thanks for the painting, Mom. See you later."

"Goodbye, sweetie." Pam held the door for her and waved as Marni put the painting on the passenger-side floor in her Miata, climbed in and drove off. Pensively, Pam shut the door and went back to the couch. She sat, cradling her face in a sudden rush of tears.

"Dear Father," she said brokenly, "I love Marni and Sammy so much. They're dear, sweet children of yours, and I can't imagine any couple who could give a baby more love. Oh dear Father, since you are the Giver of life, can't you give them a baby? And dear Lord, please make it a boy who looks just like Sammy."

Marni pulled into her parking space and unloaded a sack of groceries and the painting. Awkwardly, she carried one burden in each arm up to the courtyard gate. She had to set the painting down to open the gate, then pick it up again to carry to her door. (The gate was always supposed to be locked, but somehow never was.)

She glanced up as Cookie was about to open her door. "Hi!" Cookie said brightly. "Gosh, you have an armful. Don't you hate having to mess with that gate every time you want to go in or out? It makes me crazy. Here, let me give you a hand."

"Uh—sure," Marni said. Running into Cookie all the time was beginning to get on her nerves, more so than the gate. Marni unlocked her door and let Cookie carry in the painting.

"What a cute little girl!" Cookie exclaimed, studying the painting. "Who is it?" She placed it on the sofa.

"Me, when I was about five," Marni replied, taking the groceries to the kitchen.

"How sweet," cooed Cookie. "You had blond hair then. Don't you hate that it darkened to that dull brown? Where did you get it?"

"The painting? From my parents' home. Sammy liked it so much that my mom gave it to him," Marni replied as she put up groceries.

"'Pam Taylor.' Is that the artist?" Cookie asked, looking at the signature.

No, that's Elizabeth Taylor's sister, dummy. "Yes," said Marni.

The door opened and Sammy came in. "Oh—hi, Cookie," he said unenthusiastically. He was carrying a briefcase. "Hi, baby." She came around the counter to greet him with a kiss.

Sammy enjoyed his kisses and ice cream in a similar manner—leisurely relishing them both—and treated himself to one of these ice-cream kisses while Cookie stood by, smiling. Then he glanced down at the portrait sitting on the couch. "Oh, good. You got it. Thank Pam for me."

Cookie suddenly interjected, "Why, Marni, did your *mother* paint this?"

"Yes, she did," Marni replied.

Cookie said, "Gosh, I'd love to have one done of me and Kevin. Would you give me her phone number?"

Sammy eyed Cookie briefly and Marni said, "She's unlisted, Cookie. Give me your phone number, and I'll give it to her." Sammy went to the refrigerator to get an apple, meanwhile glancing between the two women.

"Sure!" Cookie bent to write her telephone number on the pad while Sammy and Marni made eye contact. "Here. Now if you'll give me *your* number, then we'll be all set!" She handed her number to Marni, who folded it and bit her lip.

"Sorry, Cookie; I don't allow Marni to give anyone our number," Sammy said.

"Really," Cookie said softly, with a shrewd look.

"'Fraid so," Sammy admitted. "I'm just that kind of Neanderthal. Now, if you'll excuse us, I gotta slap her around a little." Sammy went to the door and opened it.

"Guess I'd better be going, then," she said with a smirk. "Marni, please tell your mother to call me as soon as possible." And she left.

Sammy took the phone number from Marni's hand, glanced at it, and crumpled it. "Pam is not to call her," he said.

"I know," Marni said quickly. "But I'll tell Mom about it, just not to be lying. I already told her about Cookie, and Mom thought she could wind up being trouble." She went back to putting up groceries and making sandwiches.

"That a fact. I'm going to lose my temper with her and get investigated by Internal Affairs again," Sammy said, tossing his briefcase on the table with one hand. The other held the apple he was eating.

Drawing papers from the briefcase, Sammy said, "I'm initiating the paperwork to get a pardon for Sam."

"Oh, Sammy!" Marni breathed. "Really?" She dropped the mustard and ran to throw her arms around his neck.

"I'm just doin' it to get a good squeeze out of you," he muttered, holding her.

"You'll get more than that," she promised in a throaty voice.

"Um-hmm?" he murmured, lifting a brow in interest.

"But—" Marni drew back. "How will you find him to tell him?"

"Well, we'll think about that," he said evasively. She saw that he wasn't really ready to think about that yet.

They had a nice lunch together, with Sammy enthusiastically filling her in on Pruett's latest gag at work. As Pruett was an accomplished practical joker, Sammy burned with envy to match his feats. Marni listened smiling, but could not get Sam off her mind.

So after Sammy had gone back to work that afternoon, Marni went to the bedroom and pulled out the bundle of letters she had placed in the bureau drawer. She had wanted Sammy to read them first, but he couldn't bear to even look at them yet. Hesitantly, she opened up the first letter, faded and yellow:

My darling Carla:

Well, I'm all settled in and it's not so bad. They work us all day long out on the road, breaking up rock for a new highway, and by the time we get in at night we're so tired and sore that nobody has the strength to fight. I've taken some heat for the rap, but the first guy that messed with me got his nose broken, so the others pretty much leave me alone. Listen to me—I sound like a real "tough hombre."

Darling, I understand why you didn't speak up. At the hearing, you looked so pale I was afraid you were going to faint. Are you all right? The baby should be born in— September? Oh, Carla, do come see me often so I can watch your tummy grow. They're going to let you stay at home, aren't they? Man, if they'd just let us gone and got married everything would be all right. You need a husband to take care of you now and I need you. We just need to be strong and wait them out. I found out I won't have to serve the whole twenty years, I can get time off for good behavior and cut the sentence way down. Wait for me, darling, come see me and the time will fly. It will make us stronger to pull through it together.

I'm going to close now—I'm so tired I can hardly hold the pencil. I will write again tomorrow. Please write soon.

I love you forever,

Sam

The letters continued in the same loving, brave vein, but grew more pleading and desperate as weeks passed and he heard no word from her. He reminded her of the hours they had spent together, the secret places they had met and the plans they had made. One letter mentioned a letter he had written to her parents, begging them to let her come see him. There were six or seven letters dated consecutively the following September in which he begged for information about the baby and Carla's condition.

Then there was a gap of three months in the dating of the next-to-last and last letter. The last one, written almost two years after the first, said:

Dear Carla,

By your silence all I can guess is that you have decided to pick up your life and go on without me. I wish I could say I understood, but I don't. I really thought you loved me as much as I loved you. You are nineteen now, and can do what you wish.

I don't know how many more years I'm looking at here. Sometimes I wonder if I did the right thing, waiving a trial. But then I remember the look on your face and know I could never have put you through that.

There are many days when I would just like to end it. It would be hard, but it can be done. I could have done it last night. Something stopped me, though—I don't know what. Maybe just the thought that I have a child out there somewhere, and maybe someday I will know who it is.

This is my last letter to you, Carla. A little part of me hopes that you will answer this one, and we can have a life together yet. But I know that won't happen. One good thing about this miserable place—it brings you down to earth real quick, and keeps you there. Nobody dreams here.

For what it's worth, I still love you.

Sam

Marni hung over the letters and cried her heart out. She bundled them back up reverently, trying to keep her tears off them so as not to blur the already faded writing.

The doorbell rang, and the first thought that crossed Marni's mind was that Sam had returned. She ran to the door and flung it open. Cookie was outside the door. She looked in alarm at Marni's tear-ravaged face and demanded, "What's wrong?"

"Oh, hello, Cookie," Marni groaned. "Nothing's wrong. Really. I was just reading some old love letters from Sammy's father to his mother, and they were so beautiful, I couldn't help crying." Reluctantly, she added, "Uh, come in."

Cookie entered, saying, "I was just wondering if you had a chance to call your mother about the portrait. Since I don't have your *number,* I had to drop by to ask."

Marni sighed, still profoundly moved by the letters. "No, I haven't yet. But I'll call her right now, if you like."

She picked up the telephone and dialed her mother's number. "Hi, Mom. Um, Mom, my neighbor Cookie is here right now; she saw the portrait you did of me and she was wanting to know if you would do one of her and her husband." She listened, patting her eyes dry with a tissue, then said, "Okay, I'll tell her. I have her phone number when you need it. Thanks, Mom. Love you, too."

Marni hung up and said, "She said she's sorry, but she's got a backlog of about eight months' work. She'll call you when she can take new commissions."

"She must be very good," Cookie observed.

"Yes, she is," Marni replied, looking for a suitable spot to hang the portrait.

"May I ask you something personal?" Cookie said suddenly.

No! "Uh, sure," Marni said.

"Did Sammy knock you around after I left?" Cookie asked.

Marni burst out laughing. "Of course not! He just says things to get a reaction sometimes. He would never hit me. But if he did, I wouldn't be standing here telling you about it. I'd be flat on my back in the emergency room."

"He's strong," Cookie observed.

"A lot stronger than he looks. He lifts weights," Marni said with some pride.

Nodding, Cookie looked around the apartment at the good leather furniture, the expensive sound system, and the vast collection of CDs, records and tapes that Sammy had amassed during his single years. Marni could see her calculating how much all this cost. "One good thing about being childless, you can blow your money on other stuff," Marni noted.

Cookie appraised her. "Do you work?"

"Off and on," Marni replied, then said, "Look, Cookie, let me level with you, okay? Sammy is working, but his job is in a very sensitive area and we can't talk about it at all. I'd like to be friends with you as long as you understand that I can't tell you anything about Sammy's work."

"I see," Cookie breathed, wide-eyed. And Marni immediately saw how that was a mistake, as Cookie now appeared more curious than ever. Marni knew from experience that this curiosity would not just evaporate away.

"Aren't you working today?" Marni asked.

"No, I'm taking a few days off to get ready for the baby," Cookie admitted, sitting on the couch.

"Already?" Marni asked, sitting herself.

"Oh, sure. There's just a ton to do. You have to get on a waiting list for preschool—the good ones are *so* hard to get in, you know—and then you have to select a nursery theme and decor, the layette and all the accessories—why, I'd never get it all done if I waited till I got pregnant," Cookie explained.

"You mean, God can make a baby in nine months but that's not enough time for you to get ready for it?" Marni asked mischievously.

"Not if you're going to do it *right,*" Cookie said, missing the humor. She regarded her salon manicure. "Any idiot can produce a baby. Getting everything just so takes an incredible amount of planning. Maybe you'll understand that when you get ready to have your own."

Marni stared off into space. "Some babies come without any planning at all . . . without any love, or nurture . . . then for some reason only God understands they turn out to be the most handsome, loving, wonderful people, who do the most incredible, heroic things just because God put them there. . . ."

Cookie stared at her. "What are you talking about?"

Marni lowered her eyes, which had begun to form tears against her wishes. "Some people who were never shown love and compassion as a child are so full of it themselves that they just have to pour it out on any child around, even though they'll never have one of their own." She put her head down to weep again.

"Who . . . ?" Cookie murmured, perplexed.

But the door opened and Sammy stepped in. Seeing Cookie, he allowed a look of irritation to sweep across his face before he said, "Hello again. Marni! What's wrong?" He let his briefcase drop to the floor.

She jumped into his arms. "I love you. I love you so," she whispered, holding his neck.

Her embrace jostled his sports coat, and Cookie saw the holstered gun he wore. "I think I need to go," she said, walking out around them.

Sammy shut the door behind her with his foot. "Marni, what's wrong?"

"Oh, nothing, really. I read the letters your mom gave you," she murmured, wiping her nose. Sammy gave her his handkerchief, and she blew her nose vigorously. "They are so beautiful. He was a beautiful, loving man, Sammy—so very much like you!"

In distress, Sammy stroked her knuckles, then looked aside at the picture window. "I know I should read them, but I . . . just can't, yet—"

"I read them for you, Sammy," she said, resting her head on his chest. "He loved her even though she never came. He wanted to kill himself sometimes, but he didn't, because he knew he had a child out there somewhere—"

"Let's talk about something else, Marni," he said abruptly, turning to rest his hands on the window sash. "I'm doing all I know to do." He saw Cookie outside talking with someone in the courtyard. When she casually glanced toward him at the window, he closed the miniblinds.

Marni nodded and fell silent. Just for the distraction, she picked up the portrait and held it up in several experimental spots on the wall. Sammy continued to stand at the closed window, head down.

A few minutes later there was a knock on the door, and Sammy went to open it as if he were expecting someone. "Ah, Vicki. Thanks for coming."

A woman in a blue suit stepped in. "Happy to, Sammy." She carried a ledger under her arm, and she and Marni looked at each other while Sammy picked up his briefcase.

"Okay. Let's go," he said, motioning to Marni.

"Where to?" she asked, glancing at Vicki with the ledger.

"To see dear ol' Mom," he announced.

thirteen

Sammy, Marni, and Vicki went on out to his car and got in. Sammy was too preoccupied to explain matters or even introduce Vicki to Marni. So the short ride to Carla Bowers's house was a quiet one.

They pulled up to the brick house and Sammy hopped out briskly. The women trotted behind him as he strode to the door and rang the doorbell. For a few minutes nothing happened, but Sammy continued to ring. "She's here," he said.

The door opened a crack, and Carla's apprehensive face peeked out. "What do you want?"

"I need your signature," Sammy said cheerfully. "If you'll let me in long enough to sign this affidavit, you'll never have to see me again."

Reluctantly, she opened the door and stepped back. "What is it?" she asked.

Sammy came in and sat on the couch in the tidy little front room, patting the cushion beside him. His mother sat down at least two feet from him, and he drew a single-spaced, one-page document from his briefcase. Vicki sat on his other side and opened her ledger.

He explained to Carla, "I'm petitioning the Board of Pardons and Paroles to pardon Sam. This paper is a summary of what you told me the other day. I want you to read it, make any changes you want—initial the changes—and sign it. Vicki here is a notary who will witness your signature."

Carla looked at the paper in horror. "You wrote all that down? You want me to sign it?"

"Yes," he said. "It's essential to getting Sam pardoned."

"But," she said, "that will make me look like a—a liar."

Sammy opened his mouth, then said, "I think anyone who's familiar with the case will understand that you were young, and frightened, and under tremendous pressure. But now you have the opportunity to do the right thing."

"But—what good would it do now, coming so late?" she asked, drawing back as though imperiled.

Sammy patiently explained, "It will clear the stigma Sam's been living with for the past thirty years. It will enable him to get a decent job, and credit, and start his life over again."

"I can't sign that," she shuddered. "My family—"

"Mom, your parents have been dead for years," Sammy said through clenched teeth. "They won't have anything to say about it anymore. But it will mean a whole lot to Sam."

"Patsy, and Ralph. . . . What will they think?" she murmured.

With superhuman restraint, Sammy swallowed and said, "They will think you're all grown up and able to make your own decisions now." On a sudden thought, he said, "You defied them enough to name me Samuel. Do it one more time. Do this much for him."

"I can't," she shook her head rigidly. "I—can't. It's all in the past. It needs to stay in the past."

Sammy wiped his mouth and calmed himself with a few deep breaths. "Mom, there's a man out there who's living in a present shackled by the past. You're the *only one* who has the power to free him. If you ever loved him, Mom, do this for him now!"

Grasping her arms protectively around her, she turned her head away and uttered, "No."

Stupefied, Sammy gazed at her. Marni breathed a little prayer for him, as she feared what he might do. He looked down at the table and stroked his brow. Then he pulled a business card from his coat pocket and wrote on the back.

He tossed the card on the document and picked up his briefcase. Vicki closed her ledger. He said quietly, "If you change your mind, you can mail it to me at my home address. It has to be notarized when you sign it." He held the door for Marni and Vicki, and the three of them left in his car.

Pulling up to the apartment complex, Sammy parked and opened the door for Vicki. "Sorry to waste your time, Vicki," he said.

"That's all right. You couldn't force her. See you later." As Vicki climbed in her car to leave, Marni started to get out but Sammy said, "Stay put. We need to go somewhere."

"Where?" Marni asked.

"I don't know where. Anywhere. I just need to drive and think," he said, sitting and starting the car.

Marni watched him as he steered the car into the street. Sammy loved this old Mustang convertible. It was a suitably distinctive car—lime green, with a white top and white interior. He always drove with the top down, unless it was raining. Marni wondered if he had any idea that his father used to own a car just like it.

"Why wouldn't she sign it? *Why,* Marni?" he exploded.

Marni sighed, holding her hair from being whipped in her face. "Sam isn't the only one chained by the past," she said, feeling drained. "Your mother can't free herself from her family's disapproval. But you did the right thing. After she's had a chance to think about it, she'll probably sign it." Marni yawned, laying her head back on the seat.

Sammy shook his head, glancing in the rearview mirror. He did a double take, then picked up his car phone and dialed a number. "Hey, Poteet. Kidman. Get me a make on a Texas plate 607-BBZ. A blue Taurus." Marni looked over inquiringly and he said, "We're being tailed."

A moment later he said into the telephone, "That a fact? Which one? What's the address? Gotcha." He hung up and turned the corner. "It's registered to a private investigative agency," he told Marni, and she lifted her head.

Sammy turned west on LBJ, then exited to an office tower. While he parked, the car behind them pulled into a parking space about three slots down. Sammy pretended to start into the building, then made an about-face, sprinting to the Taurus to yank open the door. The driver startled, and Marni rose up in her seat to watch.

Flashing his badge, Sammy said, "What's your game, pal?"

"Oh-oh," the investigator said. "I didn't know you were a cop. I just dropped the case."

"Who're you working for? What did they want?" Sammy asked irritably.

"You'll have to get a court order for that, *sir*," he replied with a touch of sarcasm. "But I give you my word that I'm off the case."

"That doesn't mean a thing," Sammy observed, glancing up at the tower that housed the investigative agency. "But this you can bank on: if I so much as smell anybody from Dunbar & Smith around again, I'll eat your license for lunch."

"I'm sure you would," the investigator replied, and Sammy turned back to the car where Marni waited.

"Who was he working for?" she asked.

"Nosy neighbors, probably," he grumbled, starting the car.

"You think *Cookie* hired him?" she asked in alarm.

"Ah, I don't know. Her or Carla. Or somebody I once put behind bars," he muttered.

"Oh." She leaned her head back on the seat and closed her eyes.

He glanced at her, slightly peeved. "Don't get all upset about it, now."

"Sammy, please . . . take me home," she murmured.

"Sure," he said, glancing at her in some concern.

When they got back to the apartment, she dragged herself upstairs without a word. Sammy paused to get a soft drink from the refrigerator, then went upstairs himself. He looked into the bedroom to find her stretched out on the bed, fully clothed, sound asleep. Wonderingly, he kissed her on the forehead and went back to work.

When Sammy came home from work four hours later, the scene was unchanged. The painting still sat on the sofa, and there was no hint of dinner in progress. With mounting concern, he went up to the bedroom. Marni was still asleep.

He sat on the edge of the bed and kissed her. She mumbled something and rolled over. He kissed her again, a little more insistently. "Marni—baby—it's almost seven o'clock. Why don't you get up now? Marni! Aren't you hungry?"

"Uh huh." She opened her eyes and sat up, weaving slightly.

He eyed her with wrinkled brow. "Baby, you haven't taken to the bottle, have you?" he cracked.

"That's not funny, Sammy," she mumbled reproachfully, pushing back her disheveled hair. He watched incredulously as she slowly got up and stumbled to the bathroom.

"Are you feeling all right?" he asked, following her.

"No, Sammy, I'm not," she said, exasperated. "I feel awful. Okay?"

"Better take you to the doctor," he murmured anxiously.

"I don't want to go to the doctor," she said, then looked up. "I want a double cheeseburger and a chocolate shake."

"You want a double cheeseburger?" he exclaimed. "Marni, I don't think I've ever seen you finish a regular hamburger!"

"What does it take for a person to get a double cheeseburger? Do I fill out a requisition, or get a court order, or what?" she cried.

She started crying, and Sammy stared, dumbfounded. He held out a hand. "Don't . . . move. I'll go get one right now. I'll be back in five minutes." Hustling down the stairs, he muttered, "Shiminy *Christmas,* what's the matter with her?"

In fifteen minutes he had returned with the food order. Marni was seated at the kitchen table, holding her head. Sammy carefully set the cheeseburger and shake in front of her. "Thank you," she said, unwrapping it. Sammy retrieved his soft drink and sat across from her to eat his hamburger.

"Garrett got a tip on a chop shop today. We raided it this afternoon and recovered four vehicles before they were destroyed. Made six quality arrests," he noted.

"That's nice," she mumbled. Burger in hand, he watched in growing amazement while she devoured the cheeseburger. She sipped half the shake before rejecting it: "Too sweet."

"You ate it *all,*" he marveled.

"Yes, and it was good," she said, getting up from the table.

"D'you feel better now?" he asked hopefully.

"Yes, I do," she smiled at him. "Thank you, Sammy." She leaned over to kiss him lightly, then went back upstairs.

"Good," he said, quickly finishing his own burger. "She's okay."

He went upstairs to find that she had changed into her satin nightshirt. "Ooh, yes," he murmured, washing his face and hands as she turned down the covers and got into bed. In short order he had stripped and joined her under the covers. He kissed her softness and began unbuttoning her nightshirt.

"No, Sammy," she said, and rolled over.

He halted in shock. No? She said *no?* She hadn't told him no since they were married! Not ever! He sat up in frustration and dismay. "Okay, Marni, you want to tell me what the problem is?" he asked, aggrieved. ". . . Marni?" He leaned to look over her shoulder. She was asleep! Sammy sank back to his pillow, one unhappy man.

The following morning Marni began to stir as Sammy was getting ready for work. He glanced over at her curled up in the rumpled sheets. "Well, good morning, Sleeping Beauty. You only slept fourteen of the last twenty-four hours."

She moaned, shifted, and then suddenly retched. "Marni!" Sammy gasped, springing to her side with his tie half-knotted. She covered her face with the sheet and retched again, but her stomach was empty.

"Baby!" he cried, tugging at the sheet. "I'm calling the doctor," he declared, turning to the bedside telephone. "Who's our doctor? Wait, you need a gynecologist. Would this be a gynecological problem?" He sat helplessly staring at the phone in his hand.

"Sammy," she whispered, pulling the sheet from her face. "Go on to work. I'm fine."

"Are you sure? Oh, Marni, you're white as—as—" Not a sheet. The sheets were bright pink.

"I'm sure, Sammy. I think I've just got a touch of the flu. It's one of those things that has to run its course," she explained weakly.

"Marni, I can't leave you alone like this," he protested.

Truthfully, she said, "I wish you would. I'll call you if I need you to come home."

"Promise?" he said with some relief.

"I promise," she tried to smile, and he gently kissed her forehead, pausing to feel for fever. "Besides, I'm sure you've got a ton of paperwork to fill out on those quality arrests yesterday."

"Yeah," he admitted. "Garrett is beautiful on the street, but he's an idiot when it comes to reports."

"Go on." She pushed him gently off the bed.

"I'll come check on you at lunch," he said, and took up his coat with his tie askew.

Any movement sent another wave of nausea rolling over her, so Marni waited until she heard the front door open and close before she got up. Staggering to the bathroom with her eyes half closed, she was inattentive as to whether the door was open or closed. As it happened, the door was half open, so that Marni stumbled right into the edge, face first. Stars jumped across her sight and she sat down on the floor abruptly, half crying, half laughing.

"Oh, for pete's sake," she moaned, holding her eye. She dragged herself to the bathroom and looked in the mirror. There was an angry red indention across her face and a small cut just above her eyebrow. Muttering to herself, Marni splashed cold water on her face and went downstairs to get something to eat. A light breakfast helped her feel better. By the time she had showered and dressed and put on some laundry, she was beginning to feel like a regular human being again.

Some hours later the doorbell rang. Marni looked out the peephole: It was Cookie. Marni sagged against the door and considered not opening it, but she had the stereo playing, which Cookie was certain to hear. Sighing, Marni opened the door. "Hi, Cookie."

Cookie took one look at her and exclaimed, "What happened to your face?"

"My face? Oh, no," Marni muttered. She ran upstairs to look in the bathroom mirror, and saw a dark purple circle forming under her right eye. "Oh no!" Marni moaned and laughed, shaking her head.

Cookie had followed her upstairs. "Now, Marni, whatever has happened I want you to tell me the truth. Did Sammy hit you?" she asked in a hard voice.

"Sammy? No!" said Marni, shocked. "I ran into the door."

"You ran into the door," Cookie repeated, unconvinced.

"Yes, I ran into the bathroom door. I wasn't feeling very good this morning, and I got up without watching where I was going, and I ran smack into it," Marni said, turning her head to study the bruise.

"Well," said Cookie, making a show of brushing it off, "I came over because I'd like to get your opinion on some baby furniture." Marni then saw that she held a slender catalog.

"Cookie, don't you work?" Marni asked, distracted.

"I told you, I'm taking a little time off to get some of this lined out," Cookie said in a businesslike tone.

"Oh," Marni said in disappointment.

Cookie held up the catalog. "The Jenny Lind is the most popular model, I'm told, but Kevin prefers the bare, clean lines of the Modern. This is interesting—Chippendale reproductions. They're expensive, but they would become heirlooms, of course."

Holding the catalog, Marni sat on the unmade bed. Cookie glanced inconspicuously around the bedroom. There was a cozy fireplace, a cat bed, and the usual bedroom clutter. Marni's cat was playing with the laces of a pair of men's hightops on the floor. And on the bureau was a dusty trophy inscribed: "Sammy Kidman: MVP DPD Softball League."

"My mother still has the bassinet I slept in," Marni murmured, and Cookie turned back to her. "She always said she was keeping it in case—I wanted to use it someday." To her dismay, tears quickly filled her eyes.

"I appreciate it, but we cannot use hand-me-downs," Cookie said firmly. "Too many old things have lead-based paint." Marni brushed away her tears and Cookie added, "I'm sorry if I upset you." Privately, she noted the pink satin sheets on the bed.

Marni waved it off. "Oh, that's not it, Cookie. I don't know what's wrong with me. All of a sudden I cry at the drop of a hat. Sammy has just about had it with me." It was an exaggeration, of course. Marni decided she needed something to eat, so she got up and went downstairs to look in the freezer for ice cream.

Cookie followed her down. "Well, what do you think of the furniture?"

"If I were buying for me—" Marni paused and bit her lip— "I'd get the Jenny Lind. I think it's the prettiest, for the money."

Cookie pursed her lips, dissatisfied. "I suppose if you have to consider the cost, that's what you'd get. But Kevin and I don't want to settle for what everyone else gets."

"Get what you want, then," Marni shrugged, scooping out ice cream. "Want some?" she asked, licking the scoop.

Cookie raised a brow. "Uh, no thanks."

The door opened and Sammy came in. "Mar—?" He caught sight of Cookie and his shoulders sagged, saying plainly, *You again?*

"Excuse me; I have to run. Got a million things to do," she chirped, heading around Sammy for the door.

He nodded, then looked up and gasped, "Marni!"

"What?" Startled, she dropped the bowl of ice cream, which shattered on the tile floor. "Ohhh!" She got so mad she stamped her foot and burst into tears.

Sammy put his hands to his head in utter perplexity. "What—what is the *matter* with you? What are you doing to yourself? What happened to your face?" he demanded.

"Don't you holler at me!" she shouted, stamping her foot. "That's all you care about! How I look! Well, don't you think that it matters to me one little bit about what you think about how I look!" And she ran upstairs, crying.

Sammy stared after her, stared at the mess of broken pottery and melting ice cream, then put his hands on his hips and shook his head. As he stepped around the disaster area to get the trash can, he looked up at Cookie still standing by the door. "Yes?" he asked pointedly, and she slipped out.

After cleaning up the kitchen floor, Sammy went upstairs to find his wife sprawled out on the bed, still crying. Grasping for patience, he leaned down on his elbow beside her and kissed her shoulder. "Marni, you know you mean a lot more to me than just how you look," he said softly. "It just looked like you'd hurt yourself. Turn your head up, baby; let me see your face—Marni! You've got a black eye! What happened?"

She sniffled, "I ran into the door."

"You ran into the door?" he repeated, pained.

She nodded, sniffed, and then started giggling. "It knocked me flat on my bottom."

"On your bottom?" he smiled, relieved at her giggling, and rubbed her derrière. "Did you hurt your bottom?" he murmured.

"Um hmmm," she replied, still giggling. Then the giggles tapered off and she reached up to kiss him in sudden passion.

He accepted her favorable mood, no questions asked. By the time he got up to get dressed for work again, he felt sure that everything was going to be all right now. And when he got home from work that evening, he was relieved to find Marni awake and tractable, though he did have to call in pizza for dinner.

But the next morning, Wednesday, was a different story. As soon as Sammy got up, jostling the bed, Marni began retching. When he tried to see if she was all right, she ran right past him into the bathroom and locked the door.

"Marni!" He knocked on the door. "Marni—baby—*please* open the door." Then he pounded. "Marni! Open this door right now!"

"Go to work!" she shouted from within.

"I *can't*, baby doll, until you let me in so that I can get ready!" he explained.

"Too bad!" she shouted.

Sammy paced the room wildly for a moment. It was a very simple matter to get the door unlocked—blowing the door off the hinges would be a simple matter, compared to handling the female within. What was a man to do?

There was only one person to turn to in a crisis like this. Only one person could guide him through this mine field. Resolutely, he sat on the bed and dialed a number. "Hello?" she answered.

"Hi, Pam. I'm sorry to call this early, but—I've got a major situation on my hands here. It's Marni. She—she's just gotten crazy on me, Pam. She sleeps all the time, except when she's crying—she throws fits like a kid, and she starts retching when she hasn't had anything to eat. I don't know what to do," he pleaded.

"Oh, Sammy, that happened to me when I was about Marni's age. It sounds like just a little hormonal imbalance," Pam said calmly.

"Will anything help?" he asked anxiously.

"Well, a little time, and therapy. Tell you what—I know this great doctor who will lay it all out for you. Let me give you her number. Make an appointment for Marni with her as soon as possible, and she'll be her old self in no time."

"What's the number?" Sammy asked, digging for a pen in the bedside drawer. Pam found the number for him and Sammy thanked her profusely.

"You're welcome, dear. Keep me posted on how she's feeling." Pam hung up the telephone, then sprang from her bed and began a joyful execution of a combination Texas two-step/classical ballet. Clayton raised up sleepily. "What on earth has gotten into you, woman?"

"Nothing, nothing. Thank you, thank you, thank you!" she sang, dancing around the room.

fourteen

Sammy wound up getting ready that morning in the downstairs halfbath. He went in to work grumpy, unshaven, and clutching the doctor's telephone number. He called as soon as her office was open, but the earliest he could get Marni in to see her was a week from today. Gritting his teeth, he resolved to endure out of sheer love.

Marni felt terrible remorse after he had left that morning. She knew she was acting irrationally, but felt helpless to right herself. In penance, she began cleaning the apartment even before getting ready herself. She knew she must look frightful with her black eye, unwashed hair, and slovenly t-shirt, but she had no intention of going anywhere today. So she started by dusting everything, her least favorite chore, then pulled out the vacuum cleaner.

The doorbell rang. "Cookie, *go away,*" she muttered, and opened the door before looking through the peephole. She blinked at the two men in business suits standing outside. Why wasn't that outer gate ever locked like it was supposed to be?

"Mrs. Kidman?" one asked.

"Who are you?" she asked coolly, though inside she was quivering.

They showed her their badges. "Dallas Police Department Internal Affairs," the first said. "May we come in?"

Marni's stomach coiled up. "Is this about Sammy?" she asked faintly.

"Yes. May we come in?" he repeated.

Haltingly, she stepped back and pointed to the couch. They sat, pulling out a notepad and tape recorder, and Marni almost passed out. "What is it?" she asked tremulously.

"How did you get that shiner, Mrs. Kidman?" the second asked with a glimmer of humor.

Marni raised a hand self-consciously to her face. "I ran into the bathroom door," she whispered.

The officers looked at each other. "Mrs. Kidman, it's extremely important that you tell us the truth."

"But that *is* the truth!" she cried. "I've been feeling so awful, and I'm sick and cry all the time—and poor Sammy just doesn't know what to do with me—and I got up and wasn't watching where I was going and ran smack into the door! He wasn't even here at the time! Who told you that Sammy hit me?" she asked angrily.

"We got an anonymous complaint that Detective Kidman might be abusing you," the first said.

"That's—that's—" she was so angry she could hardly speak. "That's just garbage! Sammy loves me and he would never hit me! How dare you investigate him on the basis of an anonymous call?"

"We have to," the second shrugged. "We have to investigate any complaint, regardless of where it comes from—" Thoroughly distraught, Marni collapsed in tears.

The two looked at each other uncomfortably. "Don't let it bother you, Mrs. Kidman; we'll put it down as baseless and that'll be the end of it. He won't be affected by it."

She continued to cry while they got up. "We'll see ourselves out, ma'am. Uh, have a good day." They left while she was still crying.

After a moment she calmed down and went to splash cold water on her face. The turmoil still swirled inside her—she felt herself a cauldron of emotions—but now she forced them down so she could think.

That complaint could only have come from Cookie. She was the only other person besides Sammy to have even seen her black eye. But that meant she had to have known he was a cop, to have called Internal Affairs. The private detective who had been following them found out that Sammy was a cop. But why in the world would Cookie go to the expense and trouble of hiring a private investigator?

Protect Sammy, Mom had said. "You were so right," she muttered. What if Cookie got suspicious next about his nice clothes and his nice sound system, and complained that he was on the take? Even though there was nothing to find, investigating that would be a long, painful process that could permanently taint Sammy's career.

Marni gazed into the bathroom mirror with the calmness of purpose. "You made a mistake, Cookie."

She showered, set her hair, and carefully applied makeup so that the bruise hardly showed and her eyes were clear and bright. She picked up an advertising circular from that morning's newspaper, tucking it under her arm as she went to ring Cookie's doorbell.

Cookie looked surprised when she answered the door. Marni smiled, "Hi! I just saw this ad from Baby World and wondered if you had seen it." She handed the circular to Cookie and went in, looking around.

The apartment was in perfect order, meticulously decorated in glass and chrome. There were some correct, coffee-table environmental books (which portray humans as villains on a ravaged earth) and an air purification system. "How's the baby-making process coming?" Marni chirped.

"Fine, as far as I know," Cookie replied slowly, closing the door.

"How will you know when you connect?" Marni wondered. "Do you have to wait till you miss a period or two?"

Cookie laughed, "Oh, no. Don't you watch commercials? You use one of these." She showed Marni a home pregnancy test kit. "You can get one at any drugstore, and they're accurate just days after conception."

"That's interesting," Marni murmured, studying the box. "Well, I'm so excited for you. Have you decided on a decor?" She handed the kit back to Cookie.

"We're still looking," Cookie sighed. She pointed to the kitchen table, where catalogs, price lists, and brochures lay strewn about. Marni went over to sit down and look through them.

"It's such a complicated process," Cookie confided. "I do like the Chippendale reproductions, but those require pastel colors in the decor. However, primary colors are most strongly recommended for early visual development. The primary colors look fine with the Modern lines, but all they have is ash and I did want oak," Cookie said in dissatisfaction.

"What happened to pink and blue?" Marni wondered.

"Marni, *no one* decorates in gender-confining, sexist colors any more," Cookie said scornfully.

Marni looked up dreamily. "My mother decorated my nursery in yellow. She sewed everything by hand—the bumpers, the quilts, even the pad on the changing table—all bright yellow. It was like a room full of sunshine. I still remember waking up in the mornings and seeing the breeze blow through those yellow gingham curtains," she mused.

"That was fine back then, but development specialists now recommend two or three main colors to enhance visual discernment," Cookie informed her.

Marni smiled. "You certainly are well informed."

"I wouldn't *consider* having a baby without doing the research," Cookie said, pointing to a stack of magazines targeted toward new parents with annual income levels over $100,000.

Marni looked past the magazines to a personal computer sitting in the next room. "What did you say Kevin did?"

"He's a communications consultant for Intrax Network," Cookie replied.

"That sounds very interesting. Does he travel?" Marni asked.

"Yes, quite a bit," Cookie said, and then fell silent.

That was strange behavior for a garrulous person. Marni looked at her. "Tell me about it."

"Well, he flies all over, and consults with clients about their communications systems," Cookie replied vaguely.

"I see," Marni replied.

Cookie's doorbell rang, and she went to open it while Marni remained seated at the table. Marni heard Sammy's voice: "Uh, hello, Cookie. I was wondering if you had seen—" Marni came to the door smiling and he looked vastly relieved.

"Hi, Sammy; want some lunch? Talk to you later, Cookie," Marni said brightly on her way out.

As she and Sammy walked back to their apartment, she sympathetically stroked his bristly face. "Aw, poor baby, didn't even get to shave this morning. I'm sorry, Sammy. I don't know why I've been such a pill."

He eyed her cautiously. "Marni, I've made an appointment for you to see a woman doctor next Wednesday at nine. I'm going to take the morning off to drive you."

"Okay, Sammy. If you think I need to go, I guess I should," she said, most tractably. He looked slightly heartened. "Sammy, what do you know about Intrax Network?" she asked as they went into the apartment.

He thought it over. "Never heard of it. Come on up while I shave."

She followed him up the stairs, saying, "Cookie said Kevin works at Intrax, as a communications consultant."

"Then he probably does," he said, taking off his coat and tie. He opened his shirt and took out an electric razor.

Marni sat on the bed and picked up the telephone. She dialed Information, requesting the number for Intrax Network. She listened, then hung up. "Information has no listing for this company. It must be very new, or—nonexistent."

Sammy glanced at her, running the shaver over his face. "What do you care?"

"Just curious," she murmured.

"Curiosity killed the cat," he reminded her.

"But satisfaction brought it back," she returned.

He hung his head. "Marni, I do not like this weirdness. Will you please snap out of it?"

"Yes, sir!" she came to attention and saluted.

Tight-lipped, he replaced his coat and tie and held her shoulders lightly to kiss her. "I'm going back to work. I hope to see you all normal by tonight." He turned out of the bedroom and went downstairs. Marni watched him from the top of the stairs, then went across the landing to the second bedroom, where their computer sat.

She found no website for the company. The Better Business Bureau had no information on it. The public library had no listing for it in any of their business directories. "Something's fishy here," Marni advised herself. She logged off the computer and was considering her next step when the pangs of conscience seized her.

"This is not right," she murmured. "It's not right to harass her just because she's harassing us. Sammy's right. Oh, Lord, please just don't let her ruin Sammy with her wild ideas. And please help me understand why I'm being such a dingbat all of a sudden."

Marni decided to forget the whole thing and go back to doing the housework, as she should. She smiled as she unwound the cord on the vacuum cleaner. Sammy was blind to dirt and clutter, but she knew that secretly he wished she would be a little stay-at-home wife. Even though they would not have children, he wanted to coddle and protect her. He *said* that he didn't want her to get a regular job so she would be free to accompany him on assignments, but she strongly suspected that he hoped she would get used to staying home and cooking. He was absolutely enthralled by the idea of coming home every day to a wife and a home-cooked meal.

She turned on the vacuum and heard a loud *flapflapflap*. Dismayed, she turned it off and unplugged it, then turned it over to find that the belt had broken. "Ohhhhhh!" Now she'd have to go get a replacement package of belts.

Rather than run across town for just that, Marni decided to append it to her list of errands and borrow Cookie's vacuum for now. Accordingly, she went to Cookie's door and rang the bell. When she answered, Marni said, "Hi, Cookie! My vacuum cleaner just died. Mind if I borrow yours for a minute?"

"Why no, not at all," Cookie replied brightly. "I'll get it."

"Thanks," said Marni, stepping inside to wait. As Cookie went to a closet for the vacuum, the door behind Marni opened. She turned as Kevin came in. He startled briefly when he saw her. "Hi," she said briskly. "We're cleaning house."

She turned back around as she heard Cookie in the next room, but Kevin suddenly grabbed Marni's arm and dragged her into the kitchen. "I don't think so!" he snapped. To compound her astonishment, he pulled a serrated knife from a drawer and placed it at her throat. Then he dragged her back out to the living room. "All right, Kidman!" he shouted. "Come here and we'll talk!"

Marni held perfectly still as Cookie ran in. "Kevin! You idiot!" she screamed. "He's not here! She doesn't know anything! She came to borrow the vacuum cleaner!"

He stared at Cookie while Marni looked away, thinking, *So I was right. Lotta good that's going to do me now.* "She—doesn't know anything?" he repeated weakly. "This isn't a raid?"

"No, you moron!" Cookie cried.

"I knew they were trouble! The minute they moved in, I *knew* they'd be trouble!" he vented, waving the knife while keeping a firm grasp on Marni. "You and your 'friendly neighbor' routine! As usual, you overdid it!"

"Look who's overreacting! Now shut up and let me think!" Cookie pressed her hand to her forehead. "Okay. Internal Affairs should be acting on that tip real soon. This is an abused wife who ran away. . . . Take her upstairs and watch her. I'll be right back."

Cookie left the apartment and Kevin shoved Marni upstairs to the spare bedroom. She looked out the window toward the street, and he went over to close the blinds. In the moment before he did, she glimpsed a figure leaving the courtyard through the gate. It was Sam.

In about fifteen minutes Cookie returned, carrying Marni's suitcase. "Okay, she's all packed." Then she put a sheet of Marni's stationery on the bedside table, and placed a pen in her hand. "Okay, Marni, you're going to write a note to your husband, telling him that you can't take it anymore and you're leaving him. Got it?"

Marni nodded and took up the pen. *Dear Sam,* she began. "Uh uh," Cookie objected. "I know you call him Sammy. Change that."

Dear Sammy, Marni wrote, *I now understand the fear your mother felt. I can't take it anymore and I'm leaving. Marni.*

Cookie read it and smiled ironically. "He was beating you after all, huh? Is that why he didn't want us to know that you two are married? I knew you were lying when you said you ran into the door. Well, that just helped us out a lot." She took the sheet and told Kevin, "Go get something to tie her up."

He went downstairs and came back in a moment with a roll of duct tape. "Tie her up good—I've got to go ditch her car somewhere." Cookie then took Marni's suitcase and the note downstairs. Marni heard the apartment door open and close while Kevin pulled her hands behind her back and wrapped them. Even had she the strength to fight, he had her immobilized before she could so much as raise her hands.

This is getting redundant, she thought as Kevin pushed her onto the bed to wrap her ankles. He tore off a piece of tape and put it over her mouth. Marni took it calmly because she was sure Sammy would pick up the hint about his mother. Carla was frightened by all the people around her, making her say something she did not want to say.

The minutes passed very slowly. Kevin fidgeted nervously and paced between rooms until Cookie came back, then they discussed their options. Marni pretended to go to sleep so that they would drop their guard and speak more freely.

Sure enough, she heard bits and pieces from the other rooms: "At least you're not walking around with that in your briefcase—Jennings won't discover anything missing—" . . . "I know two likely bidders for it, and the Japanese companies are always looking for an edge—" . . . "Now, if they come around looking for her, you say—" But that's all she gleaned, because, oddly enough, she really did fall asleep.

When she awoke the room was dark. The tape chafed her skin and her left arm was numb. She struggled up to a sitting position, working her stiff arms. *Okay, Sammy, you can come rescue me any time now.*

She began to worry about Smoky, not being fed all day. Then she wondered what Cookie did with the Miata, Marni's graduation gift from her parents. *Then* she started worrying that Sammy might be thrown by the note, at least at first. Or worse yet, chalk it up to her weird behavior and assume she really did leave. That gave her cold chills. Finally, she realized that Sam must have come to the door, knocked, found no one home and left again. That made her saddest of all.

She worked her wrists to loosen the tape somewhat. Then by sitting very still and listening, she discerned Cookie and Kevin's talking downstairs. In a few minutes, they came up to her room and turned on the light. Marni blinked.

Cookie sat on the bed and Kevin stood in the doorway. She began to explain to Marni, "We just wanted you to know that we're not really criminals. This whole thing is so crazy. We've never done anything illegal before, but now we're in too deep to back out. It started with Kevin bringing work home on his laptop—but then he stumbled onto some secret new programs his company was running. He wasn't supposed to have that information, but when he told somebody about it, and they told him how much *money* he could get for it—"

"There you go again! You don't have to tell her our life history, Cookie!" Kevin interrupted irately.

"Well, anyway," she continued with a shake of her head at him, "we got suspicious that the company was on to him, and when we saw you two move in—well, you just looked too perfect. It didn't help finding out that your husband's a detective. Now—" the doorbell rang.

Cookie and Kevin looked at each other. "You go down and answer it. I'll stay here and make sure she keeps quiet," Cookie said. So Kevin went. Cookie turned to watch Marni while they both listened to him open the door.

With the bedroom door ajar, they heard Sammy's voice clearly. "Uh, hi, Kevin. I was wondering if you or Cookie has seen Marni tonight."

"No, Sammy, I haven't. Cookie," he called up the stairs. "Have you seen Marni tonight?"

"No, I sure haven't," she called from the door. Then she looked back quickly to make sure that Marni did not move.

"Sorry, Sammy; neither of us has seen her," Kevin said sincerely.

"Well . . . hmmm," Sammy said. "This is kind of strange. Uh, do you mind if I use your phone?"

"Not at all," Kevin said.

Several seconds later Marni heard: "Hi, Pam. I'm looking for Marni. Has she been out that way today? . . . No? Well. Hmmm. Thanks anyway." A moment later he said, "She hasn't been out to her parents' house either."

"Maybe you should call the police," Kevin suggested.

"Oh, no need for that," Sammy answered hastily. "I'm sure she'll show up. Uh, thanks, Kevin."

"Hope you find her." There was the sound of the door opening, and Sammy's reply was indistinct. The door closed.

Marni sagged on the bed. He didn't get it! He thought she had actually left! Now she *really* began to worry.

Kevin came up to the bedroom. "He's gone. Now what?"

"We have to get her out of this apartment," Cookie said resolutely. "The question is, where?"

"Well," he said, eyeing Marni, "there's the Trinity River." Marni's eyes widened and she shook her head pleadingly.

"Kevin, stealing company secrets is one thing. Murder is another," Cookie said sternly.

"Honey, I'm looking at a prison term either way!" he protested. Marni shook her head vigorously.

"Well," she sniffed, "do what you have to do. I don't want to know anything about it." And Cookie left the room.

Marni stared at Kevin wide-eyed. He sat down beside her, trying to think of a way to make a clean job of it. But having botched the lesser criminal act of company theft, he was totally inadequate to carry out a proper murder. He put his hands experimentally around her throat. She stiffened, throwing her weight back against the headboard. The headboard banged resoundingly on the wall, which was shared by the apartment next door. "Oh, you're going to make a lot of noise, aren't you?" he muttered anxiously.

I'm sure not going to make it easy for you, she replied in thought. He picked up a pillow and put it over her face. But he was not pressing hard enough to cut off her air entirely. Marni kicked and thrashed, sending the lamp on the bedside table crashing to the floor. He let go of the pillow, and Marni breathed in deeply through her nose. "I'll have you know that lamp was hand thrown!" he hissed irritably.

Marni heard the doorbell ring and Cookie call quietly, "Kevin! Someone's at the door!"

He rose from the bed. "Well, guess I'll have to wait till later in the night, anyway." He turned out the light and left the room.

fifteen

As soon as Kevin left the room, Marni began earnestly working the tape on her wrists. In no time she had it off and began picking at the tape on her ankles. Since her feet were wrapped more securely, that took longer. As she worked, she listened to Kevin trying to get rid of a persistent salesman who insisted on showing both husband and wife his product. Marni paused to pull the tape off her mouth, wincing.

Then she heard a light tapping. She froze. There it was again, from the window! Marni threw her feet on the floor and hopped to the window, pulling up the blinds. Sammy, outside on a ladder, pointed to the window lock. Marni unlocked the window and raised it a few inches. Sammy grasped it and hoisted it the rest of the way up.

He patted the sill and she sat on it, throwing her bound feet over to the ladder. He gripped her around the waist with one arm and guided her as she hobbled down the rungs. She glimpsed a fireman on the ladder beneath him.

As Sammy hopped to the ground, strong hands lowered her past the last few rungs. A paramedic produced scissors to cut the tape from her feet, and Marni looked around in awe at the firetruck, ambulance, and patrol cars clustered on the street, out of sight of the Paynes' apartment door. All these emergency vehicles had approached in utter silence. Uniformed officers held curious onlookers back.

"Marni," Sammy said, "if you felt like I wasn't paying enough attention to you, all you had to do was tell me."

"If I—!" she was so flabbergasted she could hardly respond. "That *I* felt—! Sammy Kidman!" She stamped her foot in anger. "He grabbed me and tied me up because he thought *you* had come to raid them and he was talking about throwing me in the Trinity River and *you* accuse me of setting all this up to get attention—"

While the firemen calmly put away their ladder, one shook his head and muttered, "She sounds pregnant to me." Marni was struck silent by the lightning bolt of comprehension.

Sammy put his arms around her. "I know, baby; I know. I couldn't resist razzing you. The minute I got home and found your note, I smelled a setup. But since your Miata was gone, I didn't know where you were, and that part worried me."

"How did you find out where I was?" she asked.

"Sam told me," he smiled.

Her jaw dropped, but then the very Sam appeared beside them. "I got ten dollars for one jar of bottled water," he said, holding out the bill in satisfaction.

"Sam!" she cried, throwing her arms around his neck. He staggered back in surprise, then put his arms around her, then held her tightly. All the while she squeezed his neck.

"Hey," Sammy muttered. "Wait a minute. I'm the man you love."

"Did you see me leave the apartment?" she asked Sam, still holding his neck.

"Yeah," he admitted. His lined face was full of wonder and gratification. "I was watchin' your door, trying to get up the courage to go ring the bell again. I saw you go into the other apartment, and not come out again."

"He stayed around until I came home," Sammy said, drawing her ever so slightly out of Sam's arms. "About the time I asked God where you were, Sam rang the doorbell and told me. He had been watching for hours for you to come back out."

"But I saw the other woman go in and out of your apartment, and it didn't look right—especially when she drove off and then came walking back," Sam said.

"My car—" she turned anxiously to Sammy.

"—was found in the parking lot of the apartments down the street," Sammy said, jerking his head. "We'll go pick it up a little later."

"Thanks," Marni murmured in relief.

She turned to glimpse Kevin and Cookie being placed in the back seat of a squad car. Suddenly she felt very sorry for them. All that social correctness and still no morals. And no baby for a while, either. Marni turned back to Sammy. "Then—when you came to their door—"

"That was just to pinpoint your exact location. I ascertained that you were not on the ground floor, so you had to be in one of the two upstairs bedrooms. I guessed they had you in the second one," Sammy in his professional voice.

"But—all this—just for me?" she asked wonderingly. They even had a tactical unit on hand.

"Procedure, baby," Sammy said. "We didn't know what they wanted with you. Rather than storm the place, we agreed to try to sneak you out. So Sam provided our distraction." Sammy clapped a hand on his father's shoulder, who smiled slightly. He was still holding Marni, and she him.

"Now, what was that about a raid?" Sammy asked. Another detective and several officers hung nearby to listen.

Marni explained, "I went over there to borrow their vacuum cleaner, and Kevin walked in thinking you were searching their apartment. They were the ones who hired the private investigator *and* called Internal Affairs."

"Internal Affairs?" Sammy muttered uneasily.

"Turns out Kevin stole some company secrets and was trying to sell them—that's all. But he got so paranoid about it, he thought we moved in just to catch him," Marni said.

"Well, he's got something to be paranoid about now," the detective observed. The emergency vehicles began leaving and Sammy turned to wrap up the details with the officer in charge.

Marni turned to Sam. "I'm starving. Are you hungry?"

"Sure," he shrugged.

"Then we'll get Sammy to take us out to dinner," Marni said, laying her head on Sam's shoulder. He looked rather overwhelmed. Sammy kept glancing over.

"I . . . don't understand why you're being so nice to me," Sam said.

Marni held his hand. "I read your letters to Carla," she whispered.

"She kept them?" he marveled.

"All of them," Marni replied softly.

Sammy came over and put his arm firmly around her. "Hi, there. I'm your husband. Remember me?" he said testily.

"Yes. You're taking us to Tony Roma's," she said.

He blinked. "Marni, you never eat ribs!"

"Don't make me throw a fit, Sammy; I'm too tired. Just take us to Tony Roma's," she said patiently.

He did, and they had a wonderful time. They stopped by their apartment for Sam to clean up and borrow some of Sammy's clothes to go eat out. (He firmly declined to wear Stan's.) Then it was on to the restaurant.

Sam wanted to hear every detail of their lives, and Sammy told him while Marni ate a half loaf of onion rings and a whole order of ribs by herself. And she listened and watched with silent gratitude while father and son caught up on the past thirty-two years. They were so similar—in looks, in mannerisms, even in the way they laughed. Marni enjoyed being the dinner date of two good-looking men.

"The thing I regret most," Sam said slowly, "was missing you grow up. I really wanted to be there for ball games, and report cards, and buying new shoes. I'd think, 'Well, he's ten now, startin' to notice girls and throw spitwads.' Then, 'He's sixteen now, startin' to drive.' And here you are, a grown man. I missed all of it. I try not to be bitter, but I feel like those years were stolen from me and I'll never get them back. I'll never get to hold you as a baby." Hearing this, Marni suddenly blushed and put her head down, smiling. The men did not notice.

"Maybe there's somebody for you yet . . . Dad," Sammy murmured.

Sam shook his head. "I'm not interested. All I care about now is my family, and a steady job."

As Sammy paid the tab and they went out to the Mustang, he said, "Well, several people owe me favors. We'll see what we can come up with."

"Did you tell him about the pardon?" exclaimed Marni. Sam looked up quickly and Marni said, "Sammy has started the paperwork to get you pardoned!"

"That's dead in the water, baby," Sammy said in a low voice as they sat in the car. "Patsy called me at work today and chewed me up one side and down the other for going to see Carla with the affidavit. She said Carla would never sign it, and they'll file a harassment complaint against me if I ever mention it to her again." Sammy started the car and pulled out of the parking lot.

Sam looked away. "Doesn't matter," he said from the back seat. "I've got my son, and a daughter-in-law, and that's a lot more than I ever thought I'd have. Sammy," he said suddenly, tapping his shoulder and pointing. An older woman stood in a parking lot beside the raised hood of her Lincoln Town Car. Sammy quickly changed lanes and pulled into the parking lot near the disabled car.

Sam hopped out and walked toward her. The woman backed up fearfully against her car, but Sammy followed, flashing his badge. "Police, ma'am. Would you like me to call a wrecker?"

"Yes, please," she said in relief.

"Let's see what's wrong with it first, Sammy," Sam suggested, grasping the hood.

He leaned over the engine and Sammy leaned beside him, whispering, "Uh, Dad, I don't know anything about a Town Car engine."

"Sammy, it's nothing exotic, just a four-point-six liter, V-eight engine. I see you've got automatic overdrive, sweetheart. Has that been giving you problems?" he asked the woman, who had drawn near.

"It's dead. It won't do anything," she complained.

"Oh, well, look. You've got a loose connection." Sam reached in and screwed two connectors together. "Try it now."

The woman sat and turned the ignition key. The engine promptly turned over. Sam watched it run a few seconds, then shut the hood, satisfied. "These all-electronic cars are great, until you get one loose wire that shuts the whole system down."

"Thank you. Thank you very much," said the woman. "Let me pay you something." She reached for her purse.

Both men stopped her with nearly identical gestures. "We can't take anything, ma'am. You just drive safely," Sammy said, glancing at his dad. Sam nodded and returned to the Mustang. Marni sat back in the seat. There must be a way to get this man a pardon.

When they returned home, Sammy and his dad retrieved Marni's Miata from the complex down the street. Then they stayed up talking long after Marni had gone on to bed. Sam slept on their couch that night, and the following morning Sammy decided to take him to Mavis's. Sam did not want to stay at the apartment while his son was at work, so Sammy reasonably figured that Mavis could find plenty to keep him busy.

Before they left that morning, Sammy stopped in the bedroom to tell Marni goodbye. She was still curled up in bed, awake, but afraid to move for the relentless nausea. Sammy stroked her hair. "Oh, Marni, I wish you would be all right. This is killing me," he murmured.

"I'm okay, Sammy," she whispered. "I just need a few minutes to pull myself together. You go on to work now."

"I'll be at my desk all day, so call me if you need me," he said, bending down to kiss her.

"Okay, Sammy." Marni waited in bed until she heard them leave, then she forced down the nausea to get up and get dressed.

Marni had several errands to run that morning. She got vacuum cleaner belts, some groceries, and a home test kit like the one she had seen in Cookie's apartment. She rushed home and performed the test before she even put the groceries away, then let it set according to the instructions while she put up milk and ice cream.

After the proper amount of time had elapsed, Marni nervously went back to the bedroom to check the results of the test. The reading was negative. She slumped on the bed and cried.

At Mavis's house, Sam worked all morning cleaning and painting exterior woodwork. Mavis coaxed him in for lunch at noon, then he went back out to paint some more. While he was out front working, Dolly Threlkeld arrived in a cab. She got out with difficulty, as she had arthritic knees, then handed the driver a bill. "You will wait, won't you?" she demanded.

"Sure, lady," he said. As soon as she stepped away from the cab, he took off.

"Oh!" she exclaimed angrily. "It is *impossible* to find good help nowadays!" Sam glanced over, but made no comment.

Dolly came up to look over his work. "You're not doing the gutters," she noted.

"Miss Mavis didn't want them painted, so I'm doin' it the way she wanted," he replied.

"Well, that's a miracle. Someone who does what he's asked," she huffed, then went to bang on the screen door. "Mavis?"

"Dolly? Well, hidy, honey; come on in," Mavis said. She carried a toddler in one arm as she opened the door with the other. She was a large woman with a dazzling smile or a thundercloud scowl, depending on the situation.

"I'm glad to see you're getting the house painted. How much are you paying him?" Dolly asked in her usual brusque manner.

"Not a dime, honey, but for the paint. That's Sammy's daddy, and he's doing it for nothin'," Mavis replied.

"Sammy's father?" Dolly exclaimed. "Doing it for nothing? Where does he work?"

"Well, that's the problem. You want some tea, Dolly? I just made a pineapple cake," Mavis said.

"Yes, yes. What's the problem?" Dolly said impatiently.

"He was in prison on a bum rap, Sammy said. When he got out, he worked for years as an auto mechanic, till the owner died. The son sold the shop and Sam was out on the street. He's had trouble getting steady work since then," Mavis explained, setting Dolly in the front room with cake and tea.

"Would you object if I hired him?" Dolly asked, taking a bite of cake. "Why, Mavis, this is delicious."

"Thanks, honey. No, I don't mind—I can't pay him nothing. But wait till he finishes paintin', if you don't mind," Mavis said.

After cake and conversation, they went out to inspect Sam's work. It was not a very big house, and he was more than half done. He patiently went over missed spots they pointed out, then Mavis made him take a break for a glass of iced tea. She herself went back inside to check on the children.

As Sam rested, Dolly observed, "Mavis said you're Sammy's father."

"Yes, ma'am," he murmured.

"Yes. I see the resemblance. Do you know anything about cars?" she asked regally.

"A little, ma'am," he replied.

"How would you like to come work for me?" she asked.

He placed a hand on the ladder and looked down. "Ma'am, I spent ten years in prison for rape."

Dolly regarded him silently, then said, "Never mind," and turned back to the house.

An attractive woman in a red dress walked into the Police and Courts Building—the old one. Dallas taxpayers had built a brand-new, $60-million facility for their police in south Dallas. However, due to a combination of airtight construction and carpet adhesive fumes, people were fainting in the hallways, so move-in had been postponed until the problem could be addressed.

The woman astutely surveyed the lines of people waiting to pay fines at the row of windows, then spotted a police corporal seated behind a counter beyond the lines. She walked over and handed a business card to the corporal. "I am Jasmine Reynolds of Intrax Network, Incorporated, here to see Detective Kidman, please."

"Oh, sure," said the corporal, a woman. She looked up as a smoothly dressed black man came off the elevator. "Hey, Garrett, is Dreamboat upstairs?"

"Knee-deep in paperwork," the man replied, giving Ms. Reynolds the once-over.

The corporal returned the card. "Third floor, first door on your left."

"'Dreamboat'?" Ms. Reynolds asked, brow arched.

"Oh, don't call him that to his face. He gets p.o.'d," the corporal explained.

Nodding crisply, Ms. Reynolds took the elevator up to the third floor and opened the door of the first office on the left, stenciled with "Targeted Activity." Elegant, it was not. The large room was crowded with metal desks, computers, and old secretarial chairs. The acoustical tile ceiling was stained and one of the fluorescent lights had burned out. A trash can in between two desks had a toy basketball hoop attached to it, with a crude sign that read, "Important Memos Here."

Ms. Reynolds paused to look at the man seated at the first desk. He had a square jaw and sandy blond hair, so she inquired, "Detective Kidman?"

He glanced up and pointed at a desk in the back of the room. She saw a shaggy black head holding a telephone on a shoulder while one hand sifted listlessly through a stack of papers. As she approached, she heard, "Yes, her appointment's for next Wednesday, but I just don't see how we're going to make it till then. . . . No, I can't see taking her to the emergency room—haven't you had any cancellations—? Well, if you do, will you bump us up? Right. Okay." He replaced the receiver and looked up.

Ms. Reynolds then regarded a finely chiseled face, full lips, and bright blue eyes that looked worried and distracted. "Yes?" he said.

"Detective Kidman?" she asked.

"Yes," he repeated.

"I am Jasmine Reynolds with Intrax Network, Incorporated," she said, handing him her card. "I believe that Mr. Jennings, my superior, called you." He looked blank. "We would like access to Kevin Payne's computer, to see what information he took from the company," she reiterated. *Cute, but dumb,* she thought.

"Oh, yeah," he muttered, standing. "Key," he said, feeling his pockets. He paused as something occurred to him. "Why isn't Intrax listed in Information?" he asked abruptly.

Ms. Reynolds replied, "Intrax is still technically a division of Riposte, Incorporated, though we are in the process of spinning out. The break should be finalized by the end of the second quarter."

"Ah," he said, looking under papers stacked on the desk. Ms. Reynolds saw a framed photograph of a very pretty young woman with full brown hair. "Pruett, you got the key to Payne's apartment?" he asked.

"Nobody's had it but you, Sambo," the sandy-haired man replied lackadaisically.

"Well. . . ." he muttered, searching, while she shifted her weight impatiently. His telephone rang and he seized it. "Kidman." He sat, holding the receiver on his shoulder while he shifted through the clutter with both hands. "Hi, Pam. Yes, but I can't get her in till next Wednesday and she's not getting any better. What . . . ?" His hands stilled while he listened. "Are you sure?" he asked anxiously. "Yeah, I'll hang in there. Talk to you later." He hung up, then picked up the telephone base and found the key.

"Okay. Let's take my car," he said, standing. "Pruett, if Marni calls—"

"I'll tell her you left with a blonde in a red dress," he said without looking up from his keyboard.

"Just shoot me in the back, pal," Sammy muttered, pointing Ms. Reynolds to the elevator.

As they rode down to the first floor, she watched him drum his fingers distractedly on the handrail. "Problem at home?" she asked delicately.

He glanced at her. "My wife is sick."

"Oh. That's rough. I'm sorry," she said.

They disembarked the elevator and he pointed her to a side door. They went out to the parking lot in the cool spring afternoon. A uniformed officer called out, "Hey, Sambo!" and the detective lifted his chin in acknowledgment.

They stopped by a bright green convertible that had the top down. Sammy opened the passenger door for her, then as he sat behind the wheel, he blurted, "I don't understand these women things. How can I get her to stop crying?"

Jasmine looked over sympathetically. "You just hold her and tell her everything's going to be all right," she said.

He looked dissatisfied. "That doesn't solve anything."

"Trust me," she said. "Just hold her and tell her you love her." Sammy sighed and started the engine.

Marni worked like a whirlwind that afternoon. The first thing she did was empty the trash, so that Sammy would not find the test kit. Then she tore through the apartment cleaning. She resolved to shove aside her crazy symptoms and do whatever made Sammy happy. After an industrious hour and a half of nonstop work, she sat on the couch to rest and promptly fell asleep.

About that time Sammy arrived at the apartments with Jasmine. He let her into the Paynes' apartment and stood over her while she searched his computer files. It did not take her long to find the hidden file, discover the password (which Payne had written down) and gain access to the information. When she looked over it, she shook her head. "I don't know what he thought he had. All this information is obsolete. No one would buy it."

"Well, uh, good. You about done here?" he asked, glancing out the door toward his apartment.

"Yes, as soon as I copy this," she said, inserting a floppy disk.

"Okay. Uh, don't delete anything; it's evidence. Be right back." He went down the passageway to his apartment and unlocked the door. At once he saw Marni sleeping on the couch. After debating a moment, he decided not to disturb her and backed out.

The door closing woke her. Marni sat up, blinking, unsure of what she had heard. Then she looked out the picture window and saw Sammy escorting a woman in a red dress out to his car. They got in and drove off.

Marni cradled her head in her hands, sick to death of crying. She'd finally done it. Her irrational behavior had finally driven Sammy to the company of another woman. She dragged herself upstairs to sit on the bed and think about what to do.

Remembering the last time she had run to her mother with Sammy problems, Marni realized that was not an option this time. Was leaving an option? She could support herself, she thought optimistically; she'd done it before. But as she considered this, her eye landed on the bureau drawer. She reached over and opened the drawer, withdrawing the bundle of letters.

Talk about not having any options—here was a man whose whole life was straitjacketed by his love for a girl. Even in prison he had options, though: he had the option to hate her or love her. He had the option to let bitterness and the desire for revenge take over his life, or to bear the pain as best he could and keep going, on the outside chance that someday he would find what he had lost. Did God leave anything like that to chance?

Marni replaced the letters in the drawer and got up to start dinner.

sixteen

About six-thirty that evening, Sammy picked up Sam from Mavis's house and headed back to his apartment. When he opened the door, a wonderful aroma greeted him. Marni had been cooking!

She came from the kitchen with a tentative smile. "I tried a new meatloaf recipe. I hope it's good." The table was set for three with the cheery red ware.

"Let me wash up," said Sam, darting to the half bath. Smoky ran upstairs to hide.

"Marni!" Sammy exclaimed. "You do love me!"

"Of course I do," she murmured, looking away.

Sammy grabbed her around the waist. "I love you, Marni. Everything's going to be all right," he said. She burst into tears and he moaned, "It's supposed to make you *not* cry."

"I'm all right—it's all right," she assured him, kissing his face.

They had a few moments of intense nonverbal reassurance while Sam pulled the cole slaw from the refrigerator and checked the oven. When she saw what he was doing, she drew away from Sammy to fetch an oven mitt from the counter. "I hope it's good," she repeated.

They sat to dinner and the men heaped accolades on her meatloaf until Marni was abashed. The mashed potatoes were a little lumpy, but Sam insisted he preferred his that way. Sammy agreed it was superior to watery mashed potatoes or especially (shudder) *instant* potatoes, and all was well.

The telephone rang in the middle of dinner. Sammy got up to answer it: "Yo. Oh, hello, Dolly. No, not really." He glanced at his cooling dinner. "Oh you did? No, he didn't tell me." He glanced at Sam, who put down his fork.

Sammy listened, pinching the bridge of his nose. "Dolly, that was thirty years ago. They were a couple of kids who got in trouble, and that's the way her parents chose to handle it. That's right—she got pregnant with me. He's been out for about twenty years and I don't think he's raped anybody in that time. Dad, have you raped anybody in the last twenty years?" Sammy asked.

"No," Sam said, looking at his plate.

"Dolly, he said he hasn't raped anybody in the past twenty years," Sammy said testily. He listened a moment, then held out the phone. "She wants to talk to you." Sam looked over pleadingly, but Sammy insistently held out the receiver. Reluctantly, Sam got up from the table and took the handset.

"Yes, ma'am," he mumbled. He listened awhile, then said, "I don't have a chauffeur's license. . . . Well, yes, I suppose I could. Yes, ma'am. Thank you." He hung up. "She's going to hire me as her chauffeur as soon as I get the license," he said.

"Great!" Sammy exulted.

"But—" Sam was unconvinced. "With a criminal record, will they give me a chauffeur's license?"

"They will, or—" Sammy began darkly, but Marni suddenly jumped from the table and ran upstairs. "What now?" he muttered apprehensively.

In a few moments she returned with the bundle of letters. "These will get Sam his pardon," she announced, laying them in front of Sammy.

"The letters I wrote to Carla? How will those help?" Sam asked as Sammy turned them over in his hands.

"Anyone who reads them will understand the love you had for her. And the fact that she kept them all these years shows that she loved you, too. Read them, Sammy. See if I'm not right," she urged.

Doubtfully, Sammy opened the first letter and began reading. Sam looked at his hands, the floor, the window, then his son. It was agonizing for him to watch Sammy read the story of despair that followed his conception. It was agonizing for Sammy to read it—he kept wiping his mouth and biting his lip. But there was that irresistible desire to look through the door of truth, once opened. While Sammy read, Marni laid her head on Sam's shoulder comfortingly. He patted her hand.

Marni sighed and shifted. Her hand crept to her abdomen, and she felt a hard knot there. It was different. There was something happening inside her, she was sure. Only, she did not know if it was good or bad.

Sammy read through all the letters while the food grew cold, and Marni got up to put leftovers in the refrigerator. Finally, his head hanging over the last letter, Sammy cleared his throat and said, "This will do it—these letters, a copy of my birth certificate to prove that I was the child in question, and an affidavit that these came from my mother."

Sam looked at the floor, then uttered a dry laugh. "I'd never have imagined, writing those, that they'd clear me thirty years later."

Sammy gathered them up purposefully. "I'll get on it first thing tomorrow morning." Then he looked at Marni. "Thank you *so much,* baby."

"I'm glad you enjoyed it," she replied, busily cleaning up the kitchen.

Sammy looked at his dad with a wry smile, and Sam said, "It's my turn to clean up the kitchen tonight."

Marni opened her mouth but Sammy said, "Thanks, Dad," taking Marni's hand to lead her upstairs.

He laid her out gently on the bed and unbuttoned the loose shirt she wore. "Must be getting close to that time of the month," he murmured, kissing parts that had grown round and firm. "Umm, I love it."

Actually, I'm late. Marni stared up at the ceiling while he indulged himself, then she opened her arms and closed her eyes.

The following morning, Friday, Sammy left early to drop Sam by Mavis's before he went to work. Sammy had a lot to do that day, and went about it with zeal.

Marni woke late, as usual, and got up slowly to quash the rolling tides. She had learned to eat just a little something before she showered, then snack in midmorning when her stomach felt stronger.

This morning she ran some more errands. She stopped in the drugstore again and read labels carefully. Then she bought another test kit, a different kind than the first one she had used. And when she took this test home and ran it, she did it a little differently than she had done the first one. Then she loaded the dishwasher and swept the floor while waiting for the results.

When she checked the test later in the morning, she sat on the bed to quietly contemplate the results. Stirring, she changed from her jeans into a nice dress. She set her hair on hot rollers and put on makeup. Then she climbed into her Miata and drove to the Big Building Downtown.

She almost never came to see Sammy at work, unless it was something that directly involved her. She certainly never came without calling first to make sure that he was there to accompany her in that big, intimidating building with big red warning signs which he routinely ignored.

But knowing that he would be at his desk all day and wanting to surprise him, today she entered the building alone by the door on Main. She circumvented the lines of people waiting at the fine windows, and took the elevator to the third floor where she walked unannounced into the Targeted Activity office.

Garrett and Pruett were there, bent over paperwork. Another detective was on the telephone. And back at his desk, head bowed, Sammy was scribbling notes while he talked on the phone. One by one the men looked up at her, but Marni waited until her husband had hung up the phone. "Sammy," she said.

He quickly looked up. "Marni! Uh—what's wrong?"

"I found out what's wrong with me, Sammy," she said solemnly. The others quickly looked back at him.

He paled visibly. "What is it, Marni?"

"I'm pregnant," she said.

The men broke into grins, but Sammy had so thoroughly ruled out the possibility that he did not even comprehend her. "What?" he said.

"She's PREGNANT, stupid!" Pruett bellowed. The men roared and Marni beamed.

But Sammy did not hear them at all. He was totally focused on Marni, waiting for her to answer his question. Their laughter subsided into concerned silence when they saw him gazing at her in tense concentration. "What, Marni?"

She came up to his desk and said softly, "I'm pregnant, Sammy."

He looked at her abdomen, then up at her face. "By me?" he asked. The men looked at each other in alarm.

"Yes!" she laughed. "Yes, by you; who do you think?"

"Marni . . ." he murmured in awe. He started to rise from the desk but fell over an open drawer. He landed on his knees and stayed there, head hanging.

Primly, Marni folded her dress under her legs and sat on the floor with him. She reached out a hand to his cheek. Tears were pouring from his eyes. "I thought . . . that wasn't possible," he whispered.

"Someone decided it was," she murmured, brushing tears from his face.

Pruett came over and helped Marni up, then hoisted Sammy to his feet. "Congratulations, guy." Pruett patted his back, then threw his arms around him for a big bear hug. The other men offered their congratulations, which Sammy accepted numbly. One of the men called in the news to the division gossip, and Garrett even produced a cigar.

"I'm trying to quit," Sammy said hazily in declining the smoke, then reached out to his wife. Marni fell into his arms to congratulate him with an ice-cream kiss of her own.

"She knew!" he said, abruptly breaking off. "Your mother knew when I called her about you!"

"Of course she did!" Marni laughed. "That woman doctor she recommended is an OB/GYN in the same office as the doctor who delivered me, which should have told me something! He's about to retire."

"I can't believe it," he breathed. "Marni, you're—we're going to have a baby!"

"That's right!" she laughed.

Garrett shook his head. "Might as well take him home, woman. He's gonna be useless for the rest of the day."

Well, not exactly useless. Sammy provided an entertaining diversion for anyone at the Big Building with a practical joke or gag gift for an expectant father. As soon as Marni left to go share the news with her parents, Sammy became the helpless butt of a string of jokes. He received anonymous gifts: coffee mugs printed with dirty rhymes, a box of birth-control devices labeled, "FAULTY: Researched by Kidman, Inc.," and others too crude to mention. Dazed, Sammy took it all with a persistent, idiotic grin that finally won him enough sympathy to call off the pack.

Then, someone left on his desk a pacifier attached to a chain that plainclothes officers often used to secure their badges to their belts. Sammy promptly draped the chain around his neck and wore it like that the rest of the day. Henceforth, a steady flood of baby paraphernalia appeared on his desk, which Sammy collected like treasures.

That evening, Sam was stunned to hear the news. "I'm going to be a grandfather?" he asked weakly. He was so moved that he momentarily forgot about dinner sitting in front of him. (Marni had cooked chicken for that evening.) "I'll get to watch you get big—and hold the baby—and do all those things I didn't get to do with Sammy?" he asked.

"Of course," Marni said, her eyes tearing up again.

"I can't believe it," he said. "I thought that opportunity was gone forever. All I wanted was to find my son—and I got all this thrown in the deal. It's almost too much."

"I know what you mean," Sammy agreed, fingering the pacifier still hung around his neck.

At their doctor's appointment the next Wednesday, Marni's pregnancy was confirmed and her due date set at January 20. And Sammy walked through the next several weeks in a giddy daze. Now that he understood the reason for it, suddenly he reveled in Marni's morning sickness. Each morning before he dressed for work, he would bring up dry crackers and tepid water to calm her rolling stomach. He would chatter to her as he got ready, interrupting himself frequently to ask, "Is that better? Are you feeling okay now?" He was actually disappointed when this particular symptom subsided after the first month.

He indulged her every craving to the point of spoiling her. Marni was careful to avoid the maternity trap of making the state of her body the topic of every conversation, but she did find it gratifying that merely hinting at her desire for a particular food brought it speedily to the table. Yet even she was bemused by her overwhelming desire for Mexican food.

Sammy himself was so much the awestruck, expectant father that after they first heard the baby's heartbeat through the doctor's stethoscope, she wondered, "Sammy, why does this surprise you so much? You've been through all this before."

He shook his head helplessly. "I don't remember it like this. I don't remember any of this. Maybe that's part of what I blocked out with Meredith's death. It's all brand new to me." Secretly, Marni was glad.

Pam and Clayton were elated, of course—their only child and beloved son-in-law expecting their first grandchild. Sammy and Clayton moved the computer and weight-lifting equipment from the second upstairs bedroom so that Pam and Marni could start decorating the nursery. (By this time, Sam had obtained his chauffeur's license and started to work for Mrs. Threlkeld.) Pam retrieved the crib, bassinet, and accessories from attic storage, and she and Marni began going over them.

"You don't have to use any of this, if you don't want to," Pam said, shaking out a quilt. "We'll help you get all new things."

"Oh no," Marni murmured, burying her face in a yellow gingham curtain, "I've dreamed of using these again. Oh, Mother," she put her hand over her firm belly, "this is an answer to a prayer we never dared pray."

"Speak for yourself," Pam retorted.

Marni stared at her. "Mother, did you pray for us to have a baby?" she exclaimed.

"Yes I did, and there was no need to tell you about it—until now, I guess," Pam said. Beaming, Marni reached over to hug her mother's neck.

For Marni's twenty-second birthday that August, Pam took her shopping for maternity clothes. Magnanimously,

Sammy also handed her the checkbook and said, "Get whatever you need."

Marni recovered sufficiently from her astonishment to take him at his word. Later, as she and her mother exited one store en route to another, Marni explained to her, "It's not that he's *cheap* or anything; he just didn't understand why I needed a whole new wardrobe when I'm not even 'showing' yet."

Pam smiled knowingly. "A month from now, he'll understand." Pam then caught sight of a church friend three blocks away and hailed her down to share the good news.

After the friend had congratulated them and gone her way, Marni chided humorously, "Mother, I'm doing all the work and you're getting all the credit!"

"That's what being a grandparent is all about, dear," Pam informed her, then saw someone else she knew.

Of course, Sammy and Marni discussed names. This proved to be an unexpected source of conflict in that Sammy adamantly insisted they were about to have a girl while Marni clung to the fifty-percent possibility that it would be a boy. Thus whenever he came up with a girl's name, Marni would counter with a boy's. But when the doctor suggested they could find out the baby's sex and put an end to the discussion, both parents balked.

Marni's pregnancy progressed normally, but during her sixth month, Sammy began experiencing anxiety about the baby's health. He began having flashbacks to the nightmare of his first child's hydrocephalus and death six hours after birth. The tests that showed this baby's development to be satisfactory did not ease his mind. He would still wake up in a cold sweat in the middle of the night, reaching over to feel his wife's abdomen.

This continued for several weeks, until one Sunday morning when Marni and Sammy were sitting in the worship service at the little Bible church. Sammy was restless and inattentive up to the point that the pastor began reading the Scripture of the day, from Psalm 139:

> For you created my inmost being;
> you knit me together in my mother's womb.
> I praise you because I am fearfully and wonderfully made;
> your works are wonderful,
> I know that full well.
> My frame was not hidden from you when I was made in the secret place.
> When I was woven together in the depths of the earth,
> your eyes saw my unformed body.
> All the days ordained for me were written in your book before one of them came to be.

Sammy snapped to attention, staring at the words on the page, and the wonderful analogy smacked him across the forehead. A man sowed his seed like a farmer plowing the earth, and God made the tiny seed grow in secret, unseen by any eyes but His, until He presented the new life to the sunlight. The Master Gardener knew his business well. Sammy kept his Bible open to that psalm long after the pastor had gone on to another.

From that day on, Sammy experienced no further anxiety attacks. However, he did hire a maid to do the heavy housework, to which Marni made only a token objection. Also, Smoky was sent to stay with Pam for the time being.

Childbirth classes were required if Sammy wished to be in the delivery room with Marni, but he considered them a waste of time and went under protest. He knew all about hospital procedures, and as a patrolman had assisted in several births. Unfortunately, his unruly attitude virtually got them kicked out of class. When the instructor said, "Now, what you will be feeling during labor is not really *pain,* but *pressure,"* Sammy snorted so loudly that the whole class looked at him.

Then, when the instructor was giving directions on how to breathe during labor, Sammy raised his hand to tell how one woman he had assisted during a patrol-car birth breathed so diligently that she almost hyperventilated. The instructor complained about him to the administrator, who waived the remainder of the classes for the Kidmans.

That October Sammy and Marni celebrated their first anniversary with an intimate dinner at a nice restaurant. It was a lovely evening, though he would not allow her to have any wine with dinner. And for Thanksgiving they went to Marni's parents' home, of course.

Sam had been invited, but had to decline because Dolly wanted him "on duty." Sam had endeared himself thoroughly to her with his good looks and humility ("He's Sammy without the brashness," she had told Mavis), and he was sufficiently overcome by his sudden good fortune as to spend every dime he earned on gifts for Marni and baby until Sammy sternly set him up with a budget and IRAs.

Sam's pardon came through that fall. "It's just icing on the cake," he shrugged, but Marni saw a change in him after that. He stood up straighter, and looked people in the eye. He recovered some sense of self-worth and suddenly developed a dry sense of humor.

But when his letters to Carla were returned to him, he gave them to Marni without a glance. "They mean nothing more to me," he said, "but you seemed to like them." Marni took them and hugged his neck. He squeezed her as tightly as he dared, proudly patting her round belly.

The pardon meant something significant to Sammy as well. Upon receiving confirmation of it, he sat right down and dialed his aunt's number. "Hey, Patsy. Sammy. How're you doin'? Yeah? Well, how's ol' Uncle Ralph? Good, glad to hear it. Hey, I've got some news you might be interested in hearing. Dad's been pardoned. I said, my dad Sam has received a pardon from the governor for that rape charge that your folks set him up on thirty years ago. . . . No, we got it without the affidavit. That a fact? Yeah, I thought you'd feel that way about it."

He hung up, telling Marni, "Sorry, I couldn't resist. I just had to hear her reaction, and it was exactly what I expected."

Then it was the Christmas season, and Marni was transported back to a second childhood. They hadn't much of a Christmas last year, with Sammy just beginning to recuperate from the shooting. But this year they decorated with abandon. Sammy hauled in a real tree that they adorned with lights, garlands, tinsel, and any decoration that featured cherubs. The expectant couple walked the malls, shopping for any baby items not already stocked in their fully equipped nursery or ornaments not already hanging on their heavily laden tree.

The department had their annual Christmas party, and Marni was radiant in a deep red velvet maternity dress. She drew many compliments. But a number of those observers also remarked that Sammy's face beamed enough to make him suitable as a treetop ornament for the Christmas tree at the Galleria.

He was so full of the Christmas spirit that he volunteered to participate in the department's Santa Cops program, in which officers distributed toys and food to needy families in their districts. Sammy's involvement in such a program was not at all surprising; what did raise brows was that he agreed to perform as a reindeer for the kids' amusement along with Pruett, Garrett, and five other of the toughest, most respected cops in the Special Investigations Bureau.

Marni had great fun assembling his costume, which included antlers and a white tail. On the appointed night, the jostling, snickering reindeer were harnessed to an authentic haywagon, painted red. Then they pulled Santa Mike through the downtown streets as he handed out gifts and candy to the children. The kids went wild for it, and for a few hours on that one night, the drug trade in the area came to a virtual stand-still.

To keep it all fair, the children had been given vouchers in advance for one gift apiece. But so many poor unvouchered children showed up whom Mike could not possibly turn away that they ran out of gifts halfway through the scheduled ride. There were a few tense moments until some saint took up a spontaneous collection among the spectators, and Marni and Kerry were handed almost two hundred dollars to quickly go buy more.

While they were gone, the reindeer entertained the children with rides in the "sleigh" with Santa. It was a heavy wagon, and the reindeer grew tired and sore, but Pruett kept their spirits up with a recitation of "'Twas the Night Before Christmas" (revised): "Now Basher! Now Denser! Now Pinscher and Spits'em! On, Vomit! On, Stupid! On Bomber and Blitz'em!" His rather indelicate changes in the Clement Clarke Moore classic included specifying what gifts the reindeer left on the rooftops. Marni and Kerry returned with sackfuls of cheap toys in the nick of time.

Sammy's impending fatherhood made him so tractable that, even after this, he was moved to go caroling with a group from the church. He had to, as Marni was going, and the neighborhoods around the church were not the city's most stable. It might have dampened the group's Christmas cheer had they known that one of their members carried a loaded automatic under his jacket, but they all sang nicely, nothing happened, and Marni was happy.

Sammy was happy. He became a tornado at work, recklessly hunting down stolen vehicles until he had set a record for recoveries for October and November running. He was working toward a record for December when, three days before Christmas, Mike called him to his office.

Walking the hall to Mike's office, Sammy felt some apprehension. Mike was not about to put him on a special assignment, was he? Not this close to Christmas. Not with Marni's
due date less than a month away. Surely not.

Sammy opened Mike's door. "Hi, guy. You wanted to see
me?" he asked, casually dropping into the chair beside Mike's
desk. A nice big desk.

"Yeah, uh, Sammy." Mike glanced up uncomfortably and
Sammy tensed. "'Tis the season to shoplift, pal, and we've had
a number of complaints from merchants all over the city. We're
tapping everybody we've got for extra duty."

"Oh, extra duty. Is that all?" Sammy said, relaxing. It
meant walking around the stores a few hours each night,
watching for shoplifters and pickpockets. Besides which, it
meant overtime pay, which Sammy welcomed at just about any
time of the year. "No problem, Mike. What hours?"

"Well, you're on special duty, Sammy. Undercover," Mike
said.

Sammy groaned, "Have a heart, Mike! Marni's due in less
than a month and—"

"Look, Kidman, criminal activity doesn't grind to a halt
when it's inconvenient for you to get out. The other men and
women have families, too," Mike upbraided him, and Sammy
looked down sullenly.

"Now, I know how much you're concerned about Marni,
so I got you an assignment close to home. They've had some
trouble with groups of kids roaming West End, stealing, shop-
lifting, vandalizing, the usual stuff. Our patrol needs undercover night support out there—just through Christmas, from
about nine till five A.M. Okay?"

"Sure. Okay," Sammy muttered.

Mike said, "Good. Go home and take a nap, then, 'cause
you're scheduled to start tonight."

seventeen

Marni was happy to join Sammy for a nap that afternoon, though he did not sleep much. Mostly, he wanted to play. He couldn't keep his hands off her belly, and when she got up to go downstairs to fix supper, he went right with her. "Sammy, you're supposed to be sleeping!" she chastised him.

"I'm not sleepy," he said, putting his arms around her. "Gee, how much bigger can you get?"

"I don't know," she sighed. "I feel like a cow. The baby's shifted. It feels different," she murmured.

"Listen, if you don't want to cook tonight, we can go out," he offered.

"Again?" she said dubiously.

"Why not?" he said. "We're celebrating."

"Isn't that a little premature?" she asked.

"Baby, I've been celebrating since April," he grinned, rocking her.

So they went out for a bite of Mexican food, but Marni found that she was not very hungry right then. So Sammy ate for both of them. They returned to the apartment so that he could start getting ready for that evening's assignment while Marni put a Christmas CD in the player. She sat on the sofa, put her feet up, and gazed at the Christmas tree. Then she put a tentative hand to her abdomen. She felt strange.

Sammy came down the stairs wearing stiff jeans, a couple of t-shirts, and a black leather jacket. He hooked the dangly silver earring in his lobe as Marni struggled up from the couch.

"Sammy, is that all you're wearing? It's going to get cold tonight."

"I can't look cool all bundled up, baby," he reminded her. "If I start hurting, I'll go inside somewhere. There are a few places open all night."

He bent down to kiss her and she saw the pack of cigarettes in his pocket. When she opened her mouth he just shook his head at her. "They're for show, Marni. Or, if I get really cold, I'll use them to set fire to my jacket."

"Be careful, Sammy," she murmured.

"Piece of cake," he said. "Listen, I'm wearing my beeper. If you need me, you call the beeper number, okay?"

"I know, Sammy," she said. She watched out the door while he climbed on the Harley-Davidson he had brought home from the department, waved goodbye, and roared off into the night.

"Just another day at the office," she sighed, closing the door. Then she smiled, remembering the first time she had ever seen him. He was on that motorcycle, wearing leather—the sexiest thing she had ever laid eyes on. She rubbed her tummy, still smiling.

Sammy rode out to West End Marketplace—a section of shops and restaurants built in and around old renovated warehouses. It was a highly profitable area of downtown that the city was anxious to keep clean and trouble-free for the tourists. "*Shi-kung*," Sammy said, mimicking the sound of punching a time clock as he parked the bike.

He lit a cigarette and let it dangle without inhaling as he walked around the crowded streets. There was a lot going on that night, with only Three Shopping Days till Christmas. All the stores were still open, and a free outdoor concert was in progress, which featured groups from the conservative end of the music spectrum who could belt out the evening's fourteenth performance of "The Twelve Days of Christmas." The ice rink was crowded as well, with skaters ranging in skill from Olympic qualifiers to first-time klutzes.

One middle-aged couple near Sammy was discussing which restaurant to go to for a late dinner. They'd already suffered through a Planet Hollywood experience and wanted some real food. Sammy piped up, "Try the Italian restaurant. You might have to wait for a table, but the service is worth it."

They looked at him in surprise, then the man said, "Why not?" and headed in the direction of said restaurant.

Sammy stayed on the fringes of the crowd listening to the music and looking around. Seeing one uniformed officer, he nonchalantly wandered over until, pretending to be watching the band, he bumped into the officer.

The policeman turned. "Oh, excuse me, officer," Sammy said with slight sarcasm, then looked down at his jeans pocket, where he held the badge on the chain just barely in view. The patrolman saw it and nodded. Sammy wandered off. Primary rule: undercover cops always make themselves known to police on the field.

Three Shopping Days till Christmas! Sammy stopped dead, dropping his cigarette. He had been so focused on this baby that he had completely forgotten about getting Marni anything for Christmas! He groaned, slapping his forehead. That was grounds for divorce. He'd have to do something quick.

He turned in one building and scanned the shops. There was Victoria's Secret—a lingerie store—on the first floor. Sammy eyed it, thinking. Why not get her something that had nothing to do with the baby? Something that she would wear *after* it came? His lips parted in a smile, and he went in. The salesgirls were very happy to help him make a selection, and in a little while he walked out with a flouncy pink teddy, gift-wrapped.

Tucking the slender box tied with a gold lamé ribbon under his arm, Sammy mingled in the crowds. He was walking, and looking, when he spotted someone who made him foolishly forget the most fundamental rule of undercover work: preserve your cover. "Jill!" he exclaimed. It was Marni's former roommate, who had been her honor attendant at their wedding.

She quickly turned around. "Oh—it's you," she said in a strained voice, looking at his clothes. Sammy barely noticed the man standing three feet from her who also turned to look; even so, Sammy did not remember him—but that man was Jill's brother Mark Reid.

Mark had been in love with Marni long before Sammy, and he also recognized Sammy. Mark remembered how Sammy had lured Marni to work in a sleazy restaurant and had humiliated him deeply when Mark went to try to bring her home. Then Sammy had married her right out from under him. Oh, yes—Mark remembered Sammy.

"Jill, did you know Marni's pregnant?" Sammy asked happily. "She's due in January."

"Marni? Pregnant?" Jill marveled. "That's—amazing. She always told me she didn't want kids, not for a long time." Working his jaw, Mark eyed the box Sammy held, then turned back to watch the band.

"We're so excited. You gotta come see her. She looks so cute with this big round tummy," Sammy grinned. Mark squinted at the band.

"I'm sure she does. Of course I'll come see her," Jill said faintly. She turned back around, glancing at her brother.

Smiling, Sammy moved off. Mark looked after him, then said, "It's getting late, Jill. Time to get you home." His face was so dark that she did not dare argue.

Sammy took the box to the motorcycle and locked it in the storage compartment. He was about to return to the concert area when he paused. A group of teenagers was huddled in a corner of the parking lot. They might be just hanging out, but

Sammy decided to watch them awhile. He leaned against the bike and lit a cigarette.

It was starting to get chilly, and Sammy's chest began aching after a few minutes. He decided to go find someplace a little warmer and got off the bike. Then he spotted two teenaged girls sashay into the parking lot, laughing and swinging their purses. The gang watched them. Sammy watched them. Then the gang left their corner and began advancing. Sammy threw down the cigarette and ran toward the girls.

The two girls hesitated as he approached them, and so did the gang. Sammy displayed one of his knockout smiles and put an arm around each girl's waist. One laughed, "What do you think you're doing?"

"Hey, I'm the Parking Lot Safety Patrol, and I'm here to see that two hot babes get to their car okay so they can come back and see me tomorrow night," he said. While they giggled to each other around him, he glanced over to the gang, which was still paused.

He walked the girls to their car and stood by while they got in. "What's your name?" the girl behind the wheel asked.

"Sammy. Buckle your seatbelt so you don't mess up that pretty face," he said, leaning down in the window.

"I'm Kim and this is Stirling. Are you really gonna be out here tomorrow?" she asked.

"Really and truly," he said, glancing at the gang standing off.

"See you tomorrow, Sammy." She winked seductively, started the car, and peeled out of the lot.

Sammy breathed in the cold air, wincing, then looked over the lot at the gang. They stood watching him. There were five of them. Sammy stood his ground, spreading his feet, then took out a cigarette with a deliberate, practiced flair and lit it. This little routine sent a certain unmistakable message that the gang received. They turned and walked off.

At home, Marni turned off the CD player and the Christmas lights and climbed the stairs to her bedroom. She paused at the top of the stairs, holding her abdomen. She still felt strange and she didn't know why. Every now and then, little quivers started at her back and ran around her abdomen to the front. It couldn't be labor, she reasoned, as she wasn't due for a month yet. She thought about calling Sammy, but, not wishing to whine, just changed into her nightgown and crawled into bed. Then she lay on her side to try to go to sleep.

Sammy continued to walk around and watch people. He stopped in a café, right before they closed, for a cup of coffee. When he turned out, he became aware that the gang from the parking lot was shadowing him. He surreptitiously studied their black jackets and red bandannas, quite willing that they should follow him around. As long as they were trailing him, they weren't bothering anybody else.

Someone else drove into the parking lot at that time. He parked near the black Harley hog and studied it a moment. Then Mark Reid walked through the lighted streets of West End, looking for someone.

Home in bed, Marni was sleeping fitfully. She could not get comfortable but was not awake enough to do anything but thrash around. She was dreaming incoherently of Jill, who was angry at her about something—what, she never quite understood.

Sammy strolled around, keeping an eye on the boys behind him. The concert had ended, so a number of people had gone home. Those still here were the sort who wanted more excitement than trolley cars and Christmas music, and they were willing to make it happen. They were rowdy and aggressive, and the patrolmen on duty had their hands full breaking up fights and arresting a few for public drunkenness.

Sammy watched one cop grapple with a very drunken, uncooperative woman to get her into his patrol car without hurting her or himself. Then Sammy realized that he had not seen the bandanna gang for a few minutes, and wondered where they were. He began to look for them.

As he passed a dark alley, he heard distinctly, "Sammy." He stopped, peering into the alley. It was too dark to see anything more than a form. But he heard it again, in a low whisper: "Sammy."

His mind rapidly weighed the alternatives. A dark alley screamed *setup,* but whoever it was knew him. Holding his breath to listen, he ascertained that there was only one person in the alley shadows—not a group. Which one of a hundred people that he had sent to prison was looking for revenge tonight? Or was it someone with a tip who was too afraid to say it in the open?

Sammy made the decision and stepped cautiously into the alley, not speaking, only watching. He drew up to the man, taller than he, and squinted at the obscured face. "Who—?" He barely glimpsed the blur the instant before the fist smashed into his face, sending him reeling back onto the pavement. He landed directly on his beeper.

Marni suddenly woke, seized with pains. Gasping, she got out of bed and stumbled to the bathroom. There, a sudden flood gushed from between her legs to the tile floor. The pains brought her to her knees. "No . . . it's—too early—" Even as she cried out with another sudden jolt, she pulled down a towel from the rack to soak up the puddle of water.

Shakily, she went to the telephone and called Sammy's beeper. The signal it sent back was truncated, but she went ahead and dialed in her number. Then she sat on the floor, trembling, waiting for him to call back.

Minutes passed and he did not call. Then a new, more intense pain gripped her around the abdomen and she cried out again, knocking the telephone from the table. When the seizure subsided enough for her to control her hands, she righted the phone and dialed her parents' number. "Mother," she gasped, "it's started—and I—I can't get Sammy—"

He wrestled with the figure in the alley, struggling to defend himself without resorting to the gun in his boot. The guy was alone and unarmed, looking only to use Sammy's face and body as a punching bag. Sammy took six or eight blows before he was finally able to get an arm around the guy's neck and bring him to his knees in a chokehold. "Okay, pal, what's your problem?" Sammy breathed.

Suddenly Sammy was tackled from behind and knocked on his face to the concrete. Five guys in black jackets gathered around him, jerking him upright. Two held his arms while one readied his fist in a chain. Mark got up calmly and turned out of the alley.

Pam and Clayton careened up to the hospital's emergency entrance carrying a groaning, sobbing girl in labor in the back seat of their car. As she was laid on a gurney and taken in, she grabbed at her father's arm. "Find Sammy. Daddy, please find Sammy!"

While Pam accompanied her daughter to the labor room, Clayton went back out to the desk. "My son-in-law is Detective Sammy Kidman of the Dallas Police. He is on duty at West End tonight, but he is not answering his beeper. Please help us get hold of him to tell him that his wife is in premature labor."

A sharp-eyed patrolman saw Mark leave the alley. Something did not seem right about it—the guy looked as though he'd been in a fight. As the cop started toward him, Mark glanced up and sprinted away. "Wait! Stop!" the cop shouted, but Mark kept going, dashing around the corner. The policeman then had to make the instantaneous decision as to whether to pursue the suspect or check the alley.

He ran to the alley and shone his flashlight in, which revealed a cluster of guys beating the tar out of somebody. At the light they scattered—the patrolman managed to reach out and snag one before the others got away. The officer shouted for assistance, and his partner came running.

The others had disappeared, but the policemen cuffed the one they caught and then checked on the guy who was slowly picking himself up from the pavement. "Need an ambulance, buddy?" the first cop asked.

"I need information," Sammy gasped, sitting and clutching his stomach. "The first guy who left the alley—did you see the first guy?"

"Yeah," said the cop. "About six foot, a hundred seventy pounds, blond hair, clean-cut lookin' guy."

Breathing and blinking around the blood, Sammy sat and tried to place his assailant. The other cop produced a first-aid kit with medicated wipes and a cold compress for Sammy's face. "You're the one who bumped me. Who are you?" this cop asked.

"Kidman. TAS," Sammy muttered. "This guy knew me. He called my name." Sammy closed his eyes in deep concentration. The guy must have seen him earlier, so he began mentally retracing his steps that night—the parking lot, the concert, the store, Jill—Sammy stopped and opened his eyes. Blonde, clean-cut Jill Reid. And the blond man who had looked over—

"Mark Reid," Sammy whispered.

The first officer returned from the patrol car. "The punk's not saying who the others are."

"Does that mean he wants to go down alone on assaulting a police officer?" the second asked.

"You a cop?" the first asked Sammy. "You Kidman?"

"Yeah," Sammy muttered, getting to his feet. "No problem. I know just where these rodents like to hide, and I'll be able to identify every one of 'em. Give me two hours and I'll bring 'em all right to you."

"Sammy Kidman?" the first repeated. "You got an urgent call-back over the radio."

Intent on his purpose, Sammy dismissed it, reasoning that it wasn't Marni because his beeper had not gone off. "When I'm done here, I'll call," he grumbled, sore in body and sore at Mike for giving him this assignment.

So Sammy went hunting. He spotted a manhole cover out of place and found one thug right off, hiding in the sewer drain. This was a gratifying catch, being the one with the chain.

Sammy dragged him back to the patrol car, which had been joined by another. "Kidman, your sergeant's looking for you," an officer said.

"Tell Mike to sit on it," Sammy replied recklessly, angry and hurting.

He continued his search in the bars and hangouts of Deep Ellum. Bruised and bleeding, breathing vengeance, he found anybody he collared quite willing to give information on the whereabouts of certain black-jacketed, red-bandannaed persons.

Sammy flashed his badge at a bouncer and walked into a nightclub. Spotting two of his prey at a table in the smoky dimness, he went over and seized them by their black collars, dragging them bodily off their chairs. They were too astonished and intimidated to resist when he threw them to the floor to frisk them.

By the time he got them back to the patrol car, the other officers had found the fifth, whom he identified. Yet another officer began, "Kidman—!"

"Got one more to take care of," Sammy said, turning away.

He went to a telephone stand, hoisted the directory, and looked up REID. There were three "M. Reids," but one listing for "J. Reid" on a street that rang a bell from their October wedding. This number he dialed.

"Hello," Jill's voice answered sleepily.

"Hello, Jill. This is Sammy," he said cheerily. "I'm sorry to wake you, but I have to ask Mark an important question about something that happened out here tonight. May I have his address, please?"

"Uh, sure," Jill murmured. "He lives at 1613 East Maple."

"Thank you, Jill. Sweet dreams," Sammy said, and hung up.

He climbed on the hog and roared out to East Maple. It was a street of small tract houses in a transitional neighborhood. Sammy went up to the door of 1613 and rang the bell. In case it wasn't working, he rapped loudly.

The porch light came on and the door slowly opened. Sammy looked in, regarding Mark's cut lip with satisfaction. "Hi, pal. I wasn't through talkin' to you," Sammy said in savage friendliness.

"All right!" Mark shouted, backing up into the small front room. "You get in here and we'll finish it right now!"

Sammy accepted, stepping in and closing the door. But as he regarded the fury in Mark's face, he paused. "Just for the record . . . why are we beating each other to a bloody pulp?"

Mark flushed deeply. "You took her right out from under me. I almost had her, until you came along."

Sammy gazed at him. "Marni?" he said. "This is about Marni?"

"Who do you think, scumbag? Come on, I wanna knock out some teeth!" Mark shouted.

"Marni," Sammy breathed, tentatively fingering a chipped tooth. "Well, sure. Yeah, you came to Juju's and we fought over her, and she made you leave to protect me. Then me going on to Jill about Marni being pregnant, so you wanted to beat the snot out of me. Yeah, I can understand that."

He looked up in comprehension and Mark lowered his fists. "Okay, pal. We're even," Sammy said. He opened the door and left with Mark staring after him.

"Marni," Sammy muttered as he climbed on his bike. "I should have guessed that was about Marni. . . ." Suddenly cold chills rippled down his spine and he grabbed his beeper, shaking it. It was dead.

He started the bike and gunned it toward Baylor Medical Center, praying that he was not too late. The streets were mostly empty, so within fifteen minutes he was roaring up to the emergency entrance.

Running inside, he demanded of a nurse at the desk, "Marni Kidman . . . is she here . . . in—what's the word—is she having the baby?" he exclaimed.

"You must be Sammy," she said, looking him over in mild disgust. He was a bloody, sweaty, dirty mess.

"Yes!" he cried. "Where—"

"You're not going anywhere near her until you wash up and get in scrubs," she dictated.

"Take me!" he pleaded of her five-foot highness.

In ten minutes Sammy, scrubbed and gowned, was led past Clayton in the waiting area to the delivery room—a formidable, sterile room with bright lights and Craftsman tool chests. He heard her gasping and moaning, then knelt beside her so she could see him. "Sammy!" she cried.

"Hi, baby. What's going on?" he asked. He looked up at Pam, winking, and she eyed his face under the mask.

"The baby's crowning," the obstetrician said, and Sammy looked back. "You can push now, Marni." She threw her head back and pushed, gasped, and pushed again, clutching her mother's hand.

Sammy stepped beside the doctor. "Hold the head—quickly now—here it comes," she said.

With one more push the baby slid into Sammy's hands. The doctor rapidly suctioned the mouth and nose, then the infant turned its little head, coiled its fists and began to cry.

Sammy gazed down at a son with a healthy head of black hair. He held him in awe while the doctor cut the umbilical cord, then laid him on Marni's chest. "It's a boy, Marni," he whispered, sinking to his knees beside the table.

She was crying. "Hello, darling," she said shakily, stroking the black head while the baby writhed and cried. Sammy laid his head near Marni's to look up at the newborn's face.

"Merry Christmas," Pam murmured, her mask wet with tears.

The baby was taken away for a moment to be cleaned and weighed. "What's the name?" asked an intern with a clipboard.

Sammy, totally blank, looked at Marni. "Samuel James Kidman, Jr.," she said, tired but triumphant, and he grinned weakly.

The doctor returned with Sammy Jr. wrapped in a blue blanket. "Six pounds, five ounces," she announced. "Good color, good lung development. Born at 4:10 A.M., December 23. Congratulations." Sammy put his head down on the delivery bed, overcome.

They had a wonderful Christmas. Marni healed up and Sammy healed up, relishing the jokes about how Sammy Junior had come through the birth less battered than Sammy Senior (who also received a correction for failing to promptly check in). However, he could not get an appointment to get two cracked and chipped teeth repaired until after the holiday.

By Christmas Eve the apartment was packed with visitors, food and gifts. There was so much food, in fact, that it would have taken six months for the little family to eat it all. Quietly, Sammy took some of the excess over to Mavis.

Mike and Charisse came by with their children to see the baby, as did Dave, Kerry, and Chris. Sammy was nervous about all these hands touching his tiny son, but Marni smiled, "They have only good germs."

On Christmas Day, Sam brought Mrs. Threlkeld by to meet his grandson, and Marni would never forget the look on his face when he first held little Sammy. The sad, fruitless years rolled away as he regarded the image of his own son. Dolly presented her gift to the baby in the form of a savings certificate that would amply see him through college.

Privately, Sammy and Marni exchanged gifts. She was thrilled with Sammy's present to her, and he congratulated himself until he unwrapped her present to him—a fur-lined leather jacket. Then he was chafed that she spent so much.

The sparkling, candled Christmas dinner was at Pam and Clayton's house. It was bitter cold outside, so a cheery fire crackled in the stone hearth across the large family room. Preceding the meal, Marni's father bowed his head and thanked the Father of lights for His incomparable gifts. Sammy, holding his son, suddenly felt the need to excuse himself from the table.

When Marni came looking for him a few minutes later, she found him in the gameroom, crying. "Sammy?"

"I don't deserve this, Marni," he whispered over the sleeping baby in his arms. "God should know better than to entrust so much to an idiot like me."

"Gee, I don't know about that, Sammy," she murmured. "What one idiot can't do, maybe two can."

He bent his head down to give her a wet kiss. "I love you, baby."

"Do you?" she purred, and he looked at her in surprise. "Then Mom wants to talk to you about doing a portrait."

"Marni—!" he said threateningly.

"We just want to talk about it," she said, cutting her eyes up at him.

"We'll talk," he grudgingly conceded, and Marni turned away victorious. Sammy paused to whisper to his son, "Watch out for the women, Sam. They're trouble every time." Then he followed her back to the dining room.

(The story continues in *Sammy: Working for a Living*.)

Printed in the United States
21993LVS00001B/22-30